THE SHADOWING OF COMBFOOT CHASE

THE SHADOWING OF COMBFOOT CHASE

Hillard Morley

The Book Guild Ltd

First published in Great Britain in 2022 by
The Book Guild Ltd
Unit E2 Airfield Business Park,
Harrison Road, Market Harborough,
Leicestershire. LE16 7UL
Tel: 0116 2792299
www.bookguild.co.uk
Email: info@bookguild.co.uk
Twitter: @bookguild

This work is entirely fictitious and bears no resemblance to any persons living or dead.

Early versions of some episodes in this text have been previously published
as short stories online and in literary journals:

'A Little Folding of the Hands' won the *OWT* Short Fiction Prize 2018
'The Hand Waxed Short' appeared in *Literary Yard* in August 2018
'Away from the Body and at Home' appeared in *Switchback* in October 2019
'Times in the Open Square' appeared in *The Sheepshead Review* in March 2020
'A Living Dog Is Better than a Dead Lion' appeared in *The Literatus* in October 2020

Typeset in 11pt Adobe Garamond Pro

Printed and bound by CPI Group (UK) Ltd, Croydon, CR0 4YY

ISBN 978 1915122 728

British Library Cataloguing in Publication Data.

A catalogue record for this book is available from the British Library.

For James, whose belief and support makes so much possible.

And Lay Low the Ruthless

We're safe, as long as we avoid the tyres and bumpers in the car park. It's not that we've got itchy feet, although we've ventured far and wide, but that the dark has made us brave; we've heard the wake word and selected Combfoot Chase to start our observations.

You wonder why. You think there's not much here of note, only a kebab van parked up in the furthest corner of the lot. The van is tucked beside a fence, the one supposed to stop the suicides from jumping off the cliff. A sign is tacked on every picket with a number you can phone if you're in trouble. They want it to stand out to anyone who's lost their bearings, so they've made it luminous and yellow. It tells you plummeting is frowned upon, but stretches out a hand of hope. Someone's waiting on the line, it promises. Someone's there to give you their attention. Although in fact the scheme's not worked. If you lean over – careful! It's a long way down – you'll see the teddy bears, the weather-beaten cellophane and dog-eared remnants of dead flowers heaped up at the bottom of the cliff. It's too far off to read from here, but there's a message stapled to a small bear's ear which says, 'Be Kind'.

Beside the van, in the shadow of its awning, a queue has formed. We'd like to take you for a closer look. It's curious; the queue's composed of men who line up, face each other's backs, identical to unschooled eyes in trackies, hoods and baseball caps. They make a neat, oblivious assembly. We wonder if they came to leap and if food eaten from a polystyrene carton – or wrapped up in a bit of butcher's paper – is suitable for anyone's last supper. From time to time another man arrives and glues himself haphazard to the far foot of the row. The queue steps forward in obsessive fairness, acknowledges each turn, the fleeting right to give an order through the service hatch. We can't tell who's hell-bent on self-destruction as these drifters all look much the same. The tantalising scents of roasted meat ooze from the van over the grit, insist that only feeble people would attempt to live on vegetables.

One carload fed departs the car park on the hill. Another comes to take its place. Too late to tarry very long, it pulls up, lets its driver out. The passengers stare blankly through the windscreen, will be captivated by the view only until the meat arrives. Then they'll be too distracted stuffing strips of doner in their mouths to care about a far horizon anymore.

A pause.

A window winds down and a hand snakes out. It crunches rubbish, takes aim, hurls a ball in the direction of a bin. The mark is almost always missed. The ball will bounce off or collide and clang against the hollows of the sides – the verge is littered and the bin is nigh on empty – before this car will also speed away, head off downhill. Its passengers won't notice any flowers or the stapled messages, and no one will remember to be kind.

With nothing more of interest here, we turn and leave the van behind. We weave our way between the piles of rubbish, slide behind the bin. The council hasn't mown this verge in ages and tonight the dewpoint's dipped past zero. Every blade of grass is long and crisp, is frozen solid, will remain unbending now till sunrise comes.

The tangled town of Combfoot Chase spreads out beneath the cliff. You'll see your share of bodies in this messy web of streets. We'll take you to the theatre, and we'll visit the museum and the school and dodge the floodlights on the sports pitch for all weathers. The parks and shops and sacred places wait there too. They squeeze between the jumbled rows of houses, the new and small, the older and the larger, the homes which barricade their doors in hope of keeping clear lines drawn between the public and the private space, attempt to stop the outside getting in.

The town is bounded by a blur of motorway, an orange trapline stretching off towards the stars above the reservoir. It carries all the lorries, all the travellers with any mettle past. This town is never more than white marks on a blue sign at the junction no one takes. It boasts no elegant stone circuses to draw the tourists in, no classic or refined parades. There are no posh boutiques nor tree-lined streets, for people here don't care for that. Look round the back, they say, you'll see it's only front. Instead they make the best of in-fill. When decades back the bombed-out blanks were left, the fallen walls were rebuilt using breezeblocks – quicker, cheaper – though the town still looks attractive if you squint. See how that stream of warm air rising from the sewers sets the streetlights all a-twinkling?

So where in all of this should we begin?

No one likes a spy, but we could make an easy start with Ava, who's asleep and dreams of birds. Or we could sniff the wind, pursue Marina and her whiffs of fish? Not everyone keeps pillowed eyelids closed. Mr Tombleson's awake, and so is Jem, who's plagued by thoughts that he might end today exactly where he started. Or we could head down to the river, where a silhouette's been spotted lurking in amongst the cats. Some citizens are up and baking bread or rolling pastry crusts. These characters are in it for the food and fill a pie with anything to hand. They think they won't be seen because they're clothed in night, but dawn already pokes a finger at the cliff and soon we must be off if we're to keep our cover. We've checked our cameras, sharpened pencils, prepped our apps and gadgets so we'll know if certain parties flush a dodgy item down a toilet, and we're looking for the spot where we can make our first step of intrusion.

A weary house across the town flicks on a yellow square. The light makes sudden shape in space.

"Let's go there first," I say, and so it is that we agree to go to Delia, an early riser in the suburbs. You might think that this indicates a guilty conscience, but it's better if you make your own mind up. We'll keep our verdict to ourselves – for now.

The fact is Delia's as good as anyone.

*

"It's not my fault."

We register her first words when we're huddled in a corner with her slippers. We're here to monitor her every move. It helps she never thought to shut her laptop down, nor close her curtains when she went to bed last night. Anyone could look in if they chose and Delia has no idea she's failed to keep the interlopers out for all she put a conker in the corner of her windowsill. She lies in bed and thinks she's hidden by a wide expanse of floral duvet.

"It wasn't, not at all," she tells the not-quite-emptiness.

No one's slept with Delia for years, though in the normal run of things she likes to live alone. Today, however, she'd have liked some company and wishes there were someone here to talk to. She isn't looking forward to today. It promises to jump up and attack her.

"I don't have anything to hide," she whispers to the ceiling, "but somebody is bound to cast aspersions. They'll look at me and speculate about what *really* happened."

We've learnt to recognise her voice and have to say we're interested to hear how much it's trembling.

She wipes a tear onto the frilly border of her duvet. "If I were braver, more like Ruth, perhaps," she carries on, "I'd just deny it, brazen all their accusations out." She wonders whether pointed fingers will be metaphorical or otherwise. "Perhaps it's best if I don't go. I'm not exactly up to it." She pulls the covers up above her head.

We raise the little tufts of hair above our eyes and cast a knowing look at one another.

*

Later that morning, when she's pulled herself together, we follow Delia to a substantial house – Victorian, expensive – on the cusp of what Combfootians claim to be their arty quarter.

By habit she arrives a trifle early and will have to wait until the others come. But still the front door opens when she knocks. She's herded in and saddled with a schooner of sweet sherry. She's shown through to the lounge to be confronted by the coffin which is stationed in the centre of the room. Her reaction makes it clear that she's appalled. Our auditory apparatus picks up whimpers.

"They've kept it *here?*" she says to painful stillness in the room.

A coffin, she believes, is better hidden in a hearse and only glimpsed in the far-off and departing distance, but Delia is forced to stand alone and stand right next to it. It seems too small to hold a body, though Ruth Kelly always was a tiny woman, an affectation Delia had found hard to pardon because a woman of a certain age should not be slight and slender. Ruth had come across as pert, unseemly even. She should have occupied more space as Delia and her wide and generous hips have learnt to do.

A wreath, a spray of irises, is balanced on the coffin lid. A bee emerges from one bloom, performs a waggle dance between the flowers. Boxed up whilst in the florist's shop, transported here, the bee has carried on regardless, has gathered sticky pollen on its hairs and now moves from the stamen to the stigma. It doesn't realise it's been separated from its hive and troubles no one, but this apian tribute unnerves Delia. She's reminded of the pattern on her duvet, makes a mental note to change it, to wash and iron it, to send it off quick-smart to charity. At least the coffin's closed, she thinks, that's one small mercy. She couldn't bear to see Ruth's face again. Not dead and on a body anyway.

"I can't believe she's really dead," she says, and takes a sip of sherry. "It's sudden, and I haven't come to terms with it."

Whilst she's been standing still, the lounge has filled with other funeral-goers. We mind our step between the feet and watch the mourners stand about and chat. They laugh too loudly and too much, say much too much in general. Fortunately Delia's too agitated to navigate the crowd and hangs back near the wall, where we can hear her very clearly.

"I don't want this," she thinks, although the nutty drink goes down. "I'd have chosen Fino or Amontillado, but it would've been too rude to turn it down." Besides, the glass keeps fretful fingers occupied. She's pleased she wore her hair back in a clip so she can't fiddle.

Delia suspects she may have spoken this aloud because a nearby mourner offers her an awkward smile, then turns and threads away into the looming crowd.

We write our observations down and annotate them with deductions that the mourner doesn't know who Delia is, nor what part she has played in this scenario.

A rustle at the door. The crowd makes room. Ah, watch this closely. The family arrives. Three strangers, still and dark and clothed in grief, adapting to this strange new version of their world. Delia's never met the family, but she recognises them from photographs. Ruth often used to grub her phone out of her bag and stick a recent snap under her nose, so Delia has seen these people gathered in a line or cluster around Ruth, always obedient and smiling. She remembers chins thrust out and pouts directed at the camera.

"Hilarious, isn't it?" Ruth had asked, and Delia had been forced to acquiesce. Privately she'd thought their posturing ridiculous and knew the show of harmony hid a marriage that had been unhappy.

Her friend had often moaned about a Catholic husband. Pig-headed, a misogynist, she'd said, and sometimes fiery and ill-tempered. It's funny, but these details don't fit well with what we see before us now. The man who stands here has been polished and presented. He sports a neat moustache with every hair precisely in its place. Ruth's children stand on his right hand. They hover close as though they bank on his protection, although the girl's a woman, and the boy's eighteen if he's a day.

Watch Delia in the presence of the family. Word is there's something of a question mark over the part she played in Ruth's demise and there's a chance she'll come clean, get what happened off her chest. It's possible that what we've picked up on the grapevine is just gossip, but Delia's behaviour is arousing our suspicion. One moment she'll be craving for the family's attention, the next she wants to claim the right to be forgotten.

In search of a distraction, Delia focuses her curiosity on Ruth's son. He slopes over to the sideboard where the sherry and the whisky bottles stand and pours himself a hearty measure, a remedy for feelings of exclusion and distress. He takes a tumblerful and leans his back against the wall.

"Poor whelp," thinks Delia, "he doesn't know where he should put himself." She allows herself another sip of sherry. It's mellowed in her hand and we can tell she rather likes it now for all it's sweeter than her usual selection. We hope it won't be long before she plucks up courage to approach someone. "I'd do it now, I'd walk right up and offer sympathies, if I could just remember what he's called," she thinks. "It must be age. I never used to forget anything, was always razor-sharp." She scratches round a recess in her brain in an attempt to bring the name to mind.

We also want to know so we can add it to our profile.

"Oh, it's in here somewhere…" Ruth had talked about him often, worried more for him than for the girl. "But what in heavens is it?" Delia laments and clicks her tongue in irritation. "The girl, now she's called Brogan. It sticks with you, a name like that. So sturdy and supportive, like a good and well-made shoe." Delia shakes her head as if to loosen something but finds that nothing is dislodged. The boy's name has completely slipped away.

We record reluctant question marks and tell ourselves we must learn to be patient.

Delia tackles the remaining contents of her schooner while pondering how odd it is for adult children to come home in such appalling circumstances. Whoever they may be elsewhere, they're outranked by a parent here, will always be an infant whilst a father's in the room. The daughter, she remembers, has a job in theatre. Yes, Ruth was very proud of that. But not an actress. No. Something more technical, behind the scenes. The boy has yet to find himself, has only just gone up to university. "I'd like to ask him how he's getting on," she thinks, "to hear his first impressions of his course." In fact she's keen to know what choice he made and if his parents let him do the choosing for himself, or if they did it for him as her own had done. It used to be that life was handed out to you, the plot, the part you played directed by the older generation, as though your story must be told in just one way. "He'd have had free rein, though, he's a boy…" thinks Delia.

We wonder whether she's aware that times have changed and people get to make things up themselves? Of course she must. His generation studies anything, as long as it can pay, though Delia begrudges all the options open nowadays. She recalls a dim and distant student who had opted for Oenology.

"I'm gonna have a wine shop, Miss," he'd said one day when she'd been filling gaps out in his UCAS form.

She'd laughed at him, "I thought that he was joking!" and had been astonished when he'd got defensive, even narky.

"I'll send a case," he'd said, "and then you'll see."

He'd sworn he'd not forget, but Delia had not seen him again once term came to its end, nor any trace of any promised wine. "I don't know why I was surprised," she'd mourned the loss to Ruth a few years later, "when such enterprises very often fail."

They'd been out walking on the hills above the town, had gone much further than they'd planned and conversation – like their feet – had wandered. They'd called a pause to catch their breath.

"Oh, what a view!" Ruth had exclaimed. "Let's stop a mo and grab a coffee from that van."

"I'd rather not…" Delia had flashed an edgy look towards the van. "I've heard it's rather dodgy here," she'd said.

"Oh, Delia, what on earth d'you mean by dodgy?"

"Well, a meeting place for shady types…"

"Don't be ridiculous. And nothing happens in broad daylight."

Ruth's attitude had riled her. She'd been convinced that Ruth had lingered longer once she'd realised Delia was ill at ease. She'd spent an age rummaging beneath a fence, had seemed to scrutinise each individual blade of grass. Delia had checked off minutes on her watch, had stamped her feet and huffed in irritation. "What *are* you doing?" she'd asked at last.

"Looking for grasshoppers," Ruth had said as though this were an obvious answer. "I want to try them deep-fried. They're supposed to have a salty, crunchy flavour." Ruth had always had a penchant for peculiarity, had confessed to disappointment when her son had dared to tread traditional paths. "He told me that he wants to study law or medicine," she'd scoffed. "I can't believe a child of mine could be so *boring*."

"You should be pleased," Delia had argued. "Only the best can aim for doctor or solicitor."

"He's not intelligent enough to see it through. He should have chosen something less conventional."

Delia surveys the young man who's before her now. He's hogged the sherry bottle for himself and swigs from it, tops up his glass. His back slides down the anaglypta until he's in a crouched position.

We hurry over to be near him – just in case he needs support – and kick our heels against the skirting board.

Perhaps Ruth had been right, thinks Delia, and he had overreached his competence. Perhaps he foolishly supposes himself wiser than he is because a place at university's no exception nowadays, not like it was when baby boomers like herself had gone, oh, many moons ago. Delia suspects that most establishments will let you in and take your money, even if they're not quite sure you're up to it. Too much is offered far too lightly, she believes, and no one has a backbone anymore.

"You can't blame kids for changes in society's expectations," Ruth had barked when Delia had dared to speak her mind. It had been breaktime in the staffroom. "What a modern course might lack in depth, it makes up for in breadth."

Delia is unconvinced that this is true. Ruth, like many other teachers at their school, had often spoken lots of woolly nonsense, and once such sentiments were said aloud they tended to take hold and gain a patina of truth.

Ruth, convinced of her own rightness, had dismissed Delia's opinion out of hand. "You're such a fusspot," she'd said, "such a fogey and old-fashioned."

"I simply think that youths should be accountable for their own good fortune," she'd reiterated.

"The difference is you've never had a child," Ruth had declared. "It's not surprising that you're out of touch with all your students."

The comment had been waspish and it still stings now, though with Ruth being dead and all, Delia acknowledges she ought to let it go. You're not supposed to speak ill of the dead at funerals, however much their criticism rankles.

At least the son had been brave and defied his mother. "And he chose tradition, not because he'd had it foisted on him, but because he *wants* to be that sort of person. I'm happy with convention too," she thinks, "there's nothing wrong with that." The boy has got a floppy fringe, just like the student who'd not heeded Delia when she'd warned against Oenology.

One of us picks up a camera, is about to snap the boy in blurred and sorry state, when we remind each other just in time it's better to avoid an obvious intrusion. Best let him think he's still got rights to safety and security at home.

Delia lifts her glass and drains the last drops of her sherry. Would it be discourteous to help herself to one more glass, she wonders? The son has commandeered the only open bottle, but we think it might be all right if we twist another lid.

"I wish he knew what happened to his mother wasn't any of my fault." Delia accepts the refilled glass from us and gives a tiny hiccough. "Say what you like, but I'm the only one round here who knows what *really* happened. Any decent lad would take a bit of comfort in the chance to chat to his late mother's greatest friend. And that's exactly what I was. I was her best chum in the world."

That's quite a statement and we'll have to fact-check its veracity. There's no doubt she and Ruth were closer in the past few weeks, but claiming an unrivalled bond goes far beyond the evidence we've seen. We'd better look for other links and sources, measure Delia's opinion against consensus in the room. Ruth's here, we realise, not just as a body in a coffin, but as a person in a whole host of bereaved imaginations, so we listen in to snippets of surrounding conversations.

"I'd describe her as spontaneous…"

"More maverick, you mean…"

"I suppose you couldn't *always* bank on her…"

"Although she was a laugh. She'd brighten any room…"

"I have to say she scared the daylights out of me…"

It's not straightforward to define a complex character. We don't know what we should believe or even if it matters if we write a falsehood down. We hedge our bets and keep the phrases in quotation marks. That way we'll show the judgements are subjective and maintain a little doubt and distance.

"Nothing would've happened if she'd only listened to me…"

Ah, that's Delia again. She's standing by the sideboard and we're pleased to see she's got the opened sherry bottle in her hand. She's near the boy and looks as though she's talking to him. Oh shit, we hope we haven't missed something important.

"A short delay was all I asked for, but oh, no! Ruth had to rush off without any hesitation. You probably know she moaned about her marriage to your father, but I don't get what vexed her – hic – And when I dared to ask, she only blurted out, 'Hell, plenty!' and announced that she was leaving him. You'd barely left the family home before she'd knocked it down behind you. Did you know your exit was the spur to end your parents' marriage? Well, I think you must have done. That's why you're drinking so much, I expect…"

Although to say it now is rather gauche, the point that Delia's making has foundations in the facts. No one denies that Ruth caused pain to others in her final weeks. It's common knowledge and the story featured on the website of the local paper: *Disgrace As Teacher Ruthlessly Abandons Classes*, it proclaimed. Mr Tombleson had left a comment. It wasn't a surprise in his opinion. The Mrs Kelly he had known had been a flighty piece of work back when she'd taught his daughter years ago. Respect for others used to be ingrained, he said, but folk had got too selfish nowadays.

Even with such public condemnation Ruth had gone ahead and quit both job and marriage. An online search brings up a blog in which she details plans to live alone and be a writer. We've found a haiku that she posted with a photo of her feet on Instagram – her musings on the need to walk away – and all the family assets had been duly divvied up.

Her first move was to relocate, to buy a new-build cottage on the edge of town. It's newness was a shock to Delia, who thinks a house should prove itself before it's called a home. We've got a photo of it here along with all the floorplans and the video tour is still available online. Nice place. Three beds, two baths. You interested? It's up for sale again, of course, though with a price tag several thousand less than when Ruth paid for it. Some people want a house like that, something with a suspect history, but the market's fairly niche according to our research.

And Delia's not wrong about the timing either. Ruth did skedaddle only three days after she'd deposited her son in halls. "There's no point in divorce," she'd said with brazen disregard for others' feelings, "because I've no intention of remarrying." Delia had had a notion that a Catholic husband wouldn't grant one anyway. "Quite honestly, I can't be bothered. No point in procrastinating and there's no time left to waste."

The irony's not lost, neither on us nor Delia, who rolls fresh glugs of sherry round her tongue. She picks up hints of raisins, which she'd not noticed before. She might stop by the supermarket on her way home and acquire some. She tries to memorise the name and notes the blueness of the bottle so she'll be sure to buy the correct brand. The sherry makes her bold enough to ask Ruth's son for absolution. "If I explain my side of things, you won't hold it against me," she says.

We freeze, our pencils poised. We can't shake the suspicion that some blame must fall on Delia, that no one is completely innocent, as she claims. If smoke is smelt, a fire must smoulder somewhere, and only guilty people need a pardon.

"Can't you leave it for a few more days?" Delia had stood outside this very house and cast a furtive look over her shoulder. "I don't feel up to this today," she'd wheedled feebly. "I tripped this morning and I think my ankle might be twisted." That was pure exaggeration. Although there'd been a bitter frost, she hadn't fallen, and she simply didn't want to lug the guts of Ruth's life over town.

"No. I can't wait any longer. You've no idea how irritating it can be to share your home with men. Besides, I need your car." Ruth had ignored all arguments and scorned appeals to caution. So they'd staggered back and forth, had carried one box then another from the house into the car, and then from the car into another boxy house.

"I urged her to be careful," Delia persists. "I even salted all the paths to try to stop us slipping…"

Once each package had been heaved into a new hall, Ruth had set about the gleeful task of tearing off the lids. She'd pointed this way, that way round the cottage, issued her instructions, her commands to Delia to set the contents in each designated room. If ankles hadn't ached before they certainly had done then.

"My error was to pick a box she hadn't opened…" Delia explains. The sherry works its magic and sees off a few more inhibitions.

We check our angles, make sure we can get the money shots. We've promised not to miss it when she gives up vital information.

"…'What've you got there?' Ruth asked me and she wouldn't let me go until she'd seen what was inside. 'Ah, books!' she said, and grinned at all the spines exposed in grave-like rows. 'Well, give them here, I'll take them to the library.' All I wanted was to get the job done, to go home and run a nice hot bath, but Ruth couldn't resist the chance to have a dig. 'But they're far too heavy with your injured ankle,' she said and smirked at me. And after everything I'd done! 'I'm more than capable,' I told her and I made a crisp turn, started up the stairs. I knew that what she meant by library was in fact a bedroom and I thought she had no need to be so grandiose…" Delia stops. The son's mouth hangs ajar and even with her stomach lined with sherry, she has tact enough to halt before she says how Ruth had caught up on the turning of the landing, how she'd laid hands on the box and had begun to grapple for control.

"They're mine. I want to do it," she'd screeched like a petty child. "I don't want you to go to any trouble."

As if the whole day hadn't been an inconvenience.

"She was unkind to me," thinks Delia as she gazes at the shrinking amber liquid in her glass, "and always made me feel inadequate." What had ensued could only be described as an ugly tussle. Each woman had held her corner while the box had been thrust to and fro. "To my credit I was first to view the situation as ridiculous. 'Oh, have it then,' I said, and let it go…"

It's possible she gave the tiniest of shoves. It's this doubt that is dogging Delia.

For a second Ruth had looked a little smug. Delia remembers a face lit up with triumph. She'd probably started to compose a victory poem, had planned to post it later on the internet, though she'd have claimed to do it tongue-in-cheek. Almost anyone with any sense of humour knew that Ruth was funny because she always said, 'I'm *joking*,' when she wanted you to think she meant no harm.

But then the wobbling had begun and her attitude of conquest had been overtaken by alarm. Delia has spent the last weeks trying to forget the horrid faltering, the falling and the flaccid, crumpled body at the bottom of the stairs. She stares into her polygraph-glass. "It was an accident, you see…" she whispers to the son and to herself. "She misplaced her foot and then she fell. That's all…" A tear wells up and spreads across the surface of her eye.

We can't help feeling sorry for her and place some tissues on the side for her to find.

She doesn't touch them. "How long till we need to leave for church?" she says to no one in particular. "Do I have time for one more refill…?"

Screw you, we think, and stuff the tissues up our sleeves.

Delia's determined that she won't say anymore. To speak out can be risky and the son might have a morbid streak, might want the death described in all its dismal detail. What, for example, would she say if he should ask to hear his mother's final words? She can't tell him that Ruth had cried out, "Oh, for fuck's sake!" as she'd tottered. News like that just makes distressing circumstances worse. Perhaps she should replace expletives, substitute them with a hint of piety? 'For God's sake' captures all the sense of waste whilst being much more optimistic. That could offer him a little hope. Delia is pleased with this solution. A tiny fib, but meet and right to do. She rubs away a tight sensation in her chest, picks up a sherry bottle, makes her way around the room, purports to top up other people's glasses. In doing so, her elbow bumps with someone in the crowd. "Oops, very sorry. I apologise," she says. A hiccough and an ill-timed giggle bubble up before she can suppress them.

"Quite all right…" A pleasant, lowish voice. Good Lord, she's only gone and jogged into the Catholic husband. Of all the people to come up against! She gulps and hiccoughs while he smiles, all generosity and kindness. "…Ah, Delia, I'm so glad you came," he says, and makes a show of checking that her glass is full.

"The least that I could do," she squeaks out of a tight neck. She pants and puts a hand out, reaches for his arm to stop herself from toppling. It's clear now that she's very close to him that Ruth was quite, quite wrong about this man. He seems so sensitive, considerate, attentive, Delia thinks. To take the time to speak to her, when on a day like this he must be feeling dreadful!

We watch her dry heart swell with pleasure and with gratitude.

"But then again," she thinks, "I did do everything that could have been expected when Ruth fell. No one can criticise me on *that* score."

The facts are reassuring. She'd stayed calm though she'd known from the beginning Ruth was lifeless. The angle of her neck was a dead giveaway, but Delia had completed all the checks as per instructions from the operator on the phone. She'd sought an absent pulse, had hunted other vital signs, but with no luck. No evidence of life remained and all hopes of revival had evaporated.

The paramedics had been slow to reach the scene. "They left me there," she mourns. "I had to sit there with a body." For a long half hour Ruth had remained flung upside down, one foot between the balusters, the other kicked out on the fifth tread of the stair.

The hall had been an utter mess. Delia had looked down on the pile of battered cardboard which had sailed above Ruth's head as she had tumbled. It had strewn its cargo, splintered books across the chequered floor. "I had the good sense not to move a thing," she thinks, and takes in all the charm of green and Catholic eyes. "I managed to resist the urge to tidy up…" It's harder to resist the thought that technically this man's no longer anybody's husband.

As Delia updates her terms of reference, the Catholic husband raises up his glass and clinks it against hers. "Well, down the hatch!" he says. Is it just imagination or does he smile at her? Wrinkles appear around his eyes and Delia becomes light-headed as she returns his toast. Her glass is brim-full and the sherry slops about precariously. "Oh, no more spillages, I beg," joshes the Catholic husband.

Everyone in earshot chokes and it's Delia's turn not to know where to put herself.

"Oh, Adrian, you're such a card," she hears somebody say, though she can't say she finds it very funny. Her memory spirals back to Ruth in deadly tangle at the bottom of the stairs. Her only comfort is she'd kept a proper vigil. She'd picked a careful way through all the debris, quite determined not to touch the corpse again, not even by mistake. She'd perched her ample buttocks on the edge of an unopened box and waited. No one here knows just how horrid it had been to sit and watch Ruth's blood sink out of her extremities. The twisted face had quickly turned a pale and waxy grey.

The paramedics had arrived at last, hot on their heels a young policewoman who'd firmly taken Delia's arm and led her to the kitchen. "We'll let the paramedics do their job without us getting in the way," she'd said.

Delia had thought this was a good sign. If the scene could be disturbed, it must mean everyone was satisfied with her account of what had happened, for simple tales are oftentimes most easily believed.

The young policewoman had introduced herself as Diana, had found the kettle and an ugly mug, and had presented Delia with hot sweet tea. "You've had a shock," she'd said – Delia had thought the gesture kind, although she hated sugar and wished she could have had a cup. "You take me through it when you're ready," Diana had said. "Really, take your time."

Delia had kept her cool, had relayed all the points she thought were pertinent and now, standing here before the Catholic husband, she thinks he'd probably appreciate a partner with more discipline and self-control. Ruth never equalled her in that. Even before the accident, she'd made her deathday very trying. There'd been unholy scenes when she had quit this house. Delia had not been party to the row itself, was in the car outside, had ducked behind the steering wheel when doors had banged and spoons had flown into the street, but thinks the fuss Ruth made was foreign, far too fiery to be decent, especially in a person of advancing age.

We, on the other hand, surmise a quarrel suggests passion yet to fully run its course.

"Of course he'll need some time to come to terms with being unattached," Delia thinks as the Catholic husband puts a hand under her elbow and steers her through the crowd. "One has to get accustomed to a life alone, the life that *I* have led."

We recognise a solitary creature, in stark contrast to Ruth, who'd always been intensely sociable and revelled in a jolly row. The day she'd died, Delia had watched her through the windscreen as she'd gone back time and time again to lob more allegations at an ever more defensive husband. The dashboard clock had ticked away the best part of an hour before Delia had had the nerve to hint enough might be enough.

Ruth had only grinned and said, "Not on your nelly!" and had scurried straight back to the skirmish.

Our notes make reference to the fact she'd called her husband both an 'arsehole' and a 'spider', but we can't see much arachnidan about this man. He knows his brood care. Look how he shepherds Delia and all the other guests towards the door, makes sure they know the closeness of the hour, the need for imminent departure.

Reprieve had only come when Ruth had paused to bring some object from the house, to load the heavy dregs and leftovers of marriage onto Delia's backseat. The car had grumbled with the weight.

Delia wishes now she'd not been forced to take Ruth's side. The warm sensation of the husband's fingers cupped beneath her elbow makes her yearn to spin this moment out. She remembers him leant up against the doorjamb on this very spot we're passing. He'd seemed shell-shocked, looked as though he didn't want to cross this threshold, as though he'd been betrayed by all the steps that ran up to his door and should have kept him high above the filth down on the streets. She'd thought he'd caught her eye deliberately, had not attempted to conceal his anguish. Then Delia had known that she was on the side of wrong and longed to be invisible.

"Well, that should fucking teach him," Ruth had crowed, and slammed the door of Delia's car behind her.

Delia hadn't meant to rev the engine, nor to crunch the gears as she'd pulled off. She thinks that Ruth had gloated and that that had made her nervous. With the benefit of hindsight she can see that Ruth was not as kind as she had always claimed to be. She'd crowded and fatigued in equal measure and her husband had been made to suffer that for more than twenty years.

Delia sneaks a sidelong glance at her attractive guide and notices a fulsome head of hair. He might not see it now, she thinks, but one day he will recognise the value in the sudden snuffing of his wife and will be able to enjoy his new and unexpected liberation. She feels despondent when he frees her at the bottom of the steps.

Outside the house, arranged beside the pavement, waits a cavalcade of funeral cars.

"I'll stay here, shall I?" Delia asks in tones intended to imply compliance.

The Catholic husband turns, goes back to herd the other mourners from his house.

She assumes no answer is as good as yes.

We watch the gathering assembly, amuse ourselves by picking out the people whom we think will qualify to take up places in the limousines. We spot Ruth's daughter, Brogan. She's important. You can tell because she's decked herself in jacket, pencil skirt and sky-high red-soled heels, and that, we know, is not her usual garb. Our records show she orders tough and easy clothing sourced from multinational online companies based out of Seattle. They understand her needs and will deliver almost instantly. We have to say she's coping pretty well in her restrictive, unfamiliar attire and even keeps her knees together as she climbs into the car. We notice that she disregards a thin and unconvincing smile from Delia. Perhaps she thinks that Delia's irrelevant, is just a sagging woman in an old black dress.

The cars fill up and then the coffin is brought out, prompting a stream of memories from those who've gathered here today. Some, we're surprised to say, are recollecting steamy afternoons between Ruth's legs, though Delia can only see her in the blank bare kitchen of a new-build home.

"The bastard!" she'd exclaimed, as she'd pulled fragments of her precious china out of boxes. "He's only gone and smashed up all my favourites."

It's clear that much was broken on that day.

A gust of air had blown open the kitchen door, exposed the tableau round Ruth's corpse. The necessary photographs had been taken and the body strapped onto a stretcher, hoisted onto the paramedics' gurney. The bag containing broken pieces of her friend had looked so tiny.

"Someone ought to tell her husband…" Delia had said, had thought it better coming from herself but had capitulated when Diana had insisted it was not her place. She'd not been trained, the young policewoman had said, and didn't understand the way to break bad news. This is Delia's one regret. She would've liked to be the one to update Adrian and to watch the change of weather in his face.

Instead she'd let Diana drive her home, had nodded off in the backseat, had woken up embarrassed in the hope she hadn't snored. She'd been too tired to notice that the neighbours photographed her coming home in a police car but had felt the full humiliation when they'd posted it on Facebook. Since then her little house has seemed so vast and quiet and empty. She's never minded solitude before, has thought herself innately antisocial, but as the coffin slides into the hearse Delia admits that there's allure in company.

She stands beside the curb and waits until the last car has departed. Disappointment curdles in her stomach. She'd really thought she might be worthy of a seat inside a car. Though strictly speaking not part of the family, her status as the last person to see the wife alive might have afforded special dispensation, she believes, but clearly that is not to be. Like us and all the others, she will have to walk. She's glad the swelling in her ankle has subsided and she's worn her sensible flat shoes. One has to stand around a lot at funerals. It won't be long before Brogan regrets her choice of footwear.

Delia has planned her outfit carefully and is satisfied with what she chose. The funeral card demanded that she don bright colours – in homage to Ruth's lust for life – and nearly all the mourners have obeyed. Nearby a bright lime green umbrella and a lilac coat belie the grief we're all supposed to feel, and one brave soul has risked a suit from top-to-toe in orange. This goes far too far, thinks Delia. She'd feel a fraud in such a vulgar get-up. She smooths her plain black dress against her legs. She's pleased she thought to grab a scarf last minute and to tie a loose loop round her neck. It had been bought on a school trip which she and Ruth had led to London many years ago. They'd visited the National Gallery and Delia had been tempted by a range of yellow souvenirs inspired by the paintings of Van Gogh. Peer closely. You can still make out the faintest outline of a sunflower. The scarf – although much faded with much washing and much wearing – had been very daring at the time, so no one can accuse her of completely disregarding Ruth's instructions.

Persistent January drizzle dampens all the pavements. Delia sets off at a fierce pace, heads the procession which makes its way along the street, is confident in grippy rubber soles. "No foolish trips for me," she thinks.

In spite of rain Ruth's followers are out in force. They shout and beckon to each other, so much so that we wouldn't be at all surprised if someone were to raise a banner and set them all off singing. The numbers bulge until the swell of chatter is so great we hardly hear ourselves or others think.

Delia keeps her head down, doubts her funeral will be anything like this. "A more demure, sedate affair would be appropriate for me," she thinks. This cheerful atmosphere is fake, though she expects that it will carry on in church. The priest is likely to encourage it, will tell the congregation not to mourn Ruth's death but celebrate her life.

The walk to church leads past an ugly laundrette, a trendy café on a corner. We'll come back later. It's not the right time yet, and there are lots of other dots we must connect before we get back here. We've never been inside a Catholic church before and will admit to being curious. The outside's bare, utilitarian, as though the money ran out and the architect was told to cut the decoration. You'd be forgiven if you thought it cold and soulless. Perhaps the inside's more appealing, though? We'd lay a bet a massive crucifix is hung above the altar. One of us suggests the cross will be backlit by panels of stained glass, another speculates there'll be a spotlight hidden somewhere in the rafters. We could have fun with that, we think. We could cast shadows which would freak the congregation out. Of course we won't. We'll keep the drama subtle, just the faintest glow of focus on the coffin.

We enter in and soon track Delia down. She's chosen quite a humble pew towards the back, but as she's sitting in the spot next to the aisle, we have to scramble over her and then we grumble to each other because we haven't got the greatest view.

"The front's reserved for family," says Delia.

I catch my breath and look a little nervously towards my colleagues. Does this speech imply she's spotted us too soon? We're not yet ready, haven't finished our incursion.

"But never mind, the back's a better place for watching other mourners," Delia continues. She shows no other sign of knowing that we're here but – to be on the safe side – we think we'd better sit in total silence.

As it turns out she's quite right and this position gives a clear view down the aisle towards the pew, where the Catholic husband takes his seat, is flanked on either side by his two children. Three divine mops of bright hair, all in an angelic row. Delia notices the son and father have a similar hairline. It grows to a point at the nape of the neck and sends an arrow down beneath the collar. She licks dry lips. She likes the way these men both bow their heads, avoid the false and cheery chat which fills the church behind them. Brogan's hair is too long to distinguish if her hairline matches with the others'. She's bolt upright, inhabits thin and scraped-out looks, seems tense and ill-prepared for what she faces in the coming ceremony.

Elsewhere in the church a catalogue of Combfoot Chase has set itself in formal forward-facing rows. Reporters from *The Chronicle* get their pens and cameras ready to record that several representatives of the council have arrived. The council members sit down next to Mr Locke, the current head of the town's only comprehensive school. As former boss to Ruth he has been asked to do a reading. He rustles his script and props it on the shelf that lines the back edge of the pew.

Delia allows her eyes to rove around, spies many faces from her past, the colleagues, parents, students and voyeurs who've come to pay their last respects to Mrs Kelly. Delia has also spotted Mr Tombleson, who's sitting a few rows ahead and is accompanied by both his wife and daughter. She pretends she hasn't noticed them, because Sandra was a little shit in class and Delia would rather not renew that old acquaintance. She's shocked by all the people who have outlived Ruth. "She wasn't old," she thinks. "It isn't right she was the first to go."

A woman in a sober suit is standing far off in an aisle. We clock she keeps one eye on Delia and deduce they must've met before, but from the way she shuffles we'd say that Delia can't place where or when. She'd need to get her specs to have a closer look but is afraid that to retrieve them – and to put them on and stare – would be too rude. The woman gives the faintest nod and Delia nods back though shuttered tightness has begun to tug her chest. She fiddles with her handbag clasp and mourns again that age has ushered in forgetting.

It's a relief for everyone when organ music pipes into the air and then the coffin's carried in.

The service puts us through our paces. Unaccustomed prayers and hymnody pose challenges for us but seem to cheer up Delia. She's calmed by structure, is soon able to return to contemplation of the Catholic husband. He conducts himself so admirably, she thinks, and wears such well-cut clothes. His suit is snug across his shoulders so she guesses it was made-to-measure. That's not the norm, not from what we've seen so far in Combfoot Chase. You only have to look around the church to see the evidence. Ruth should've realised when she'd got it good.

How little Delia had understood the inner workings of Ruth's mind, although she has high hopes for greater intimacy with her friend's family in the future. When they lead out, she thinks, she'll simply slip into the aisle and quietly merge with them. She's glad she's not in glasses after all, because it isn't possible to offer proper comfort and condolences behind a lens. To give her credit, this plan almost works. She does step out and does her level best to nudge in at the head of the parade, but somehow all the other mourners sweep her far back in the line and when she leaves the church she's still near us, amongst the hangers-on and also-rans.

Unperturbed she tackles the walk back towards the house with something of a new spring in her step. We have to flex our legs to match her pace, but even she can't travel fast enough to stop herself from being caught by Mr Tombleson. She wonders if she could discourage him by feigning interest in a poster in the window of the laundrette. "But that will never work," she thinks. "He knows I'm not the type to wash my linen in a public place." She faces the reluctant fact she's stuck, will have to listen to his belly aches.

Ruth had often mocked him as a nimby. Whilst Delia had sometimes said a word in his defence, now that she has to walk with him she realises he's every bit as bigoted as her friend had said and tolerates nobody but himself. She's glad to reach the house and slip away into the dining room, to have the chance to melt into a boisterous crowd which quickly picks up steam in preparation for a roaring send-off.

Throughout the house noise rises steadily, aided in no small part by a stream of freely distributed sherry. A good choice, Delia thinks, taking a welcome sip. She's partial to it now because it stands up better to a warm room than a white wine would and fends off dampness from a winter church.

There's no sign yet of any Catholic husband, nor of the son, but Brogan can be spied beside the sideboard. She's eased her feet out of her high heels and is massaging a blistered toe. Poor girl, thinks Delia though in truth the thought is laced with told-you-so. She wends her way across the room with plans to offer insights into Ruth's last moments to the daughter but is brought up short by Brogan, who looks up and says, "Oh, bugger off, why don't you, Delia?"

The moment is an awkward one for everyone.

Delia is stranded, skewered, crushed.

The other mourners pretend a sudden fascination with their feet.

"I'm really sorry. She blames you, you see." We're stunned that Delia's rescuer is none other than Adrian, the Catholic husband. He appears as if from nowhere and this time we've no doubt that he's smiling. "She thinks that you're the bitch who told Ruth she should leave me," he says, and he makes his eyes grin crinkled-green and then he laughs out loud. "In fact it was the best choice Ruth had made in years."

The low voice tickles Delia's ear and makes her catch her breath.

"No doubt we should have split up yonks ago," he carries on, "and growing up with us must've been bloody miserable for both our children. Please, Delia, don't upset yourself." He throws his head back, knocks his sherry off. "The fault is mine, it really is." He pats her shoulder, disappears again into the throng.

Well, this is quite a turn-up for the books and not at all what we'd projected. Delia looks flushed and seems to feel much braver than she has all day. Encouraged by his kindness she gulps down her sherry, sets off in pursuit of more, is startled when she bumps into the woman in the sober suit. "I know you, don't I?" she blurts, and squints in vain to place the face.

"Oh, yes, we've met." The woman smiles and sets her glass of sherry on the sideboard. Unlike Delia's it's hardly touched, though there's the faintest trace of lipstick on the rim. "No one ever recognises me out of uniform," she says.

The voice is recent and familiar. A link is formed to black and checkered hats, to images of walkie-talkies and to crisp, sharp collars.

"Oh, it's you!" says Delia, and pants and sways, regrets the recent run of sherries which has left her memory clouded. "Are you here to represent the force?"

Diana – for it is Diana – again lays hands on Delia and steadies her. "Something like that," she says. "I've got some questions I'd quite like to chat about. A few things don't add up. It won't take long. If you can spare a moment?"

Delia's breath is tight again. She makes small circles with her fingers on her chest, tries once more to soothe her fluttered conscience. She wishes she could get away, retreat once more underneath her floral duvet and never ever surface. "Oh… of course…" she flounders, "yes, I'll help… in any way I can…"

In other rooms a shout goes up. The legs of chairs are pulled back and make scratches on the floor. What do they think they're doing, Delia wonders? This lot show flagrant disregard for what's appropriate and they'll spoil the parquet if they're not too careful.

"Da-a-ancing!" sings the voice of an exuberant ex-husband, and loud music pumps out of a distant stereo.

We have to question whether this would be a fitting tribute even for a person who never knew how to behave.

"Yes, I promise we'll talk later… but not now," gasps Delia, who through ostensible compliance manages to shake Diana off. "Not here… I'll pay my last respects and then I'll meet you in that café down the road… a little heartburn… glass of water… yes, that's what I need…" She clutches at her glass and reels towards the hubbub in the other room. She stumbles, has to put her hand against the wall and makes her way towards the kitchen, almost crawling. The route is blocked by colours, by the swirling bodies of the other mourners. They keep on shifting, changing their configurations, make the house much harder to negotiate. It's wild, she thinks, disorganised and dangerous.

"Deeee-liiiii-ahhhh!"

All of a sudden she's clasped around her sturdy middle and swept into the heart of rioting. She's caught without consent, is dizzied, dangled and unbalanced. Somewhere in a darkened corner of her mind the hazy notion lurks that it's the Catholic husband who has swept her off her feet.

It's such a pity. This would be the stuff of Delia's dreams if horrid knots of indigestion hadn't soured the sweetness of the moment.

An anxious stab goes from her jaw down to her abdomen. She tries to force her lips to smile but only manages to bare her teeth as she is twirled around the centre of the room.

The blurry grin of Mr Tombleson whirls by time and again.

A hungry circle forms around the dancing pair. It stamps and claps and jeers, but Delia hardly notices at all. She grimaces and coughs and staggers. The crowd assumes that all her frowns, her scowls, the ugly twists, contortions of her face, are triggered only by embarrassment.

"She always was uncomfortable in social situations," heckles Mr Locke, and everyone who hears him laughs.

No one thinks the pain is punishing. Unable to imagine her destruction, they think it's funny that she's forced to put on a performance when she's clearly so distressed.

The dance is shattered by a glass deep at its core. Delia's hands are limp and far away. The schooner slips between her fingers and its shards bounce up from the parquet, turn a caper to a blood-sport with the nasty threat of cuts to any ankle that's nearby.

The crowd which has ignored her cries is now made helpless in the face of the attack. They stand by motionless and watch as Delia falls and falls. She hits the gap between the chairs and drops, a heavy price to pay.

"For fuck's sake," are her last three words.

The room is still.

It hums and blinks.

"You might call this a glitch," one of us whispers.

One Bull for a Burnt Offering

Outside, on the top step near the front door of Ruth's house, we regroup and watch the mourners drift off into public space. They came to celebrate a death but haven't got the stamina for two. "So what the hell just happened?" one of them is heard to ask.

No one has an answer.

Most of them don't know or don't care, more or less in equal measure.

They skulk away, troop down the steps, disperse along the street in both directions.

The rain has stopped but skies stay leaden. A thick grey quilt casts shadows over Combfoot Chase. God knows what it could hide because the clouds look heavy and malevolent. Any second there could be another downpour to make web-crawlers dive for cover. This avenue still boasts a tree so – if we need to – we can shelter there. It's one of very few which have survived the council's programme of inspection. A spokesperson on local radio announced that there would have to be a cull. He'd calculated forty per cent of trees across the town would have to go. He blamed ash dieback, said the council had no choice; they had to chop the whole lot down. Of course nobody likes it, he protested, but the trees pose risks to highway users. They might appear completely healthy on the outside, but if truth be told they're riddled with infection.

Combfootians are convinced the council uses the disease as an excuse to get rid of the trees. Without the trees nobody has to pay to sweep up leaves, nor will their branches be a threat to roofs and cars in winter storms. A questionnaire revealed that most inhabitants would guess that more than half the trees have gone already. Of course this estimate is an exaggeration, but we can see why they'd believe it. The stumps and emptiness along this road are obvious. One lonely tree remains, the solitary souvenir of what was once a grove. The tree stands close so if the rains do come we'll hide in there, climb up into its web of leaves and make sure that our hair stays dry.

"We've not lost everything, though, have we?" I dare say at last. "We've found out quite a lot of data and we've got new information stored." I'm trying to be positive, but the rest of us look doubtful. We're not sure if the details we've collected will be any use now Delia is dead. How can a lifeless profile help us shape an animated future? We've made mistakes beginning with a person who was obsolete. She's just the sort of character we're trying to replace. "We ought to look for someone younger and more with it," I suggest. "It can't be very hard." A lot of people make their lives available. The owners leave them lying round; it ought to be a breeze to pick one up, to get our setules onto someone else so they can carry us along.

As if to reaffirm our new growth mindset the clouds part and a patch of blue appears. It's tempting to believe the fallacy that the weather is intelligent, that it can know and understand our every thought and feeling. An aeroplane emerges from the haze. It's so far off it looks as though it's weightless. The benign dot floats across the sky, no longer part of this world down below. It's hard to fathom just how huge it is, to comprehend how powerful, to compute how much sulphur is emitted from its vapour trail.

Behind us the front door to Ruth's house bangs and gapes. Two bodies tumble out onto the steps. We recognise her children, the boy drunk, propped up by his sister.

"Oh, for Christ's sake, Mattie…" Brogan has been left to bear the weight of family and needs both hands to complete the job. She jettisons her heels and chucks them in a fit of anger to the bottom of the steps.

We scatter, would prefer it if we didn't end up skewered by stilettos.

Brogan groans and hoists her brother up. "Can you at least get yourself into the car? I couldn't park much closer… I know you're used to being carried, but you're not a baby… Jesus, why d'you have to get so shit-faced…?"

What luck, we think, and congratulate each other on an opportune encounter with some savvy kids who won't mind sharing.

*

The young so often get a bad press. In certain quarters of the media, they're labelled yobs and louts and thugs. You'd be forgiven if you thought that youth today hung out on corners and expressly looked for opportunities to cause the utmost trouble. *The Combfoot Chronicle* once ran a competition targeted at the older generation: spot three hoodies in a row, it urged, and you could win a camera. A brand-new digital affair, state-of-the-art with lots of buttons, dials, devices. We'd have given our eye teeth for that, especially as it had a really powerful zoom. In fact it went to Mr Tombleson, although he's never used it. He doesn't know what all the knobs are for and doesn't like to read instructions.

Although we don't believe there's nothing good about young people, Brogan's driving makes us wonder if there's any truth in claims they're inconsiderate. She puts her foot down, swoops out into traffic, follows speed with slamming on of brakes. We brace ourselves and close our eyes. If there's a crash, we think, it's better not to see it coming.

Her brother's in the back where she has strapped him in and shoved a plastic bag into his lap. "If you throw up, for God's sake, do it into that," she said.

To be honest we're beginning to regret our choice to sneak into her car. We've stowed ourselves in footwells, in the boot, in all the secret spaces where we won't be seen and no one will disturb us. A couple of us had a go at hiding in the glovebox, though it didn't work. It was too small and all our legs hung out. The rest then had to haul us out and only got us out of sight just in the nick of time, before Brogan climbed into the driver's seat. That was a close shave, no mistake. She bumped the engine into life and set off round the corners far too fast and far too frequently so all our stomachs turned a shade of green.

"It's not just Mattie who might need a sickbag," I said as a gag.

From my position on the parcel shelf I open half an eye and catch distorted glimpses as the town of Combfoot Chase speeds by. "It's funny," I say in a low voice to my colleague who's a little younger than I am, "but it wasn't very long ago you'd only have to pick up speed, go over forty, thirty maybe on a hot day, and there'd be insects splattered all over the windscreen. When you turned the wipers on their bodies smeared in arcs across the glass." I crane my neck, peek over Mattie's shoulder, sneak a look round Brogan's headrest. No, there's nothing, nada, nichts, nieko, not one small smudge of mangled leg, only some dust in corners where the wiper blades can't reach and dried-up winter leaves trapped in the pivot, flapping in the slipstream. "Where have all the bugs gone then?" I wonder to myself aloud. "Have they really disappeared or have they just got smart enough to stay out of the way?" It's odd that in a few short years they've vanished so completely. It's really very sobering.

My colleague looks at me as though he doesn't have the foggiest. "What *are* you on about?" he says.

I turn away and I close my eye again.

Soon we notice changes to the motion of the car. This, plus the duration of the journey – too long, however long it is – makes us think that we've probably reached the motorway. Now the car will hurtle round the outskirts of the town, will make its way towards the modern block where Brogan rents a little flat. In fact, we realise, she lives not so far from Mr Tombleson. His house is just a bridge away from hers, though he and Brogan don't share social circles and we're pretty sure they never get together.

It's often quicker if you use the bypass and avoid the ins and outs of Combfoot Chase. The town was built for horses and its narrow streets can't cope with modern day-to-day congestion. All the residential roads stand double-parked and drivers have to squeeze between the vehicles, blindly hope they'll miss the wing mirrors on either side. It's common to spend more time waiting or reversing than in going forwards, though this fact doesn't inhibit Brogan, who shows an utter disregard for other travellers. She occupies the outside lane, clings to the bumper of the car in front – an ugly Nissan – and nudges out towards the central reservation in a bid to peer around its rump. She flashes all her lights and bangs her knuckles in frustration on the steering wheel. "You bastard road hog!" she exclaims.

We note her dicey style and recommend that it's reflected in a raised insurance premium. Such poor performance makes us question if there's something other than a dead mum on her mind, especially when we take into consideration the conversation that she'd had last night with Mattie and her father when they'd been told that Ruth had left them both a bit of money.

"Quite a sum, in fact," her dad had said, though he'd been downing whisky at the time and Brogan's not sure if it would be daft to take him literally. Mum was both a spendthrift and a teacher. There's not a cat's chance she'd have managed to be rich. She'd watched Dad gulp his drink and raise his empty tumbler, turn it upside down and place it on his head. A solitary drop of whisky had made its way along his parting, traced a route across his forehead, then lost itself amongst his eyebrow hairs. Dad had cackled. What a twat. And anyway, what did he mean by 'quite a sum'? The term is vague and mightn't mean enough to make a difference, particularly split between herself and bloody Mattie. Brogan wishes she were home and on her own, so she could think it through in solitude.

Brogan's flat is nothing to write home about, one bedroom and a balcony which isn't noted for its scenery – unlike the house of Mr Tombleson and all his wealthy neighbours, who have great views of the river. No, this flat faces quite the other way, enjoys a panoramic view of all the traffic on the motorway. To be fair this does mean she gets it cheaper. If Brogan rented on the other side where the apartments enjoy vistas of the older part of town, she'd have to shell out several hundred more. Perhaps, she thinks, Mum's money will enable her to move to a location where she doesn't feel like such a loser? Or to buy the one she's in and get a proverbial foot upon a rung? It's an appealing thought, although she warns herself she mustn't get her hopes up. No one in their twenties catches breaks these days.

The traffic on the motorway grinds to a halt. All three lanes are chock-a-block with no way forward, no way back. Brogan snarls in irritation. She's in a hurry, wants to scoot around the flat, decide if it is worthy of investment. There'd been a letter from the landlord last week which suggested she might like to buy, but when she'd seen the asking price it had so many noughts she'd not considered it, had put the letter straight into the bin. She wants a lot, but at a price she can afford. Well, perhaps today might mark a change in fortune. Fingers crossed she hasn't taken out the binbag, can dig down beneath the plastic packages and fag-ends, find the letter, take another look. Whatever she might do with it, she thinks, the money will be put to better use than would've been the case if Mum had lived. She'd just have wasted it on books or fancy clothes, and would've gone too frequently on lavish holidays.

Or given it to Mattie, who is useless.

"But you don't *need* my help, my darling," Ruth had said the one time Brogan had been bold enough to ask her for a sub. "You're such a coper. Always have been." Mattie, on the other hand, would only have to blink and Mum would give him almost anything. "Just to get him on his feet, my darling…"

Brogan glances at her brother in the rear-view mirror. He's fast asleep, head back, mouth open, seatbelt cutting lines into his cheek. Everything is always handed to him on a plate. Poor Mattie, five years younger, needing incubation. Brogan hadn't planned to bring her brother home with her, would rather not hang out with someone floppy and pathetic. A mummy's boy, he'd always lapped up the attention, had spent today in mournful poses angled at preposterous spinsters at the wake. Such women seemed to think that death was harder on a man. And none had had a thought to spare for her. If Mattie thought there was a chance she'd give her bedroom up, then he could think a-bloody-gain. For one night only she would let him stay, but he'd not get one step beyond the sofa.

His presence sends her evening plans awry and it's a crying shame. Last night, when cooped up in the unchanged setting of her childhood bedroom, she'd plucked up courage and had sent a private message to a girl she knew from work whose name was Ava. *Can you come tomorrow night?* she'd said. She'd tried to play it cool, had worked on Ava's instinct for commiseration. *It's bound to be a bloody awful day…* She'd lain back in the narrow bed and conjured up a medley of dark intimacies. Yesterday her night-time fingers had been limited to toying with the Ava of imagination, but today she'd hoped for access to an actual body, one delicate and ripe, alive and lined with warm and humming blood, spread-eagled and available. She'd let herself explore the possibilities of flesh, then afterwards, once she had hollowed out each tiny bone, she'd thought she would be liberal and buy them both Chinese. The news of an inheritance has made her generous. "I'll pay for it," her future-self will say to mind's-eye Ava. "It's my treat and you deserve it, darling."

All that's now up the spout, of course, since Dad has charged her with the care of Mattie.

The wake had fallen still. Delia had dropped, a stone in water, and the circled crowd had rippled out, had distanced itself from the body.

Dad had shoved his hands deep down into his pockets and insisted loudly that he hadn't touched the woman, though everybody knew in fact he had.

"Of course you didn't, Adrian," Mr Locke had said.

An official-looking woman in a charcoal-coloured suit had stepped up, taken over, ushered everyone out of the house, and Dad had looked relieved, though it was obvious he hadn't got the faintest clue who she might be or why she might be there.

We remember that she'd squatted down and Delia was shielded from our view so she could twitch her final twitch in private. That was very disappointing as we'd hoped to see if real life measures up to snuff.

Brogan also thinks about Diana's crouch and how it stretched the grey skirt taut, and how the fabric rode up just enough to show the shape of muscled calves and brawny thighs, the evidence of one-too-many plyometric lunges. Brogan hadn't taken any notice of the woman through the day, though she had seen her idling by the sideboard, had thought her just another partial stranger come to ogle. But she's glad she had that glimpse of thigh, is grateful someone else took charge and no one called on her to shine a light in Delia's empty eyes.

"Just get Matt out of here, please, will you?" Dad had pleaded. She could tell he'd had a lot of sherry because his eyes were bloodshot and his words had come out slurry. "Can't you take him back to yours? Oh, what a frigging mess…"

It's not that Brogan wanted to have stayed. Another night surrounded by the past – albeit one that's feathered with the sweet figment of Ava – was better to be missed. And Dad had no desire to keep her either. He might not clear her room, nor take down all the posters from the days when she would buy a magazine and tear the pages out, but Brogan doesn't kid herself that that's a sign of mawkish sentiment. Dad isn't hanging on; he simply can't be bothered to dispose of her, just as he keeps ancient jars of pickles at the back of kitchen cupboards and will never erase any of his emails. Oh yes, she'd wanted very much to go, just wanted not to have to go with Mattie.

She'd made excuses, tried to wriggle out of obligation. "We've got an early call tomorrow," she'd complained. "They've done the get-in and they need me for the technical."

The failure of this protest was predictable. Dad had only arched an eyebrow. The theatre was indulgence, at the very best expendable. All arts were interchangeable in triviality and Brogan disappointed insofar as she'd refused to work in something cyber, information-based or scientific.

"*Medea*," she had pleaded. "The production is Euripides' *Medea*." She'd hoped the classics would suggest the discipline, tradition and rote-learning that she thought her father valued in an education.

In spite of this he hadn't been impressed. "It can't be more important than your brother, Brogan," he'd said pointedly, as though he'd always acted in the best interests of family.

He's a selfish shit, but she'd submitted to his wishes nonetheless. She'd loaded sottish Mattie in the backseat of her car, had dutifully driven him away. A daughter knows she ought to do exactly what she's told and is allowed to seethe only in secret.

It's five to four. The get-in will be finishing and then the company will turn its mind to getting in the drinks. They'll gather in The Cock and Bull, the pub of choice because its beer is bargain-basement and it's not far from the theatre. Soon Ava will be scooching down a bench and making space for Jason or some other bovine actor who has idled in the wings all day, has hung around and reeked of animal. If not for gridlock Brogan would have put her foot down, whizzed past all the cameras, intervened before a man could get a predatory paw on Ava.

At this point I decide to turn all our equipment off.

"What d'you do that for?" one of us demands. "That was starting to get interesting."

"We need to think before we go much further," I prevaricate. "They'll brand us parasites and ask us tricky questions."

"*And?*" she says. She's brazen, that one, you have to give her that. While I'm in knots about the ethics, worrying about a trail of sleaze and illegality, she'll get the job done, blow the lid off all my scruples.

"It's better if no one notices," I say. "It's better if we wait, lie low and play a longer game."

The look I get tells me my colleague's not convinced. She'd rather know it all and simply pay the price for everything we know.

*

Mattie's sprawled across the sofa. He's asleep, one arm flung high above his head. Bacteria are working hard to break down perspiration, so when we creep up close to him we have to hold our noses. Someone should have turned the heating down, or thrown the blankets off, or got him out of yesterday's old clothes.

Brogan is already up and in the park. We have to say that we're impressed by that. Last night she raided her emergency supplies and found a bottle of cheap brandy, enough loose change to buy a pack of cigarettes. She and Mattie drank the brandy out of mugs and twenty fag-ends stink in saucers on the floor. She woke up with no memory of getting into bed, not knowing if she'd even cleaned her teeth but with a taste like somebody had emptied half the bin into her mouth. In spite of this she's gone to join the theatre's nodding donkeys for their early-morning workout by the duck pond.

These sessions are run by one of the actors, Jason, who insists they ought to do it every day. He says the actor's body is the main tool of performance and has recently begun to film these workouts for his YouTube channel. There isn't any need for us to go. We've already subscribed and one of us will don some legwarmers and watch the session later when we've nothing else to do.

As stage manager Brogan has no reason to expect her body will appear on stage, but she's keen to join the workout anyway. She likes to keep up the illusion that the company is social. Her true motivation is the fact that Ava will be there and she wants to watch the actress limber up. On frosty mornings such as this her nose will stick out from her hood, a little naked beak. It will glow red as it grows cold. Brogan likes to look at Ava's nose and wonder what it would be like to warm it up. It's desperate, but you have to take whatever you can get and try to satisfy yourself the best you can.

Before she left the flat she wrote a note for Mattie and attached the times of all the trains which leave the station in the morning. *See you sometime,* she had scrawled, then, *You've got lectures to get back to, I expect.* She hopes he's gone before she gets home, doesn't want to talk to him again, has nothing more to say about the bloody dissolution of her family. Any details needing more discussion can be handled by solicitors.

We took a photo of that note and stored it carefully inside the same file where we've kept our records of the boy's first term at university. He's the sort who makes a good impression – a crawler just like us. When his tutor called him to her office with the bleak task of informing him about his mother's death, she'd been relieved that he had demonstrated a degree of self-control, had only shown appropriate levels of distress. The tutor had felt sorry for him, had thought it sad that one so young should lose a parent, had hoped he'd find someone to mother him now that his actual mother was factually dead.

Brogan, on the other hand, has no need whatsoever of another mother. She heads straight back to work, tries to forget the sticky silk of family which attempts to trap her. *Medea* is a strange play, but she likes it. Filicide had been a shock at first, but now she understands the instincts which could lead someone to take revenge. She sees how murdered sons might be the choice of hemmed-in women.

When we finally catch up with her, we're forced to dodge the kicks she's aiming at a skirting board. Her anger's caused by Ava, who ignored her at this morning's session in the park. The online footage shows a girl absorbed in tricep-dips and squats. It's clear to anyone who cares to view it that she didn't stop or notice Brogan, that her eyes were firmly trained on Jason. We'd say Brogan did a fair job of pretending to feel nothing. She turned away and squinted at the glass walls of the tower which borders one edge of the park and houses capital and finance businesses in Combfoot Chase. The tower's monumental, brutal as it hits the pavement and then marches to the sky. Brogan's face is hidden in the video, but it's clear that Ava's treatment made her furious, especially as she's always been profuse in her support.

"This play will be your big break," she's reported to have said last week, and slung a reassuring arm around Ava's uncertain shoulders. "*Medea*'s gonna be the making of you. No one cares the theatre looks a little dingy and depressing."

She's right that there's no buzz of glamour here, no lights to blaze a well-known name or herald famous faces on this stage. The only entrance to the theatre is a doorway snared between a shop stuffed full of branded garish plastic and a takeaway fast-food chain selling chicken by the bucket. Is this really the best that Combfoot Chase has got to offer? We hope for Ava's sake that shabby paintwork doesn't matter and that no one notices if their shoes stick to the spilled drinks on the carpet in the foyer.

Brogan's kicks scuff off more flakes of ancient paint. They lie conspicuously white against the darkness of the carpet. Brogan steps on them, grinds them underneath her heel until they're crushed to powder. The particles sink out of sight between the fibres of the pile. She hangs her hoodie – sweaty, smelly after prancing round the park – inside the kiosk. A sign above claims this is the location of the box office, but the same space has to act as cloakroom and a hat-check stand for those who are pretentious and still come to theatre in a hat. We can't see anything inside the booth except a coat rail which boasts a range of mismatched hangers and the floor is scattered with the ticket stubs of previous productions. Brogan knows she has to clear this up before the previews and the press night. The task is written on her list, but till she's actually obliged to do it then she won't be making any effort.

We follow her into the auditorium. In one short day the space has been transformed and Corinth has been built in combinations of white columns and a looming stair, a sketch in modules, a city out of nothing. The plans we've seen show how it's meant to work, how pillars or a flight of steps can truck, can take up new positions to suggest each change of scene. It's very clever, quite remarkable how once it's all in place the ugly functions disappear and leave only the illusion that it's beautiful. We'd not expected that, and even Brogan stops to take a breath.

Ava standing centre in a blood-red dress. She lifts her arms and turns, a slow rotation as lights rise and fall across the stage. A black spot fills, then empties and a cry of 'Heads!' rings out, alerts those down below to all the business of the rigging up above. We glance between the girl alight, the other lurking in the gloom and register the full force of a secret urge, so silent and invisible.

"Don't people pair up all the time?" one of us whispers. "Couldn't Fate be made to bring these two together?"

For many hopeless matters gods arrange.

I smile but shake my head towards my colleague. He's older and inclined to be a little too romantic. "Sometimes it's much better to do nothing," I contend.

Brogan collects a clipboard from backstage and starts her checks. Are trucks and treads all set correctly? Tick. And sandbags used to weight the lines? Is carpet laid to muffle footfall in the wings? Tick, tick. Uh-oh, she stalls. She's found a snag. One column isn't firmly clamped. She makes a note and moves on, tick, tick, tick. All day she waits and watches in the rising dark, will call out only when a problem must be solved. She can accept that Ava's lost but only when she's disappeared into her character, when she becomes Medea in a distant past where myth and truth have merged, and where she waits for Jason and their mutual destruction.

At last the actors reach their final marks. Ava high up on a column, two doll-bodies cradled in her arms, Jason on the ground where tragedies unfold. The ending of *Medea* is uneasy, full of wailing and confusion once the corpses have been carried on. If Brogan has learnt anything from Ruth's death, it's that real life doesn't send an ending when expected, not when everyone is ready and the tension has been built up in advance. But, she hopes, it's possible beginnings can come quickly too.

The final blackout, then a sudden unexpected interruption. Just a bleep. A screen lights up, up-lights a face within a chair somewhere a few rows from the front. Who's this who breaks the rhythm and the rules, who dares to take a seat before they've put their phone on silent and concealed it in a pocket or a bag?

The blue gleam casts an eerie light on Mattie.

"Sorry, sorry," he begins to bumble. "Let me just… that's it. I've turned it off."

"You cock," says Brogan.

Nearby actors snigger. No, don't worry, these ones aren't important, so you can relax. You don't need to remember everyone.

Ava perches docile on her pillar.

Jason squints into the dark and frowns.

Someone in the lighting box takes the initiative and puts the houselights up.

Brogan leaves the wings, heads downstage and squares up to blushing Mattie from the apron. "Why d'you come here?" she demands, then turns to Ava and the others. "I promise you, I didn't say he could."

Mattie looks up, waves apologetically, then sweeps his hand to lift his heavy fringe. "So sorry, sorry, everyone," he calls out. "I didn't think… and didn't mean to interrupt." He won't admit to anyone that he was sad and on his own, and when he'd woken to a wrecked flat he couldn't think of anywhere he'd rather go. "I only came to see where you were working," he says to Brogan, "and no one locked the door…"

"Piss off. We're busy." Brogan turns her back, but not before she sees the fluttered glance that goes from Ava to her brother. It's just a look, a beat, it's almost nothing, almost imperceptible, yet Brogan sees it's something, a beginning of communication passing from the column to the chair. A meaning flickers into life and nothing, nothing now can ever be the same. "You fucking cock," she says again. Mattie will take everything from her, she thinks, by simple consequence of being. What began with Mum will continue with the doleful flapping of his lashes towards Ava.

If she's fully taken on the message of *Medea*, Brogan could set out to seek revenge. Emotion should enable her to do things she wouldn't dream of in her usual state. We're quite excited, want to see what happens next. No doubt there'll be a ruction like in stories that are written for the television. We've soaked up all the skandi-plots, the noir in all the soaps and dramas, have never come across a plot where principals just shrug and walk away. That wouldn't make a satisfying ending, though it's true we're still at the beginning. We've got a long, long way to go before we reach the end.

"I think we ought to do something," my older partner says.

"Maybe you're right," I say.

"We can't," our female colleague says. "We're only here to gather information. We have to look as though we're innocent."

The most we can concede is that a certain younger person in our party might have accidentally brushed against that unclamped column. We were in a scramble to conceal ourselves because rehearsals had come to an end and there were people everywhere. It's possible he might have tripped or stumbled, but we will deny most categorically that anybody planned for it to topple. It's hard to prove intent and we can argue that it can't be down to us because we're far too small. It would take more strength than we've got to fell a great white shaft like that.

Later Brogan will admit she was surprised because her brother did precisely nothing. He must have seen the pillar as it fell, she'll say, and should've noticed there was danger. She'll speculate he should have had the time to get out of the way, although things happened very fast. Jason, for example, rolled away from underneath the column's path and left the scene unscathed, so why not Mattie? But her brother only raised his hands above his head and that was not enough to save him. Brogan will inform the inquest that she's no idea at all why he had failed to act, will wonder if it signifies that no one has the right to change their future.

In fact he simply thought the column wasn't tall enough to reach him. He made a calculation and he got it very wrong.

From her bird's-eye view above the stage, Ava gapes in horror and clutches tightly to the bodies of her dead doll-children.

Cast the Same Hour into the Midst

"Quick, over here!" We dash outside and make ourselves look inconspicuous. We're masters of disguise so watch the company leave unobserved.

One by one the actors and the crew are told that they can go.

Jason is the first to slope away. We note the skin around his mouth is bluish and his forehead clammy, so come to the conclusion that he's shaken by what's happened and predict he'll find it hard to free himself of guilt. No one really gets away unharmed. It's natural to reproach yourself if you have dodged a pillar when someone else did not. He'll set himself a strict programme of exercise and try to get his head around the reasons why he's saved. He leaves the theatre, makes a turning to the left. He's heading back towards the park, will run ten laps around the lake and only then admit – in some far corner of his mind – that he's quite glad to be alive.

In contrast Brogan and the lighting crew will head off to the right. They'll cross the road and drown their sorrows in The Cock and Bull.

"You coming with us, Ava?" one of them will ask. They'll poke their head into her dressing room but quickly pull back with a mind perturbed. They'll tell the others that she'd stood unmoving in a puddle of discarded dress. "I did invite her, but she said she'd sent a message to a friend, to someone she called Grace. Apparently she's made some other plan."

Please come and get me. I can't face this on my own.

"Well, that's all right then," they'll convince each other, though they'll hang around a while before they go. They'll wait until they witness the arrival of a woman. She's well-dressed and looks business-like. She'll scoop up Ava, whisk her off. And then there'll be no point in waiting anymore and so they'll go and let the frosted saloon doors click-clack and close behind their gloomy group.

In the pub Brogan will drink a bucket-load of gin before she slips up and says out loud that with her brother gone Ruth's money will be hers in its entirety. "Oh, bloody hell," she'll gloat. "It's possible I might be able to afford my flat!"

The crew – though drunk – will still be stunned into uneasy silence. They'll quickly write her faux-pas off as one provoked by grief. "It's all right, Bro," they'll say, "we know that you don't really mean it."

"But I do," she'll think, though she's astute enough to not say any more. She'll nod and somebody will pat her arm in sympathy and buy her yet another drink.

And so the company quits the theatre and the scene of Mattie's death.

Each member walks straight past us. Not a single person notices we're leaning on a nearby lamppost. I've struck a pose as though I'm waiting for a bus. Or perhaps a date. Or maybe for a likely candidate to mug. It doesn't matter just as long as I give off the vibe that I've no interest whatsoever in the people exiting the theatre. Another of us has turned up his collar and tugged down the brim of his old trilby hat. Another lights a cigarette and leaks her loose-lipped smoke in lazy loops. Another whistles a familiar tune.

"Oh, I know that one," I say.

"What is it then?" he asks.

"No. No, it's gone. Or I've forgotten."

"Far too new for you," he says.

"Oh no, I've definitely heard it," I insist. I shake out this week's newspaper and hold it high to hide my face. Quite by chance it opens on *The Chronicle*'s obituary pages, the town's last word on all its citizens. A double-spread of careful tributes catalogues all those who have departed Combfoot Chase. Half a column has been dedicated to the memory of Ruth – she made a big impression on this town – and underneath a few lines make a passing reference to Delia.

Once we're satisfied that every member of the company's accounted for, we head into the chicken shop next door. We won't wait for Mattie's body to be carried out. We've seen a corpse before, and one more won't make any difference. And besides, we're hungry.

The chicken shop has had a recent refurb. The name has changed, although the logo's stayed substantially the same. You don't now have to queue but simply pick a table and make sure you know its number when you order at an interactive screen. In due course someone in a plastic cap and mask and gloves will bring you all your food. You're no longer obliged to stand and talk to someone at a counter. We're glad because we'd rather not look anybody in the eye. On the screen are images of different buckets. You can choose from different sizes, different combinations of the secret herbs and spices. We sniff the stubborn scent of bouillon and boiling oil, can't wait to sink our teeth into a meaty leg. And how about some fries, a vat of fizzy drink to go with that, the screen suggests? No, thanks. We'll keep it simple, just the eight legs in a bucket. So you press the picture. Wow, like magic, every wish fulfilled and all your chicken dreams delivered. You only have to wait a minute; all things come to those who wait. You're promised everything you want, as long as you want chicken.

We gather round a table like the monsters of low culture. Having spent the day amongst the heightened language of *Medea* we put our feet up and indulge in easy, mundane conversation.

"Well, at least the rain has passed…"

"The forecast says another front is on the way…"

"It's only what you might expect this time of year…"

"It's mild, though, isn't it, for the end of January?"

We're not unusual. We've noticed that most people here in Combfoot Chase prefer to talk about the weather than great art. It's unpredictable enough to help them overcome their social inhibitions. As topics go it's easy to exhaust, though, so we're glad when buckets come and we can eat instead of talk.

I'm halfway through my second leg when I spy Ava and her friend, Grace, through the window. Ava buckles and her friend is forced to prop her up and let her wet the shoulder of her green, expensive coat. She holds on tight. Her fingers pat out gentle gestures that are meant to say, *It's all right, 'cos I'm here now and I've got your back.* I'm touched. It's nice to see that Ava has a friend who'll show her some affection, because not everyone is granted that these days.

"You wouldn't think they'd cast her as Medea," I say, and nod towards the scene unfolding on the street.

My colleagues turn to watch a rare display of tenderness.

"You're right, she's far too young, and much too soft."

"She doesn't look like she could be that single-minded."

"It's all an act, though, isn't it?"

"She'd have to understand the part to play it so convincingly."

"Nah, she'd just use imagination. People fake things all the time."

"Why'd a young girl want to play a part like that? It's not very attractive…"

We all agree Medea's not a very sympathetic character.

"Perhaps she wanted to improve her range?"

"I don't get why she'd kill her own kids, though."

"That's just what's written – it's a story, made-up, no one actually believes it."

We know that that's an overstatement, that everything is true these days, especially when it's not.

"Oh, look, they're coming in," I say.

"Oh, crap, they mustn't see us." My young colleague ducks beneath the table.

"Don't be daft," I say. I'm feeling bolder. "Why don't we reach out, offer overtures of friendship?"

"No, we can't do that!"

"It's far too soon."

"Oh no, I'd say the timing's absolutely perfect. And all we have to do is hold our hand out and be kind."

"She won't accept."

"We've not gone far enough."

"You're wrong. They're used to us already."

If they stop and look around my colleagues will discover that the other people in the chicken shop show no qualms whatsoever at our presence. They insert earbuds, set their eyes on smartphone screens and gobble, absently discard the bony relics of their meals into an empty bucket. No one sees us and we all know monsters only pop up in the eyes of a beholder.

"No one's looking," I say. "Not at us, at any rate."

Ava, who is pushed into the chicken shop by an insistent Grace, flaps her head out of her hood and shows a face of make-up massacred by tears. The friend prepares to fend off ogling strangers, has defensive phrases ready on her lips: "What d'you think you're gawping at? Why don't you mind your beeswax? Have you not seen anyone upset before?" so is surprised when no one bats an eyelid.

"See?" I say.

Grace scans the room. No tables left. The indoor species might be very different from the outdoor type, but with a cold snap you'll find everyone inside.

"There's nowhere we can sit, Grace," Ava gulps, the problem insurmountable.

I don't wait. "Join us, please," I say. "We're almost finished. You can have our table."

Ava doubts.

Grace comes a little closer. "Thank you. Are you sure? That's very kind," she says. She drapes her coat over the proffered seat and doesn't stop to look too closely at who's sitting next to her.

"No trouble. None at all," I say, and shuffle up, make room. "When you order, this is table number four," I add.

"Right. Thanks. You'll come and choose?" Grace asks, but Ava shakes her head.

"Just get me anything," she says.

Grace sighs and goes to order on her own. She worries for her friend, who tends to think the whole wide world's connected and it makes her too afraid to touch a screen. Ava holds the view that anything invented in a flat plane must eventually – inevitably – be brought to life. She veers away from virtual worlds – fears freaks and beasts can get her even there – and wants to hang on to conventions of reality. Unlike the others in the chicken shop, her phone is soon discarded on the table. It remains untouched whilst Ava folds her fingers one by one into an agitated ball.

"You okay there?" we ask.

She replies, "Not bad."

We know her answer's not sincere, but neither was the question.

"I got us chicken," Grace says as she drops into the chair.

Ava squeezes blood out of her knuckles.

Grace rests one hand over Ava's in a vain attempt to cover up her suffering. "So what d'you reckon then? What d'you think you're gonna do?"

"I don't know, though I'm thinking I could use a fresh start," Ava says.

A scoop, a scoop! No need to hack the voicemail when folk talk things through so openly.

"For what it's worth, I think you're nuts."

"You do? Why's that?"

"You've only ever wanted to be an actor. All your life. You've wanted it for longer than I've known you, so it doesn't make much

50

sense to me, that when at last you're getting somewhere, you decide to chuck it in…"

Ava stares at Grace's hand as though she's spotted Jesus in a piece of toast. No hand, she thinks, is safe enough. No one's really able to protect you from a fall.

"…and it's not as if you even knew him, did you?" Grace thinks her friend's empathy's vicarious. She really should get over it. "It's just plain stupid if you quit a title role…"

She's probably right, thinks Ava, but she sees a pattern, chases meanings. Instinct tells her that a life crushed ought to signal something. "Anyway, I expect they'll cancel the production…" she suggests.

"They might, but then again they haven't yet." Grace sits back, pulls her hand away and cruelly folds her arms. "You always said you wanted some excitement," she says. "Now you've got it, haven't you?"

Ava plummets, hides behind closed eyes. "I should've done something to stop it," she whispers, wraps her arms around her body, stretches them as far as they will go.

I make a note to send her ads for pick-me-ups. She's ready for a pamper box, a card that says, *Life's tough, but so are you!*

"Like what?" asks Grace. "What d'you think you could have done? Stuck on another pillar, miles away, you should be grateful that it wasn't any other column falling, that you didn't end up with an injury yourself or killed to boot."

An unseen worker sets a bucket on the table in between them. Ava doesn't move but watches all the little barbs of Grace's teeth break through the breadcrumbs, tug a string of tissue from a bone.

"I s'pose you do know that you're talking nonsense?" Grace says, swallows, licks the fat from off her lips.

"All I know is that I can't do it again."

"So what d'you think you'll do instead?"

"Dunno. I'll get some other job, I s'pose."

Ava thinks to get a job is easy, and that people should have influence over the course of their own lives. A quick search pulls up local stats – twelve thousand workless households here in Combfoot Chase. A decent job's like hens' teeth in these parts. She's lucky that I've overheard and take the opportunity to cast away my copy of *The Chronicle*. The ads for jobs – by happenstance – lie upwards and in open view. It isn't difficult to make her take the bait. She reaches out and slides *The Chronicle* towards her.

"Honestly, I don't care. I'll do anything," she says.

Grace picks a fist of fried and twisted twigs and pushes them into her mouth. "Most jobs these days will ask for some experience in cyber…" she begins.

"I'll learn, work hard, retrain, get up to speed." Ava's phone's already in her hand. She plucks a random number from the paper and converts it to a dual-tone multi-frequence signal. "Hello? Yes, I've seen your advert…" The call is brief, just long enough for Ava to confirm a date and time. The twittered timbre of the woman on the phone implies she's dealing with somebody on another line, that this call couldn't be more inconvenient. "You got a pencil?" Ava mouths.

I push one over, watch her scribble on a corner of the paper. Her hand is firm and clear but leaves the ovals open so I know that she believes in ghosts.

She compensates for her untimely call by being overly polite. "That's perfect," she coos down the line. "At three o'clock. Yes, thank you. I'll be there." She throws the phone down on the table and sits back, looks up at Grace, triumphant. "See?" she says. "It's not so hard. I've got myself an interview."

Grace runs her tongue around her mouth. "They didn't ask for any details," she says. "Don't get your hopes up. You can't expect a job like that to carry any weight."

"I'm not the same as you," says Ava. "I'll be glad not to be noticed for a while." She gives my paper back. "Thanks very much," she says.

I tear the corner off and slip it in my pocket. I can't risk making any more mistakes. We mustn't turn up at the wrong place or the wrong time, and Treasury Row is not a road we know. It must be in the old town on the far side of the river, so we'll have to look it up. We'll punch the destination into Maps and let that calculate our quickest and our most efficient route.

We slide down from the table, grab our coats and leave with all the usual inanities. "Goodbye," we say, "good luck with looking for that job."

"Yeah, thanks again for sharing," Grace replies, and I see glimpses of leftover chicken mashed with ketchup in between her teeth.

"You're very welcome." I smile as we sidle off towards the door.

"See you tomorrow, then." The older one of us is putting on his trilby and forgets that Grace and Ava don't know who we are, nor how much we're around these days.

"You what?" Ava frowns. It's possible she'll meet us once again, she knows. In small towns it's quite usual to bump into the same people, the same crowd, see the same face crop up on a stranger on a bus. Your habits mean you rarely change the pattern of your day as long as all your needs are met and coincidence is nothing more than other people's routines having intersections with your own. But unlikely it should happen very quickly, not as soon as by tomorrow, she is sure.

"They didn't mean it," Grace says as she's keen for Ava not to worry anymore. "It just slipped out. They said it by mistake."

None of us dare breathe again until we've stepped outside the door. Phew, we think, that cut things pretty close. But we were lucky and we now know where we'll be going next.

Tomorrow, then. To Treasury Row.

*

The streets are narrow here and the buildings dark and tightly packed. They lean in, hold each other up. It's rickety for all it's very quaint. The council ought to put some pictures of these streets up on their website, show them off, we think. If we'd known Combfoot Chase could look like this we'd have come sooner. With a close-up of a lintel and an image of these jostling bricks or windows squeezed in under heaving eaves, the town could be on tourist trails in no time, inundated, if they sold the place as somewhere nothing happens, nothing changes. There's a market for that sort of thing and people like to holiday in towns which claim to be historic. It gives them faith that no one can do any lasting harm.

Ava steps down from the bus. A piece of paper in her hand is criss-crossed with the lines of frequent folding and unfolding, so much so that it threatens to disintegrate. She knows what she has written on it off by heart but stops to check it anyway, can just make out directives to proceed to number 30, three o'clock.

She kids herself she'll like it here. Old-fashioned, dull simplicity is the order of the day and unremarkable routine exactly what she wants. She pictures a new version of herself, stationed at a designated desk with window blinds to shut out too much sun or too much rain, a handy strip-light substituted, no one very much concerned if flickers might affect her eyes, her brain. There'll be a stipulated time to take her lunch, she thinks, a half an hour, never more nor less – no taking five because she wants to – and best of all no more surprises, all the minutes between nine and five kept in their proper place and followed in their proper order.

She halts before a thin door wedged above two steps. *Urquhart's Solicitors* is painted in chipped letters across the square panes of a window to her right. "Yes, this can be my backwater," she thinks.

This comment strikes us as a little too self-conscious. Too strong a whiff of tragedy to suit our tastes. We'd better take it as an affirmation, as a bid to beat persistently self-sabotaging thoughts.

She lifts the dolphin knocker, lets it fall.

This place of work is not the kind of place where you can activate the lighting with a voice command. We only recognise the room behind the door is meant to be an office because it's furnished with a desk, a filing cabinet and a row of chairs, but even so it still looks very like the drawing room it once had been. Whoever Urquhart is he's only got one foot in modern times. We peg him as the type to run his business as it's always run, the type to think the past is good enough and doesn't need updating, the type to think that objects gather value simply by becoming old.

We look him up. He's not got a substantial online presence. The company does have a website, but it's no more that the outline of a homepage. When you click the link UNDER CONSTRUCTION pops up in a font we'd never recommend to anyone with any inclination to appear professional. The youngest in our party signals that it won't be easy to collaborate with someone who's not fond of gadgets, who shows no sign he's open to invention, innovation. I joke that we might spot a quill pen and a pot of ink poised on the desk but no. With some relief we clock instead an Amstrad CPC, an ancient printer grinding paper by the wall.

"Well, it's a start," I say. "Better than nothing, I suppose."

Ava enters, finds nobody there and crosses to the fireplace which dominates the best part of the facing wall. Its marble mantle is retained, although the grate has been removed, the chimney filled up with a monstrous cast-iron radiator. She stretches out her February fingers in anticipation of hot metal and warm air, is shocked to find that something which takes so much space could be allowed to stand stone cold. She puts her hands into her armpits, stamps her feet. In spite of a distinctly frosty welcome she decides this place is perfect, just the spot for her renaissance.

How curious, we think and wonder if – with time – we'd manage to grow fond of it ourselves. We like a beam, a crevice, nook or cranny just as much as anyone, and aren't old houses meant to look a little spooky? It's only what's appropriate. We'd oust that portrait in its gilded frame, though, if this place were ours. We couldn't look at that all day, some old bloke in a wig and gown who's glaring down at us, one fist a tight ball in his lap. A brass plaque tacked beneath the frame proclaims *His Honour, Peter Urquhart, Judge.* All rise! A man like that can make the sternest soul feel guilty. We cross our fingers Ava won't be interviewed by him and hope she knows that anyone she sees can't possibly be God.

"Should I call out?" she whispers.

There isn't any sign of life, except a telephone lies off the hook, emits a low and irritating whine.

"I'd wait," I say.

We queue up on the chairs and make-believe that we're potential clients.

The room gives off the smell of silvered damp. A band of broken flies is gathered on the windowsill. They all lie on their backs, their brittle legs stuck in the air. A patch of mould grows from one corner of the skirting board, creeps halfway up the wall. The paint has blistered, lifted, has begun to flake in fragile chunks. If you think Ava is put off by this, you're wrong. She tells herself it makes her feel at home. In the respect of flies and paint, then Urquhart's is exactly like the theatre.

"I'll just buy thermal underwear," she says, "if I do get the job."

"The answer's no," a voice decrees.

"I'm sorry?" Ava jumps.

It takes a moment to compute that this reply was not addressed to her. It issued from a round be-jumpered woman who has entered and is barking at the telephone. The woman clunks the handset back into its cradle, turns her glasses onto us, the tenants of the chairs.

"Milk bottle-bottoms," I think, then kick myself for being unoriginal.

"Can I help you?" It's impressive how the jumper swells up fuller when she speaks.

"Um, yes, please." Ava stands, holds out her piece of paper. "I've got an interview with Mr Urquhart. I was told to come at three?"

The bottle-bottoms swivel to a crooked wall-clock up above the desk. Its hands point five to three. We double check and are surprised to find the clock's precisely on the dot.

"You're early," snaps the woman. "Mr Urquhart isn't here."

Now that's unfair, we think. It's proper to be punctual when you want to make a good impression. We think that Ava's done exceptionally well, especially as she came by public transport which in Combfoot Chase is notorious for being unreliable.

"Oh, I s'pose I am, a little," Ava says, "though actors say ten minutes early is really bang on time…"

The bottled eyes revert to Ava. "We're never superstitious here," explains the mouth beneath the glasses, and it pinches to a circle.

From this Ava concludes that Mr Urquhart is habitually late. She considers whether she has ever met someone who's more significant than time before, decides it's probable she hasn't.

We look towards the portrait and wonder if the man will be as weighty in the flesh.

"It's not *that* Mr Urquhart," says the mouth. "The old one's dead, the more's the pity. It's his grandson, Edward, that you're here to see." Two hands stick out from jumper sleeves and pull a sheaf of papers from the filing cabinet, plonk them without ceremony on the desk.

Our youngest member pushes his specs up his nose and is about to launch into a pitch to tell this woman that the proper use of systems would enable her to free herself from paper, that a new computer or an upgrade of the hard drive and the RAM would make this office more efficient and productive, but a quick dig in the shin reminds him that he'd better keep his mouth shut. This is Ava's interview, not ours.

The jumper sits and bulges as the woman bends to review pages, perches bottle-bottoms on her head. The glasses watch us, even when the eyes do not. We force ourselves to sit still, not to fidget or to twitch. It's just some spectacles and an enormous jumper, we remind each other, so there's nothing to be scared of.

"She's probably wearing lots of layers to keep the cold out," Ava thinks.

It's generous to look at it like that. Our version ran along the lines of lonely spinster, middle-aged and overfed on custard. We'd assumed that – with no prospect of a sexual partner – she'd given up and let her waistline go. We might be right but understand it's better Ava doesn't think like that. She doesn't need to dwell on negatives, especially if she's serious about a job here.

The clock marks off another ten, then fifteen minutes.

Still no sign of Mr Urquhart.

Our ears acclimatise to ticking silence and we pick up rhythmic thumps and groans which growl deep down within the bowels of the building. Somewhere underneath the floorboards metal clangs on metal and a pipe which runs along the skirting board behind our chairs begins to glug and gurgle in a most peculiar fashion.

The jumper gets up from the desk – a skirt's attached and legs are too. It goes across the room to kick the pipe with forceful toe in robust shoe. The pipe qui-i-ivers, then falls silent. We listen more intently in the noisy hush.

What's that sound?

It's footsteps.

Mr Urquhart?

No.

A smudged young man appears as if from nowhere, takes a place beside the desk and wipes dirt from his hands with rags. We can't resist a sly glance and an elbow nudged in Ava's ribs. Ooh, cop a look at that, we smirk. There's muscle underneath that T-shirt. That's a body worthy of the firemen who post themselves on Facebook every Friday.

"Any joy?" The jumpered woman seems a little warmer and the circle of her mouth a little looser now this young man has appeared.

"I'll only say I've done me best here, Janet," he laments, and shrugs his shoulders. Oh, those shoulders. I can see my female colleague would just love to bite him right there in the deltoids. "Like I said to Mr Urquhart, nothing lasts forever, but I've done the best I can."

"You don't have to convince me, Daniel," says the woman whom we now know is called Janet. "I've been here and I've seen it. I've seen everything you've done." She takes the glasses off her head, a handkerchief from up her sleeve and starts to polish up the lenses.

"He won't listen, though, 'cos you're the only one he pays the least attention to."

Is that a splodge of pink that rises up in Janet's cheeks? If so then she's concerned to hide it in the pages of a diary that she's swift to open on the desk. The compliments of young men are such fleeting things and mustn't be allowed to hold the slightest sway. She starts to leaf through weeks and asks, "How often have you been back now?"

"Seven times in three weeks," says the young man as he tucks the rag into the pocket of his jeans.

"Oh, well! We're keeping you in business then?"

"You could say that. It might be true if he would pay me bills. That boiler's not worth half the money he's racked up on its repairs. And even if I got it going properly a new one would be more efficient. If he replaced it he'd soon have saved a fortune on the cost of fuel. He'd get his money back in no time."

"You're preaching to a convert, Daniel, as you know."

"I know I am, but he's not here to tell, though, is he?"

Ava's looking at her feet. We realise she's embarrassed to be party to this conversation, has not yet grasped that no one has the right to privacy these days.

"When he phoned me up this morning," Daniel says, "he told me it was on the blink again. He swore he'd meet me here. 'I'll talk to you about a new one,' I said, 'get it all priced up and that, and you can tell me what you think.' 'All right,' he said, 'you do that. Bring an estimate, we'll have a conversation.' 'Sure thing, Mr Urquhart,' I said, and I did it, look!"

Daniel digs beneath the rag in pocket and pulls out a list of figures. From what we can make out, he's put the numbers in a column and the sum of everything is totalled at the bottom.

"He must've meant it when he said it." Janet takes the list and reads it through, her only comment an occasional and disapproving tut. "He runs a business, after all," she says at last. "He must know what he's doing."

As though a mild defence is adequate.

Daniel reddens, scowls. "This estimate is more than fair," he says. "There's no attempt to diddle him. That boiler won't get any better than it is now. And if nothing else he'll save himself the call-out fees, though he's not paid the last few if I'm honest…"

Janet stiffens and grows crisp. "Give me your outstanding bills," she says, "and I'll make sure they top the pile."

Reproaches weaken their alliance.

"I'm sorry, but it's not that much to ask…" pleads Daniel. "You can tell him that I've got the pilot light on…"

"Well, that's something then at any road…"

"…but I can't make him any promises. It might not last another week if he's unlucky."

"What makes it go off, d'you think?"

"The thermocouple. Though I've cleaned it up, it won't stay lit. The trouble is the thing's so old they've discontinued spare parts years ago. I've told all this to Mr Urquhart, but he doesn't want to hear it."

"Right you are. I'll have a word when he gets in."

"And can you ask him *please* to settle up? I've got some bills meself I'm due to pay…"

And so the hands crawl twenty minutes more around the clock and Daniel disappears again into the boiler's den.

"How long am I supposed to wait?" thinks Ava. It's now long after the appointed hour and still no sign of furtive Mr Urquhart.

Janet snubs her from the cluttered muddle of the desk and it begins to dawn on Ava that her friend may have been right. Perhaps this interview's a mad idea. If she succeeds she'll only end up as an extra in the chilly middle of these characters' unhappiness. This place – a million miles away from the offices of imagination, which gleam with glass, and where she'd be allowed to help herself to filter coffee, to wear sharp suits and high heels and to take a liberal spritz of perfume from a bottle in the ladies' – smacks of broken toilet seats and cracked old soap. There are many things, she realises, that can be done but really better not be.

"Don't look into corners, there'll be spiders," she whispers to us, and hurriedly we tuck in all our legs.

The minute hand, by now, has climbed halfway back up the face.

Just as Ava makes her mind up not to wait a moment longer, a crunch of tyres, the creak of brakes, the coming of a car. Outside on Treasury Row a door clunks open to release a gust of furious yaps, as quickly muffled by a hasty slam. Janet pauses in the scratching of her pen, looks up, rebalances her bottle-bottoms, sighs, returns to work. Feet thunder up the steps, the outside air bursts in and sweeps the office. It's no colder out than in, but we all shrink from shock and Ava blinks as though she's been kept too long in the dark.

"Those bloody roadworks!" A tall figure stoops beneath the too-low casing, trench-coat tails in eddies round its knees. A pummelled panama is pulled from head and tossed towards the filing cabinet. It lands precarious, threatens to upset a pile of paper.

Janet barely blinks an eye. We'll have to check the footage later. It's too fleeting to be sure when we're relying on our eyes, but we're convinced she shows a nanosecond of disgust before her hand shoots out to catch the papers and the hat to stop them falling. "Afternoon to you too, Edward," she replies.

"They've dug the bloody road up yet again! The lights let only one car, maybe two through at a time! Damned nuisance! Can't get anywhere without some idiot who's digging up the bloody road!"

"It's been like that for weeks. The council notified us. They sent the details through."

"Oh, damn the bloody council! They're all worse than bloody useless! There'll be potholes everywhere again in one month's time, you mark my words! You, there! Angel's in the car!"

I'm too consumed with noting exclamation marks and how they always spoil things to perceive this man has held his car keys out and charged this task to Ava.

"That's not what I came for…" She knits her brow and looks to us for back-up.

I record a question mark and wonder if she's scared of dogs.

"It's only a chihuahua! Bloody hell!"

"I don't think there was mention of a dog, not in the advert." Ava hesitates. It's clear she's not habituated yet, not ready to be fully placid and compliant. "If I refuse, I s'pose the job is forfeit?" she enquires. "Though actually I'm not sure if I'd mind…"

Her honesty knocks everyone off guard. It's not the done thing, not par for the course.

We notice Urquhart – when he isn't talking – lets a silence fall like stones.

A cough from Janet. "She's come in because you called her here for interview."

"Ah, yes, abso-bloody-lutely." Edward Urquhart flings his coat after his hat, extends a hand and grins a tardy welcome.

Ava notices there's rocket in his teeth.

"And Daniel's downstairs working on the boiler." Janet keeps her eyes down and her pen fixed on the papers.

"Excuse me? What!"

"It wasn't working, so apparently, you called him."

"No, I bloody didn't! And you've let him in? You should *always* check with me before you let him in! Seventy quid, he charges, every bloody time! I've told you, you should smack it with a bloody hammer!" Edward Urquhart pantomimes a dive behind the desk. The drop – to throw open a low drawer of the filing cabinet – occasions his substantial rump to stick up in the air. His trouser fabric stretches taut over enormous buttocks. Ava fights the urge to laugh. He rises with a spanner brandished, waves it ominously close to Janet's glasses. "Keep this handy, then you'll only have to bloody hit it!" he bellows.

The bottle-bottoms barely move. "You know I won't agree to that. May I remind you that I did it once and told you then I'd never do it. Not again. It scared the living daylights out of me that last time and it's not my job to fix your furnace, any more than this lass wants to walk your dog." The jumper surges, billows, rolls. "Besides which, Daniel says the system can't be fixed. He says you'll have to get a new one."

"Daniel says, oh, Daniel says… Oh yes, I bet he bloody does!"

"He asked me to remind you that you haven't paid his bills."

"I would! I'd pay him every bloody penny if he'd fix it properly!"

The room begins to wheeze under the mounting pressure of the argument. Beneath the floor we hear the clang of new attempts to spark the heating in the boiler room and wonder what His Honour Peter Urquhart, Judge, would make of this. We look to him, but he remains impassive in his frame.

"All right! I'll show you, shall I? You just give the valve a bash, that's all!"

"A poor environment to work in, that's what this is, Edward Urquhart. You should count your lucky stars that I don't sue. With all this damp you should be grateful I'm not prone to lung diseases."

"D'you know what he's quoted, hmmm? Ten grand! Where the bloody hell am I supposed to find ten grand?"

"There's cases coming up. You could make it a priority."

Ava, ashen, plugs her ears. "At least Grace will be happy," she thinks, and decides her friend will probably make a begging phone call to the theatre, plead with them to please take Ava back. "I might not know exactly what I want, but I'm sure it isn't this," she decides, and having come to this conclusion, she stands and walks towards the door.

We're undecided what to do. Some of us contend that we're obliged to follow Ava, but we know there's no reward for loyalty these days and if the truth be told we'd rather stay here, watch the fireworks. They'll need some witnesses if this dispute should escalate, and we could document the whole lot on our phones and offer it as evidence. You never know, we could be lucky, end up with our picture in the paper.

"Right! I'll show him!" blusters Edward Urquhart. "He's no expert! It'll only need a bloody tap…"

Janet turns her back, refuses to be part of this debacle, while Urquhart thuds off downstairs towards the boiler room.

Ava turns the handle and is freed onto the street.

She's kind enough to leave the door ajar so we can see the battered car of Edward Urquhart has been parked on double yellow lines. Its front wheels mount the pavement, block the steps to Number 30. Ava has to clamber past, and as she does, her kneecap bumps the bumper, sends an unexpected judder through the vehicle. A chihuahua shrieks and throws itself against the inside glass, slides down into the footwell, leaves a streak of hot saliva and a blurred impression of its body, claws and teeth.

"Even his dog is bloody angry," Ava laughs. Before she goes she turns and lifts her palm to us. "Bye then," she says, "and thanks for everything."

*

We go with Janet. This is rather more by luck than judgement in the end. She happens to be last to leave when all the chaos reaches its conclusion.

Ava reads about it at the breakfast table in the morning. She's stayed the night at Grace's house. They're eating toast, are interrupted when the paper is delivered. On the front page is a photo of a ruined street. It's somewhat altered from the day before when Ava saw it, so it takes a while for her to realise that she's looking at a scene from Treasury Row. The walls are blackened now, the windows only ragged holes. A crack is clearly visible in the brickwork, snakes its way from very top to very bottom of the building. An article accompanies the photograph, explains how shortly after four o'clock the previous day a huge explosion ripped a hole through this, the old historic part of the town. No one's been able to assess the damage yet, nor can they say for sure what really happened, but someone somewhere overheard a firemen say he thought it possible the blast was caused by a defective boiler.

One fatality has been confirmed, not formally identified as yet, but named by an insider as a local man called Edward Urquhart. A young man questioned by reporters had inhaled some smoke. He'd reeked of it, reporters said, but had been able to tell paramedics he was fine, although his hair was slightly singed. Others in the building had escaped unharmed and one employee had had the foresight to bring out a notable and celebrated portrait. A dog was also liberated from a car outside and has been taken to a rescue centre near the reservoir.

"Christ, that was close," says Grace, and whistles through her teeth.

Ava's of the same opinion. She squints, peers closely at the picture and sees what – in his hurry to get the paper out to print – the sub-editor has missed. We've photo-bombed the image and have tucked ourselves inside the bottom corner of the frame. She sees our grins under our hats, our thumbs up by our collars. "Oh, so you're still here," she says, surprised.

Across the town in Janet's flat we aim a victory punch towards the ceiling, and congratulate each other with a high five.

A Living Dog Is Better than a Dead Lion

At this point in our shadowing we're brave enough to think of hiding in plain sight. It's time to ditch the skulking and disguises, to peel off fake moustaches and false beards, be less inclined to hang out in dark corners. It's not impossible to be both visible and not be seen, though it'll take an attitude adjustment. Don't fall into thinking that it's easy to be someone else for twenty-four hours every day. Your actions leak far more than any words you say and we all know what we don't say matters. No tweets for a week and someone out there's bound to draw conclusions.

To be invisible in public we're going to have to modify our gestures, even change the way we walk. We've spent a few days hidden inside Janet's flat, have taken every opportunity to watch the people on the street. People here stand square on both their feet, we've noticed, whereas we have tendencies to put our weight on one foot or another. Our stance could give the game away and mark us out as misfits or as weirdos. That's not the look we're going for, so we're trying to appear as though we come from Combfoot Chase.

One amusing afternoon was spent in passing round a beanie hat and taking umpteen selfies. We untucked our shirts and let the tails hang down below the tattered rib of V-neck jumpers, wore our trousers far too large and swaggered round with bum cracks on display. It really was a laugh. We even tried on tracksuits – grey and saggy – just the thing to blend in with a certain type here, as we've seen. These details are important because the slightest variation draws the eye. If we're to vanish in the open, we must match ourselves to local cues and do it underneath the very noses of the citizens.

We're gathered in the living room of Janet's flat because I think we've still got lots of work to do improving our non-verbal skills.

Janet's home is colourless, a temple to the various shades of brown preferred by those who have accepted old age as inevitable. As though life rusts, left long enough. I've tipped the contents of a biscuit tin onto a plate, arranged the brittle circles in an illustration of the colour palette, beginning with the palest tan and ending with the brutal dark of toast. The biscuit surfaces are lined and gridded, fat and sugar straight-laced into prudish shape. They look unappetising and I know they'll taste like shit, but still I make a show of bringing in the plate as though delivering a treat. I put it on the coffee table, careful to position it – as Janet has requested – on a doily, then I open the discussion on how best to test our gestures, how we might blend in and pass unseen when we're about the town.

"I reckon our best bet is if we start with babies and work up," I say. It's only a suggestion. I'd dispute the accusation that I think I've got the automatic right to tell the others what to do.

The female's eyes are glazed and roll like marbles.

Bugger me, I think. I can't believe I've never noticed that she's interested in babies. She's never said a thing. She's never noticed other people's kids or called them cute, or stayed up late to watch a rom-com. I've never registered a difference, never thought she'd want to swap her freedom for responsibility, but now I wonder if a bump's about to come between us. "You couldn't do this job and have a baby," I say flatly. When I watch her help herself to biscuits, I notice that she's hungrier than me. She has a tendency to snatch, to take more than is strictly her fair share.

"Why not?" she asks. "You got a problem with it?" She picks up a digestive, inserts the circle whole into her mouth. "I've got a friend," she says through muffled crumbs, "who's really high up in her company. She's pregnant and she posts the pictures of her scans on Facebook, says that women can expect to manage everything these days."

I think about the effort it would take to hide a baby. "Oh, I didn't know you had a friend," I say.

She scowls and reaches out to take another biscuit, but I quickly slide the plate away and offer it around.

The others silently avert their eyes, sit side by side on Janet's couch, each nested in their dent within the outlines of her skirts and jumpers. They face the blanked-out television but follow every shift of weight, know which of us is nimble, which is not. They'd like to move, to alter their positions, to prop their backs with trimmed and twisted cushions and to pad themselves with stuffed velour, but neither yet dares make himself so much at home.

The older man takes off his hat and worries at an itch between the bristles on his chin. He likes things as they've always been, thinks custom is the guardian of order, has no desire to pose a threat to anyone. He eyes the plate, considers every biscuit with great care, then plumps for what he calls nostalgically a squashed-fly biscuit. "I used to eat these when I was a kid," he says. He takes one, but he doesn't eat it. He wants to look at it, this relic of his past, and so he holds it some way from his mouth and keeps it pinched between his forefinger and thumb.

The younger one is busy scrolling through past chats on Signal, checking that he hasn't left a trail behind him. He's pretty sure he's set the app to make use of its self-destructing messages, is eager not to be accountable for anything he's said. He doesn't much care who's in charge, is confident he can adapt to anything, is used to change and swaps sides and opinions willy-nilly. Freedom is the outcome of his own propitious choices, he'd say, although he doesn't look directly at the plate and simply grabs whatever comes to hand. He bites and chews, is disappointed by the Maribon. The name holds an allure, it's true, but the reality is disappointing, not much of an improvement on an ordinary Rich Tea. The thyroid cartilage in his throat throbs with the effort every time he swallows.

I set the plate back on the doily, am about to take my turn among the biscuits, when the woman swoops and scoops the lot into a makeshift cradle that she's fashioned from the belly of her jumper. "Next time get the chocolate ones," she says.

"Who d'you think you are?" I say. I mean it only as a mild protest and don't intend to pick a fight; it's just that someone ought to challenge poor behaviour and it might as well be me.

"You can call me Obic," she announces as she breaks up squares and circles, shatters fragile beige until there's nothing left but flecks.

"What kind of name is that?" I scoff. I turn towards my colleagues. I'll be honest and admit I'm looking for support, though all at once they're fascinated by their knees, distracted by the sudden urge to check their legs. No one keeps allegiance anymore, I think. God, what a pair of parasites. "That's not a proper name," I say again.

If any of the others have assumed a moniker or handle, they haven't mentioned it. Well, not to me, at any rate.

The old man blushes. He's ashamed to speak the string of letters that denote him, thinks the sound is redolent of dust and obsolescence whenever it is said aloud. It's not escaped his notice that the citizens of Combfoot Chase no longer call their precious children Kevin.

The specky one smirks silently. He thinks that no tag fully sums him up nor can express his true identity. He intersperses characters with capitals and numbers, adds a symbol, varies sequences each time he writes them down, because he knows he's safer if he never stays the same, or if he introduces something random just to make sure no one else can ever be too sure of anything. If you should ask his name he's bound to lie. The best you'll get is minor deviations from the truth.

"It's not a name, more of an acronym," says Obic. "And I shall call you Arak," she continues, "like the drink." She stands and comes towards me. As I'm seated she is suddenly astonishingly tall. Her close-cropped head looms close beside my ear; a too-sharp chin lands on my shoulder so her voice is just a whispering away. "Translucent," she says in tones so low that only I can hear them. "And evocative of sweat and liquorice."

"That's *Mr* Arak," I retort, and shove her chin away. "That's *Mr* Arak, if you wouldn't mind."

She laughs at me – you pompous twat – and might as well have kicked me in the balls.

Specky also laughs, impressed by Obic. The new will always trump the old, he thinks. He doesn't worry that such changes always cause a loss, that history and customs are deleted. The aged only have to wait, he thinks, and they'll be overshadowed by the young.

Kevin coughs. "I don't think babies see that well," he says – softly, softly, not to tread on anybody. "Can they make sense of our gestures? Won't they need to hear a voice and recognise the tone?"

"Okay," I say, "let's put that theory to the test."

I wish I could put Obic and the things she's said behind me, though it's difficult to lose something deliberately. The more you try not to remember, the more you can't forget. I'd like her to be locked up in a cupboard or an attic, only taken out on the occasions when her presence might be handy, or when I've made the active choice to look at her.

I cross the room to Janet's bay and tug the cord to lift the central blind. Janet's flat is part of a conversion not far from the park and near enough to be disturbed by tinny tunes from ice cream vans on sunny days. Many moons ago this building was the workhouse here in Combfoot Chase, but Janet doesn't know its history. She could find out easily enough if she were willing to go digging. There's a dusty ledger kept safe in a glass case at the Town Hall. She's bound to know where that is as it's just a step away from where she used to work on Treasury Row, but as it's only open Tuesday until Thursday, ten till one, it's possible she's never had the chance to look around like we did.

You can go and see the artifacts for free in the Town Hall's museum. You just turn up and ring the bell. In no time a receptionist will come and greet you, invite you please to step in through its great front door. The door is straddled by enormous columns so you know you're entering a place of some importance. We spent an hour or so in marvelling over bits of ancient pottery and coins, were stunned to find that Garibaldi and the Romanovs had loose connections with the place. You'd never think they'd come to somewhere quite as unexceptional as this, but there you go. Surprises aren't so scarce if you go out and look for them.

The history team have made an effort to engage the youngsters of the town in what is classed as heritage by making this museum interactive. Beside the workhouse ledger there's a small touchscreen device. A sign encourages the visitor to type their name and then computers scan the archives, check the records to determine if a likely ancestor had ever been an inmate. We all had a go when we were there, though using borrowed names, of course. I chose to pose as Delia and was frustrated when the database turned up precisely nothing.

Anyway, the landlord knows this building's past because it's stated in the title deeds, but he's done everything he can to keep it quiet. Poverty and hardship aren't the images he's trying to project. Nor has he ever dared to test his name. He doesn't want to know if he's descended from a line of failures.

Janet's flat is on the first floor. It's slightly bigger than some others in the building, as these rooms were used as the accommodation for the workhouse master and the matron. It used to have a decent view. When Janet first moved in she'd spend long hours by the window. She could see the cliff, the river, watch the far-off lights of vehicles zooming down the motorway. That view was how she'd justified a rent which secretly she'd thought was astronomical. But that was seven years ago before the telephone exchange across the street was sold to a developer and plans were made to put a block of tiny individual apartments in its place. Connection House, they said they'd call it. They thought the name was both appropriate and funny.

She'd made complaints directly to the landlord. "I object," she'd said, and hoped the landlord had a contact in the council who could pull some strings.

The council duly sent out their surveyor.

"All these new apartments," Janet had implored the day he'd visited, "I don't think it's acceptable to squeeze another twenty households into this one street. Where will they park, for one thing? Not to mention that the architecture's ugly and a building there will interrupt my view." She'd hoped that adding her true motive as an afterthought would make her sound more reasonable, less desperate.

Just this once the landlord had decided he could back her up. "She's right, you know. If new flats go up, mine'll be devalued. Prospective tenants want a bit of light, to see the river in the distance. No one wants a lump of steel and glass across the way, nor someone peering right into their living room." He'd stopped himself before he'd said he really worried about balconies, that several tenants had already hinted at a hankering for outside space and threatened to decamp. They'd mentioned that it made more sense to live inside an ugly block and have a view of more attractive architecture.

The surveyor from the council only shrugged. "No one has rights over the view," he'd said. "You don't own that, Phil. No one does. And other people need somewhere to live. We've got to meet our targets to develop dwellings on these brownfield sites. Progress is progress; that's the bottom line. If you don't go along with it, you'll just be left behind."

The consolation for the landlord was that planners told the architect he'd have to drop designs for every flat to have a balcony. The town's refusal reflex was enough to do the job. The impact on the neighbours would be far too great, it claimed. And so they built Connection House, a tight, apologetic block of uninspiring boxes with square windows where the newest generation of less affluent Combfootians can live out their little lives.

The landlord also took the opportunity to house his mistress in a small flat there. The location is convenient and he wants her living somewhere unconnected with his name and in a block so modest that there's little risk that any other occupant will be a person known unto his wife.

Unlike the workhouse, Connection House has no chance of still standing in two hundred years from now. At least the architect has had the foresight to choose cheap construction methods so that when the building's worn and weathered it'll easily come down.

I look out on the brightly cladded rows of flats across the street. One storey is a stripe of yellow and another is a pukish pink. The gaudy colours are at odds with what we've seen so far in Combfoot Chase and don't make visual sense. I don't know what possessed the council to give it their permission. The residents have frequently petitioned to remove the cladding from the building. They complain it's ugly – and have concerns about their health and safety – but none of them can raise the sum required to do the work and as the owners are unwilling to stump up the cash, the eyesore has remained.

Mr Tombleson is furious each time he drives by and is made to look at it. When he'd wanted to convert his loft, he'd made an effort to design something in keeping with the spirit of his street, he'd thought, and was affronted when the planners said his project didn't fit well with the neighbourhood. He'd only wanted to install a dormer, but his ideas were dismissed quite out of hand. The relevant authorities said the project was too large and didn't make good use of their approved appropriate materials. To fall within what counted as permitted, there'd have to be a drastic diminution in its size. They courteously sent a sketch of what they would allow. Mr Tombleson grew red and ripped the drawing into pieces, threw it promptly in the kitchen bin. "There isn't any bloody point," he'd grumbled to his wife. "We'll not get head height for a shower if that's all we can do."

I try to turn the catch which locks the meeting rail of Janet's bay. Two hundred years of effort clogs the sashes, the last remaining traces of the long-dead inmates who once painted and repainted walls and windows in a token task to earn their daily bread. I struggle for a while before it's possible to shift and then I shove the bottom casement up. Janet hardly ever opens any of the windows. She prefers the outside out, the inside in. This early in the year the town's still coated in stale air, she thinks, as unscented and flavourless as any boring biscuit. There's no point opening anything until the odour molecules are less suppressed.

Below a young mum with a baby in a buggy attempts to bump her way out of Connection House. The building has no lift – which doesn't help – and then she always has a showdown with the double doors out of the lobby. We have to say the pram is huge, a chunky black three-wheeled affair, gifted by the father of her child. He'd meant it as a demonstration of how pleased he was when she'd announced her pregnancy. He quite forgot that something so unwieldy would be nothing but a nuisance. He spent a lot of money on it too, although he didn't tell his wife and took the money from the secret bank account that she knows nothing of. He'd wheeled it in and staged a grand unveiling in the girl's main room and felt a surge of pride at how gargantuan it was. The young mum, on the other hand, had felt dismay because the pram had taken all the floorspace in her lounge. Size matters, she believes, but not as much as he and other men might think.

"It's all right," he'd said when he'd noticed that her jaw had dropped, "there's a mechanism on the side so you can fold it flat." He'd fiddled with some catches till the thing collapsed and turned from an enormous object standing in her room to an enormous object lying on her floor.

Even folded up the pram's too big to fit into the boot of the father's flashy car. That's really not a problem because he only ever sees the mother of his child when he makes visits to Connection House. They never go out anywhere these days. It's tempting, but they both know that they mustn't take the chance now she has had a baby. Previously he'd passed her off as an employee, but now they look too like a family and he can't run any risk that they'll be spotted.

Kevin joins me at the window. We watch the young mum bounce the pram down the steps onto the pavement. She bends her hooded head against a vicious bout of gusty weather. She's too young to be a mum, she thinks, has almost done her nut cooped up with the persistent squalling of her offspring. An hour ago she sent a desperate invitation through a WhatsApp group. She said that she was getting out before she wrung the baby's bloody neck and asked if any friends would like to join her. *Please.* One or two did check their weather apps and only said no when they'd clocked the probability of rain and had remembered that a young mum isn't fun to be with anymore. So she's alone and must expect the punishment to last forever now she's had a child.

"Hey," I call out, and the sound makes mum and baby both look up. I make a deep and dreadful furrow in my glabella.

The baby's depth perception is improving daily and it frowns back, then it draws a mighty lungful of wet air and frets and boos and storms until you'd think the window glass must crack.

"You see?" I say triumphantly. "That proves it doesn't need to hear a voice to understand I'm being serious."

"Well, would you look at that," says Kevin. "I'd not have thought it if I hadn't seen it with my own eyes." He puts a friendly hand upon my back.

Kev sets a good example to us all, I think. He never holds a grudge and though he's getting on a bit, his brain's still able to absorb new information.

Obic – always jealous of success – has sauntered over and is followed by the specky one.

"You can't blame her for trying," Kev says gently, "and it's only natural that she'd chance her arm."

He's right, of course, and leadership is always art and never science.

"If she really does want one of those, she must be mental," I say with a nod towards the howling baby.

We shuffle to one side and make way for our colleagues. A flimsy concord is restored. Four heads peer down on all the stuff of human nature on the street.

The young mum leaves her fussing with the baby's blanket and looks back at us. "What the fuck d'you think you're doing?" she yells. Her voice is fissured. She throws her hood back, so we get the full force of her glare and see the tight compressions at the corners of her lips.

"Apologise!" growls Obic. "I bet she's tried for hours to get that kid to sleep. One look at you and now she's back to where she started."

"Don't see why I should." I shrug. In my opinion Obic has too low a threshold for what merits an apology.

She sticks her head out of the window. "Sorry, sorry. Very sorry," she calls down, her repetitions thick and sticky as a slick of treacle. "I know what, why don't you let me tell a story? It'll help to get your baby back to sleep." And off she goes, an offer equal to an invitation, determined to regale the baby till its swaddled in the telling. "…There was a cell once," she begins, "which first became a cluster, then a ball. The ball was covered in a root-like structure and was let loose in a garden, told to seek a place to burrow, somewhere it could find its feet. The place it chose was in amongst some mulberry bushes where the ground was drained. The earth had been improved by those who had preceded it, who'd tried to cultivate the space before…"

"I'm not sure that there's any point to this," I say. I'm not especially fond of folklore, think it's better not to trust a thing that can persuade you when you don't know that you're thinking.

76

"…'I look quite like a mulberry,' thought the little ball of cells, 'so this must be the right place to begin.' It looked around and settled in with the intention of developing a spreading habit. But it wasn't long before the ball discovered that it wasn't quite a mulberry after all. It grew, but not as all the other trees had grown. 'You're not a proper mulberry,' scoffed the other trees. 'We'll let you stay, but you can never be the same as us. You mustn't get ideas above your station…'" Obic's treacled voice drips in the baby's ear. It screws its face with concentration, halts mid-wail, its mouth hangs open, ready to suck up the syrup of her words.

"You shouldn't lie to it," I mutter. "As targets go, this one must count as vulnerable."

"…'So who am I then?' thought our little ball of cells…" Obic disregards me and continues, "…though by this time the ball had grown quite large and could have stood up on its own two feet if someone showed it how. 'And what am I supposed to do?' If it had known the words to signify its various parts, it would have known it lay upon its back. The other trees preferred it down there where they could admire it from above and it could not reach high enough to pick even their lowest-hanging fruit. They didn't tell the ball that it had grown up, had become a big and comely body, and so it never questioned its position. It thought that it was still a ball of cells and that was all that it was meant for—"

"This is ludicrous." I fold my arms and nod to Kevin, signal that he ought to do the same.

"…And then a blade of grass bent over in a breeze, began to tickle what the little ball of cells would come to fathom was its ear. It realised that some way away it heard machines, the thrum of metal turning, forcing grass against a cutting bar. 'I could do that,' said the little ball of cells. 'I could work and cut the grass, I wouldn't mind.' 'Don't be so silly,' said the mulberry trees. 'You lie back, stay exactly where you are. You look angelic in the grass. There's others better shaped to do the cutting and the forcing. No need for you to move.'…"

In her effort to enchant the baby, Obic has leant out, hangs far over the window ledge. She balances across the line that separates the out from in.

"She ought to be more careful, eh?" I say. "It'd only take the slightest shunt and she could topple over…"

Kevin blanches and he doesn't laugh along as I'd expect him to.

"…The little ball of cells thought it was lucky to be so cared for by the mulberry trees. They made so few demands and it loved the smell of grass, the cow-dung green and rich scent crawling up its unknown nose. The sun above turned new cheeks pink and unused limbs a nutty brown…"

Unlike the rest of us Specks isn't looking at the baby. He's staring thoughtfully at me, but when I catch his eye he drops it to his trainers. A lace has come undone and must be tied back up immediately.

"…But in the end the ball of cells had to admit how bored it was with lying still. 'I'd like to run and jump and swim and hold high-powered meetings round a table in a polished boardroom,' it announced. It grasped, you see, that doing nothing is equivalent to being nothing…"

"What kind of fucked-up story's this?" the young mum shouts. Somewhere deep within her lizard brain even she can recognise a revolution. "You think you're very clever, but you're only talking shite," she says. She glances at her phone. Nope, still no text from friends or baby-daddy.

"It's just a tale," says Obic. "It's meant to spark imagination, so the baby can experience things in its own mind before it has to face them in real life."

"Oh, piss off, all of you." The young mum isn't sure what has disturbed her. Perhaps it's just the oddness of the story – which is too strange to be believed – or it might be due to twenty-seven hours of silence from her baby's father. Either way she doesn't know, nor does she have the energy to come to a conclusion. As with most things she'd rather think about it later because she's very tired. Sometimes she thinks her whole life is the enemy of sleep and is preoccupied with the need to check the balance of her bank account. If that bastard hasn't paid each penny of the maintenance he owes her, she'll take a walk across the town and find his fancy house beside the river. She'll break in somehow – even climb the gates, she thinks, if that's what it'll take – and then she'll stalk along his carriage sweep. She'll nip around the back and make her way into his garden, where she'll vandalise that fucking boat he's got tied up to the pontoon he'd built at great expense. He hasn't told her his address, but he's not very careful with his LinkedIn posts. It only took a boastful photograph or two and then it wasn't hard to track him down. Right now she doesn't care that he lives miles away, nor that her shoes are wearing thin. She only knows it isn't fair that she lives here in one small room while his wife and other children have a home bar and a games room and a hot tub.

In fantasy she hunts the father down and rings his bell. She thrusts their ball of cells into the arms of whoever comes to open up the door. And then, she dreams, she dumps the nappies and the baby wipes, the sleepsuits and the frilled booties, the bibs and dummies, all the powders, pastes and feeding bottles, every rattle and cloth rabbit, even this ridiculous titanic buggy. Imagination gives it all a shove and watches as the whole lot trundles down the lawn, tilts at the edges of the bank and shatters through the pristine surface of the river. She fancies that she waits and watches as the water weighs its volume. Slowly it begins to realise that although the items aren't compact, they're far too dense to float. The river seeps and saturates each part of babyhood until it swallows everything, until no molecule of motherhood is left in sight.

When she allows herself to think like this, the young mum shakes with rage. She's desperate to be rid of millstones, at the same time loves them more than she can love herself. She's no idea how to survive ambivalence, is permanently torn between her bottomless remorse and her infinite resentment.

"Why don't you piss off back to where you came from, leave us both alone?" she shouts, her face a twisted gargoyle. She hoicks her baby from its pram and jogs it on her hip. "Yeah, shush now," she says. "Shut the fuck up, oh, for Christ's sake, *please…*"

We watch her push a rusk into its mouth.

"Well, that went well," I say, and close the window.

Kevin crinkles up his nose.

Specky thinks his shoelaces are still not tied in perfect knots.

"She got us pegged and straight away," scoffs Obic.

"I did say we need practice," I protest. "We all know real change takes some time."

"But we're in a real hurry."

Silence clatters into Janet's flat.

"We've always got our sunglasses," Kevin offers. "We used to use them, didn't we, if we had to disappear? Although" – now a confession – "it seems I've mislaid mine somewhere." He bats his sides with flattened palms, attempts to locate what's gone missing.

"No, you haven't. You've still got them. In your pocket, at the top."

"Oh, thank you, Arak. Yes, of course, yes, there they are."

"Well, put them on then." Then a pause. "That better, is it?"

"Yes, but not enough to go outside." He sighs. "I've lost a bit of confidence, it seems. D'you think we ought to hide another day or two?"

"I'm not sure Janet would put up with that." Obic moves towards the kitchen, opens cupboards, pulls out tins of beans, sticks sliced bread in the toaster. "I get the feeling she's fed up with us."

I disagree. "All things considered we've been very pleasant houseguests. We've made sure we don't get underneath her feet. We've always made the beds and folded our pyjamas under pillows. I don't think we've been taking liberties."

A mess of orange swarms into a pan and gas is lit beneath the saucy gloop.

"Anybody else still hungry?" Obic asks.

All the signs suggest that Janet's used to us and she's been unexpectedly hospitable. Her only strict rule is we have to take our shoes off and go stocking-footed round the flat. She doesn't want us tramping mud across her rugs and I've no beef with that. There's nothing worse than dirty pawprints on a carpet. They're a bugger to get out, though she once mentioned something about vinegar. "Plus lots of elbow grease," she said. "That's what it takes to shift a really stubborn stain. But better to prevent than cure in my opinion."

I assured her that we wouldn't cause her any bother. "You won't know that we're here," I said, and made sure that we helped her with domestic chores. It's also true we kept our efforts just inept enough so as not to undermine her.

She's out today, just as she has been every day. She's not lost all the habits of the days she used to work at Urquhart's. She still makes sandwiches and clips them in a plastic box, then adds a frugal apple – just enough for a lunch taken hastily – a choice driven by pragmatism more than by desire.

But on a Friday when she's feeling end-of-weekish – and sometimes on a Thursday too – she lets herself indulge her fondness for a piece of cake. For preference she'll have Battenburg. She likes its checkered symmetry, appreciates a little law and order with her dose of sugar. To me the pasty slab looks uninviting, a shuttered windowpane, but Janet loves it, and a sniff of almond triggers salivation in anticipation of first airy bites. She cuts her slices fairly thin, reminds herself she mustn't be too greedy, and sets about consumption in particular and long-established fashion. She skins the sticky peel of marzipan and nibbles at that first before she separates the pink squares from the yellow. Once the cubes are segregated, she pauses to enjoy the tidiness of regulation.

"There, that's better," she will always say. "You know exactly where you are when things aren't muddled up together."

Nevertheless she always eats comparatively, takes first a pink and then a yellow, tests to see if tastebuds can distinguish any difference.

Sometimes she thinks it's possible they can but only if she's bought the cake from Mrs Jasper at her favourite bakery.

She passes Jasper's daily, always had to on her route back home from Treasury Row, though in the years she worked for Edward Urquhart she'd finish work too late to guarantee that any Battenburg was left. It's better now she's free to get there early. Gone are the days when she has had to leave the bakery empty-handed and make do with a packaged product from the supermarket. Those plastic Battenburgs are bland and claggy, drunk with sugar, far too stingy on the jam. They taste like a pretence, she thinks, are not enough to satisfy, not even in emergencies.

The Jaspers and the bakery have been established here in Combfoot Chase for generations. Janet treasures memories of morning trips there with her grandma when she was young enough to have to lift her arm above her head to hold a hand. Once through the doors she'd slip through ageing fingers and pursue the possibilities of pattern in the tiles which paced the width of polished floor. She'd hopscotch whilst her grandma with a parted lip was parted with her money as she made her slow selection from the jewelled cakes lined up along the counter.

"Ooh, that's a good choice, that, me duck. Here, let me cut you off a little taster…"

"Oh, now, Mrs Jasper, that's a dream…"

"The secret's in the buttercream…"

"There isn't any other baker in this town who makes a cake like you…"

Janet had hopped and jumped between the morsels of their conversation. Her mouth had watered in the knowledge that some cake was meant for her. She smiles to think how dizzy with desire she'd felt when Grandma gave her emptied boxes, let her wipe up skid marks of ganache. She'd stick her fingers in her mouth and tongue their tips until she'd lapped up all the cocoa-cream. Grandma would watch over her and laugh a waste-not-want-not laugh and recognise the clicking of connection, the closing of the circuits of reward.

Of course her adoration of the bakery is much less passionate these days. It's normal, isn't it, to be less fervent, more refined as you get older? The Jaspers are still there, but Janet doesn't jump a pattern on the tiles when she goes in. The current baker is the last in line, and must be Janet's age if she's a day, although the shop's still polished and the same, the cakes still packaged in the elegant white boxes and scrolled with Jasper's monogram and passed across the counter with a hush of satisfaction.

It's satisfaction Janet's never found in anything but cake.

The bakery is held in high regard throughout the town because the Jaspers care so deeply for their reputation. The habits of the past have been preserved – their first line of defence against the whims and whips of fashion – a determination that the future will be better if it keeps a foothold in the past.

"Our recipes will never change, as long as there's a Jasper breathing."

Janet sometimes takes a risk and dares to ask the secret of their Battenburgs.

"Now that, me duck, is known only to family," says Mrs Jasper, laughing, and she taps a steady finger on her craggy hook of nose. "We can't be telling tales to all and sundry."

Janet's never got her to confess, although they've known each other since they were mere babes in arms. This is a source of constant disappointment because Mrs Jasper has the look of someone on her last legs. It's proper to be wary of potential competition, but Janet never bakes herself so it wouldn't matter if they made this one exception. "No harm in telling me," thinks Janet. "I know how to keep a secret." She fears that with no one to pick up the baton of the bakery all the recipes will die out with the present generation.

Janet cradles tenderly her chosen box of cake and walks home through the falling dark. As she goes she glances in through the lighted windows, notes how few the variations are in hearth and home across the town. How uniform the functional theme of sofa, lamp and table, though it's true some folks succumb to dubious trends and paste up noisy wallpaper around the chimney breast, or sling a flatscreen television on the wall as if it were a masterpiece. It's funny how we try to hide an object's proper purpose, Janet thinks as she walks past, as though we're all embarrassed by the things we use to help us live our lives. With everything built-in or fastened to the wall, we renounce the right to take them with us when we go. We buy new and deny we've built foundations on the past. She scores each house for loveliness, marks out of ten, gives mostly threes and fours. Her inclination is towards an air of disapproval, but even so she's disappointed if a household draws its curtains early.

Sometimes when she gets home – especially if it's cold or wet, or over hot, or far too dry – she'll grant herself an immediate piece of cake. Not enough to put her off her supper, just the merest tingle on the tongue. She eats it slowly, forces a pause between each bite of apricot and almond. A sliver, wafer-thin, of what she fancies does her good, she tells herself, although we've noticed that no matter how much Battenburg she buys there's none left in the tin by Saturday.

Specky claims he saw her when he couldn't sleep last Friday night. He'd stayed up on the sofa reading – so he said – and spied her secret tiptoe from her room as late as midnight. He describes a mouth crammed full of cake, so much shoved in she'd gagged and had to hold her head above the sink to catch the spluttering of crumbs. He paints his pictures without pity, thinks the worst of everyone. "She's got no self-control," he says. "You have to work quite hard to get as fat as that."

On Sundays Janet weighs herself, stands saddened on the bathroom scales and makes a promise that she'll stick to apples, carrot sticks and celery. She spreads the butter on her sandwich thin to start the week and at her most abstemious has been known to buy a pot of cottage cheese. She stows these paltry lunchtime items in an insulated bag and leaves them by the door so she won't overlook them when at seven thirty sharp she sets off who knows where.

We wonder if she's found another job. We know there won't be anything like Urquhart's – no one else runs businesses like that these days – but we allow ourselves to hope she's found a steady occupation. She's a strong track record of commitment and experience of working in an office, for all that it was out of date.

Obic trawls the internet for clues to where she goes.

"You got her yet?" I ask.

"No."

"Not a sausage?"

"Nope. A query twenty years ago, a message posted on Friends Reunited, but hardly anyone made contact."

"That's unusual."

"Just one reply to which she didn't answer."

"Maybe from someone she'd not remembered?"

"Or from someone that she did. I've tried on Pipl, Zabasearch and YoName, but no luck."

"We'll have to sort things out the old way then and find a phone book, visit libraries, use the records of the courts."

Kevin perks up.

Specky squirms.

"Why is it that we only follow women?" Obic asks.

"I don't think that we do."

"We have so far."

"It's not a strategy per se. It's just that women tend to share more information."

"You're saying that it's their fault 'cos they let the snoopers in?"

"Well, it's a point… No… Yes. Perhaps in part."

"So if I found a man with looser attitudes to privacy, we'd follow him instead?"

"Of course we could," I say. I'm confident no man is daft enough to share his first pet's name or mother's maiden name in answer to some online quiz.

"Hah! Bingo."

"What?"

"I've got one."

"What?

"We've even met him."

"Who?"

"It's Daniel. Look here, Daniel's got a vlog."

"You what? You're joking aren't you?"

"No, I'm not." She turns the laptop screen towards me and she's right. There's no doubt that it's Daniel. His fine physique is frozen in a moment with the frosted outline of a circle and an arrow pointing right inside his chest. Obic snorts and licks her lips. "I'd follow him, and willingly," she says.

She's changing her priorities, I think. It won't be easy for the rest of us to pick up any slack if she goes off, or makes demands for flexibility, or asks for alterations to her working hours. It would be easier if nothing had to change. The future would be better if we all just stuck to what we know. "He probably isn't worth the effort," I say.

Obic moves her finger on the trackpad, clicks the arrow.

Daniel comes to life.

A minor chord dissents and sows the seeds of my uncertainty.

*

I don't know why I'm doing this. It's not something I've done before, so you could say it's an experiment of sorts. I've told meself I'll just see how it goes. I might not post this, might not even bother. When I watch it back I'll probably think it's stupid, feel embarrassed and delete it, but we'll see. It's worth a shot, it might help with me state of mind. I've got to try and prove, if to no one but meself, that I'm not absolutely raving mad.

*

We can't deny that Daniel's good on camera. He's filmed this on a smartphone but it's one that optimises images and boasts the all-round benefits of a great post-process package. If we're not mistaken this specific model even has a lidar scanner so the night-mode function features quite impressive resolution. When he moves the camera close, we're startled by the greenness of his eye in contrast with the whiteness of his sclera. He keeps still, knows by instinct that exaggerated gestures look discordant on a small screen, but his pupils – which, of course, he can't control – are very narrow, so we understand the tension that he's been under.

*

So, me first thought was to keep a diary, he goes on, *but I'm not the sort of bloke to put me thoughts on paper. I'm not that fond of writing, as it goes. I'd rather talk, or type it at a push. At school when we got essays, I was always awkward with a pen.*

"You'll have to practise writing faster, Daniel," Mrs Kelly used to say. "You can't type in exams. You've got to learn to get your ideas down when up against the clock."

I used to think I'd be all right if they'd just let me speak it. "Can't I use a Dictaphone, Miss?" I'd ask. "You've heard me talk about these books. You know I know me stuff. Why can't they let me speak it, Miss, then they'd know that I know it all as well?"

"You've got to walk the walk though, Daniel," she would say, and shake her head. "I'm sorry, but the rules of the exam say that you've got to write it down. They seem to think that putting it on paper is the stretch."

I tried. I did. I bought a fountain pen and ink and everything she recommended, but I never got the hang of it. I think it's 'cos I'm left-handed, you see. Me hand will always trail across the ink and smudge it. Looking at those smears of blue and black I felt so slow and simple and I came to hate the tracks of loops and curves they said I had to make.

"Oh, don't be daft," Mrs Kelly used to say. "You've got an honest hand, so straight and clear." Yeah, she was really kind, but it upset me. I remember sitting there and thinking of the things about me that she didn't know, of all the secrets that I'd kept from everyone. I wondered if she'd listen if I told her.

There's not many as nice as Mrs Kelly, though sometimes kindness comes quite unexpectedly. Which brings me back to Janet.

*

Janet? Now we're all ears. Now our hairs stick up.

*

I don't remember telling Janet what's been going on, but I s'pose I must've done, 'cos she knew that I was looking for a place.

"I don't know if it's what you're after," she said, "but a room's come up in my block which might tide you over."

"Is there?" I said, and I must've sort of looked excited 'cos then she had to wave me down.

"Oh, please don't get your hopes up," she said. "I can promise you it won't be much."

"But I don't need much," I told her, so she nodded.

"Well, all right," she said. "I'll get it sorted."

And she did. Simple as that. She's arranged for me to go round there this evening, meet the landlord, check it out. It's kind of her to think of me. I don't know why she would, but I'm dead grateful. And I've got me fingers crossed that this might put an end to it, to him, to all his comings and his goings.

*

And then the screen goes black.

"Is that it? All there is?" I ask. "When did he post it?"

"About a week ago, I think," says Obic. "Hang on, there's a follow-up on autoplay. Yep, here we go."

Another tiny oblong evening. Daniel in his van, his phone propped up before him on the dashboard, filming. We can see over his shoulder to the piles of pliers, hacksaws, mole grips in the back, the evidence of hands-on work which doesn't pen him in a classroom.

*

I've just come round and met the landlord, Mr Turner, he begins. *I'm not sure what to make of him, to be completely honest. You get the feeling that there's trouble coming when you're with him. One minute he stands too close and then he turns his back on you. If nothing else I get the strong impression that he isn't patient, doesn't like folk wasting time.*

"Come on," he barked, and led me up two flights of stairs until we reached the second floor. "There's not a lift. You don't get those in older buildings, not in ones with character at any rate," he said.

I know that's nonsense, but I didn't argue. I just followed him along the landing till he stopped outside a door.

"A lovely studio, self-contained, you won't find anywhere that's half as cheap, not in an area as sought-after as this," he said, and stuck a key into the lock to let me in.

The price he quoted didn't seem that cheap to me, but that's what comes with running me own business. Cash flow's always been a problem, 'specially after what just happened down at Urquhart's. I don't expect I'll ever see me fee for that, but still, at least I'm not at anybody's beck and call. Far better to be me own boss than to follow others' orders all the time. I had enough of that to last a lifetime, thank you very much. In spite of money being tight I can't say that I'm sorry to have struck out on me own. It's been a year now, almost two, for all Dad was so pessimistic. And I've kept the business going. Just about. He wasn't pleased when I first told him what I planned to do, but then he never was.

I still see him — his disapproval — sitting in that leather chair of his. He'd ordered chips and sausage, left the packet seeping on his lap. The room fair stank of vinegar. "Most start-ups fold within a year," he said, "so don't come round to me to bail yer out then, will yer?" He shovelled meat into his mouth between each sentence.

"I'll be all right," I said, and tried to make meself sound perky. "I'm not scared of working hard. I know it's tough and will be touch and go at first. I think I'm tough enough, though, so I reckon I can do it."

He glowered, skewered lumps of sausage on his fork. "Wisdom's more than strength," he snarled, "and you don't know a thing." He lifted up the lump and tore it with his teeth.

I looked down at me plate and lost me appetite for sausage.

"I'll not support a failure, Dan," me dad went on. "I'm proud and well-respected in these parts." He peeled his lips back, poked a tine between his teeth to loosen bits of jammed-up sausage skin. "I'd sooner put me son out on the street."

Well, you can see it hasn't come to that yet, Dad. So if you're watching, it might not look like much, but I'll be paying for me own roof from now on.

When you first go in the flat there's this short, narrow passage which then opens out into a room that's big enough for one. I reckon I can easy get a sofa-bed against one wall and I spotted a TV point, several sockets in a corner. Straight ahead there's this bay window which looks out across the street. Another block of flats stands just across the road, but I can get a blind or curtain so there won't be any problem with the privacy.

"Oh, it's quite like mine," said Janet, who'd come up and joined me by this time. The landlord waited in the hall and let us view it on our own. I saw her running calculations in her head. I've never been in Janet's flat 'cos I don't know her very well. We only met through work, but I do like the thought of someone being downstairs, looking out for me, if only at a distance. I stood beside her in the window and we watched the street together. "Yes, this must be right above my living room," she said.

Anyway, there wasn't much else there to look at, just a kitchenette – not that I cook that much – and a tiny shower and toilet separate out the back.

"Well, what d'you say?" The landlord poked his head in from the landing, dangled keys for me to see. The way they clanked he might've been a jailer.

It'll do, I thought. Far better than to rattle round in Dad's old place, for sure.

Janet opened all the cupboards, scuttled round and tried the taps. D'you know, I'd never think to do that sort of thing. I might spend all me days in fixing other people's stuff, but when it comes to mine I seem to go to bits. Dad laughed at me for that.

"Yer useless, boy," he'd roar. "Not one grain of good sense in yer entire 'ead." He'd reach and ruffle up me hair like I was still an eight-year-old. He thought it funny if he messed it up and made it stand on end. I hated him for that because he kept his own brushed back and bouffy, no one else allowed to touch it.

The loo flushed and Janet called, "It's all right, Daniel, I've checked everything. It all works and you've even got hot water coming through."

"I'll take it," I said to the landlord, and held out me wodge of notes. "There should be enough there to cover the deposit and that," I said.

The landlord took the cash and counted it. He eyed me up and down as though he couldn't make up his mind about me. "You got references?" he asked.

"I'll vouch for him." Janet stuck her head out of the bathroom. "You won't have any trouble, Mr Turner." She has this knack of making herself look bigger than she is, does Janet. I wish I knew how to do that. Instead I shrink when under pressure, but she stood there, hands on hips, and I could tell he found her quite intimidating.

"I won't make any noise," I promised. I was keen to get things signed and sealed, and wished I'd changed into a cleaner pair of jeans before I came. I stuffed me hands into me pockets and tried to pull meself together. He'd still got me money so I told meself there wasn't *any need to worry. I knew by long experience with me dad and Mr Urquhart that the businessmen round here don't let their notes go in a hurry.*

"Right then, rent paid in advance, first of the month," he said at last. And that was that.

"Sweet as a sheep," said Janet.

Once the landlord left, Janet showed me all the ropes. "He's not as bad as you'd expect," she said, in part to reassure me. "He's not at all as wicked as he likes to think." She walked me back downstairs and held the door for me. As she did the streetlights blinked and came on, and me van, parked up beside this curb, reflected sudden orange.

"I didn't realise it'd got so late," I said.

"It's just the time of year, though, Daniel," Janet said, "and darkness comes too early."

*

He tells a decent story, does our Daniel. He keeps each vlog spot short and only focuses on the compelling content. There's no sign of beginner's awkwardness before the camera, which we must say is a feat – not everyone stays natural when they know they're being watched. He needs to work on outros, though. He's missing tricks by leaving out a subscribe button, by not having a distinctive logo. Still, his vlog is far more polished than we thought it could have been. The hooks are there and leave us wanting more.

When Obic looks at Daniel she might just as well have coated Janet's flat with pheromones. I'll have to pull her to one side and have a quiet word with her. It's not appropriate behaviour and I worry that her influence on Specky will be negative. He doesn't need someone to help him go astray.

"That's it for now," she says. "I can't find any more." She looks as though a new and shiny toy's been snatched away. "I'll check back, let you know when there's another post."

92

Until such time we'll while away the hours making Janet cups of tea. We like to think we're useful, like a personal assistant. We put the lights on, play her favourite music, add an item to her shopping list, check if it'll rain today, do all the tiresome little tasks so she won't have to lift a finger.

At home we realise Janet does a lot of sitting. In her favoured spot at one end of the sofa, she takes the weight off, sometimes switches on the television. Every Monday there's a magazine delivered which lists the times and channels of the next week's programmes. We tried to tell her that she doesn't need this anymore, that it's a waste of money. She only has to ask and we'll put all her programmes into schedule-view. We were surprised she wasn't very keen on that idea.

"No need," she said. "A bit of paper and a pen works just as well and there are articles I want to read." She flicks the pages of the magazines and glances at the pictures, cherry-picks a programme with a circle of red pen, puts stars against the absolutely-must-not-misses. Some habits die too hard to change her ways. "So many channels, still a lot of rubbish," she complains. We know her system is archaic but admit we still get all the necessary information to know what time we need to turn the telly on.

If nothing's on the television Janet listens to the radio. She tunes to something classical but only wants to hear the highlights, likes an aria, loves to hum along to *Madame Butterfly*. The music always calls to mind a young American she used to know. She'd met him when he'd busked outside of Urquhart's and she'd fallen for the cowboy boots, the Harmony guitar. Nothing had come of it. He'd wanted more experience than Combfoot Chase could offer and one fine day he'd set off in pursuit of better things and greater pleasures. It is bitter to remember, but Janet cherishes her few mementos of a more exciting past.

As she hasn't heard of streaming, podcasts, playlists, she doesn't realise she could download any track and listen at her own convenience. Instead she has to wait and hope, though she'd insist anticipation only adds to her enjoyment. She likes to watch for threads of smoke on the horizon, allows herself to hit the sweet spot in the middle of exotic and accessible, encounters flawlessness in one note every syllable. When the music ends she takes a handkerchief from up her sleeve and wipes her thick and misty lenses. "That was simply lovely," she will always say.

Some evenings are more disappointing. If the radio won't play the tunes she wants, if nothing stirs the chords of reminiscence, Janet turns the whole flat off and simply sits in silence. Specky ran a sweepstake, said he bet she'd knit or maybe do a bit of crochet, but so far we've not seen evidence she's doing either. Kevin searched the flat, but didn't find so much as one small ball of yarn. It's such a shame. I think she'd be quite good at it. She's patient and she likes routines and life's consistent patterns. I suggested she could make a row of novelty egg cosies and donate them to a charity, but so far she's not taken up my hints. Instead she parks herself before the window, points her slatted gaze between the louvres of her blind and waits for night to fall over the town.

Janet can't remember when she last saw any alteration from this window. The view has been the same for years, ever since Connection House went up. The details of her world are never-changing, insignificant, familiar. She's seen it all before, has long ago made peace with an accustomed blank, so it takes the abrupt illumination of a window opposite to make her switch back on.

It's dusk one day late on in February. Janet's just come home, has only just put lunchbox on the counter, is about to empty dregs of cold tea from her flask into the sink, when a light snaps on across the street and draws her eye. She's not yet shut the blind because the nights are starting to draw out again. "I try to make the most of natural light to keep my leccy bill from rocketing," she says, and comes to join us in the bay.

We watch a bare bulb make a bright box in Connection House. We see the picture whole, uninterrupted.

A man comes in and pulls a girl into the square. His arm trails like a towline, fingers make a snare around her wrist. He doesn't let her go until she's right inside, until the door is closed behind them. His grip must be too tight because the girl rubs at her joints, makes checks of all her nails. She flexes and extends each finger carefully as if to signal no harm done. Not yet.

"Oh dear," says Janet, "they must've had a quarrel. I remember moving house was very stressful." We know it's been an age since she was last inclined towards upheaval. She's dealt with what's been thrust on her and nothing more. She shoves the bottle-bottoms up her nose and moves a little closer to the window. "They don't look much like lovers," she reflects, and we agree. They're not your average couple. There's an evident disparity in ages for a start. He's clearly getting on a bit, whilst she's still at an age when time moves languidly. Janet tuts. "Father and daughter then, d'you think?" she asks.

"No, can't be that," says Obic. "Look, her clothes are far too skimpy. Any father worth his salt would say something to that."

I notice round the man's neck there is something on a chain. It bumps against his chest with every step and only when he stoops to lock the door do any of us realise what it is.

"A key," breathes Janet.

The new occupants of the flat across the street eye each other like a pair of cats.

In stillness we make studies of the girl's face. To Janet her expression is a little impudent, though when we lean in, look a little closer, we notice that it's drawn on with great care. We can't pick up their words from here and are too prone to bad lip reading to guess at what is said, but every time he speaks her brow lifts in the arc of unasked questions. The girl remains unspeaking as he unpacks words and words, and words upon more words. Whatever she might think of him, she keeps it to herself.

Time stands still.

The sky behind Connection House goes black.

The yellow square stands gaudy in our gaze.

"Oh Lord, this counts as snooping!" Janet says, and breaks the spell by drawing down the blind. "I've never spied on neighbours in the past." She flushes – we can't decide if this is caused by shame or by excitement. She hurries to the kitchenette and tries to muster interest in her supper. "I've bought some liver and some onions," she says, opening a plastic bag. "It was supposed to be a midweek treat, but I don't think I'm too hungry…" by which we understand she doesn't want to cook wet flesh. "She's so young, that's the trouble," she says, puts the quivering meat back in the fridge. "I'm not exactly used to it. Most people round here tend to be a little older. Like I am."

We've noticed it's an area where people shrink and soon become quite unappealing.

"Though that can hardly be the case with Daniel," Obic says, and licks her lips.

Nor with this new girl, I think, who's so young that she gleams. She makes us feel like old clocks running slowly, lagging far behind.

Janet boils her cranky kettle, drops a testy teabag in a mug.

*

Another evening, the time when Janet usually takes her TV magazine and browses till her chosen programme is about to start. Tonight, however, when she sits, she leaves the magazine abandoned in her lap. She wraps her hands around her cup of tea and tucks her feet beneath a cushion. Behind the blind a deeper darkness sharpens pictures in the window. One of us springs up to hit the lights, but Janet gestures no – asks us instead to push the sofa closer to the bay – and when the dusk has grown so dense that we can barely see, she slowly pulls the cord to separate the slats.

"Oh, good, he isn't there," she breathes.

It's true: the man has gone, the girl's alone. She's shed what little outer clothing she had on and stands beside the window in her underwear. She tugs a brush through strands of hair. Long strokes pull locks towards her crown. She takes a band and binds the hair so it stays high then tumbles down her back. A shaft of light from the electric bulb sends circles round the sable of her shoulders.

Janet's breathing quickens and a red rash rushes up her neck. She doesn't wish for beams to touch the torso of the girl, to glance across her hips or trace the whole length of her limbs. Instead of wishing Janet blinks and sips her tea.

Once the girl has finished brushing, she perches on the window ledge and reaches for a paper bag which must have been left on the floor. Her hand delves into it, discovers a thick sandwich. She opens the bread and peels a piece of ham from in between its buttered thighs, places it with obvious pleasure on her tongue. The bread she throws away. Again she delves and this time pulls out the perfect circle of an apple. She holds it up and turns it in the lightbulb glow before she slips below the windowsill. She crouches down, her face square to the outside so her chin rests on the ledge. We watch Janet watching, fascinated, as the fingers delicately place the apple green in the centre of the sill. The girl leans back to check that it is equidistant between the jambs. She smiles, is satisfied by symmetry.

Her gaze lifts and for one moment it seems she looks directly into Janet's eyes. This takes us by surprise and Janet is afraid that she's been caught out. A sharp intake of breath and we have to remind ourselves the room is very black. It must be nigh on impossible for anyone to see us.

The girl raises the inside pink of her hand.

And then she waves.

*

"Morning."

What, already? Oh, it's only Specky by the window. "Is it morning?" Not too early either by the look of it. It's fully light. "What day is it?"

"It's Saturday."

Thank God. Oh, don't stand up. Balloon-head bloats until it's bound to burst. I close my eyes again and lie back on the cushion. "What the blazes did we do?"

"You can't remember?"

"Pretty blurry…" A few vague shadows coming back. Oh yes. I was a fool and got upset when that girl caught us looking through a one-way mirror. "Drank too much…" But so did everyone.

"I've kept a tab on Daniel."

"Daniel?"

"He's just parked his van across the street and is about to do a livestream."

"Did we make a plan to start this early?"

"As he's come to us I thought we should. He's making it quite easy."

"Right. I'll get up then."

"And don't forget your headphones, Arak."

Arak? Oh yeah, that's what Obic called me. Didn't think the others picked it up. "All right, I'll do that, Specks, but hold on while I get a drink."

"Yeah, take more water with it, guv."

You mocking me, you bastard? "I see you haven't bothered waking Kev or Obic." How come they've both earnt the luxury of sleep? Still shrouded in their sleeping bags. I don't know why he woke me up. If I were him I'd take the chance to get one up, to find out something that the rest of us don't know. He thinks he's all that, but he's missed a chance there, hasn't he? That's not like him. It must be in his interests to have me on his side. He's up to something. Definitely. And what's that in his hand?

"I thought you might appreciate a paracetamol."

The condescending twat. Though not wrong, as it goes. My head is throbbing. C'mon, Arak. Grunt a word of thanks, at least. Yeah, that's the decent thing to do. Even though you don't know if you trust the specky git. "Ta very much." Right then, get on and swallow these.

"That better?"

Stupid question. "Hasn't had a chance to work yet."

"Well, the show's about to start."

"Okay." I only have to crawl across the room and take a pew beside him on the sofa.

"There's our Daniel." Specky turns the screen towards me. "Bet he wasn't off his tits last night. And in his tightest T-shirt too. Oh, Obic'll be sorry that she's missing this…"

*

We're here. It's moving day. I've packed and loaded up me van, have left me dad's house for the last time. If I'm lucky. Everything I need is in the back. I picked the keys up from the landlord and I'm here outside the new place, ready to begin again. I'm really pleased I'm moving on, though all me mates think I'm doo-lally.

*

"I like a man who keeps his sense of humour in a crisis," comments Specky.

*

We were in the lounge of Dad's house late last night. I've lived me whole life in that place but couldn't wait to get away from there. I didn't want to stay a minute longer than I had to. Can't stand the bloody sight of it. "Well, this is it," I said. "I'm off."

"Don't be a dick, Dan," Jason said.

"Yeah, dickwad," added Mark.

I know. What sort of friends would speak to you like that? But no, I didn't call 'em on it. Might be cowardly, but I don't reckon that it's worth it. So instead I just said, "What do I need with five bedrooms and a massive kitchen?"

"Party house!" they said in unison. I imagine they'd have talked it over when I wasn't there, thought they'd get to fill each room with different bits of skirt picked up in town. "Crank up the music, order food and lure the birds in, fuckin' pumped!" They laughed.

I tried to laugh along, but in the corner of me eye I saw me dad lean forwards in that huge reclining chair of his. He'd got his hands braced on the arms like he would pounce at any minute. I could see him snorting, growling, clear as day, and knew that if I didn't get 'em both out in a hurry he'd make mincemeat of the three of us.

"Nah, I can't do that," I said. "Not yet at any road." I said that last bit to appease 'em. "It's still me dad's house, in't it?" I said. "I'll just rent it out or summat." Then I hustled 'em away, out of the lounge and on to the front door.

"When did you become a pussy?" Mark asked. "What's it to yer dad? He's dead now, in't he? Time to have a bit of fun, get over it."

"Yeah, we'd all feel better if we got some exercise," Jason said, and gave a wink. He made those air quotes with his fingers so I knew that when he mentioned exercise he actually meant, well, something else. "And don't they say that helps with moving on?"

*

"Just wait till Obic gets a load of this," laughs Specky. "She'll be gutted when I tell her that her favourite specimen believes in ghosts."

"Oh yes," I say, "I s'pose she will be slightly disappointed."

"Though I guess it's only 'cos he's stressed. It's not unusual to sense a presence in abnormal circumstances."

"You might be right," I say, and take another slug of water.

*

I'm moving on, Dad. Yes, I am. And in me new flat there's no reason whatsoever for the likes of you to be around. I never want to have to deal with you again. I shouldn't have to trip up on the past each day and I'm relieved to get away. It can't be right to keep on seeing someone who you know is really dead.

When I first caught a glimpse of him I barely questioned it at all. I'd thought about him such a lot since stumbling back from hospital all numb, unable to believe that after all that time the worst was over. I reckoned I was just remembering when I first noticed him still sitting in that chair.

"Look what I've achieved, son," he was boasting, then he rambled on as always about the size of his house, his big gates, the long length of his drive. "Yer'll not make 'alf as much of yerself in this town as I've done."

I even asked a nurse about it.

"Not to worry," she said. "That's completely normal." She was kind and touched me arm so gently that I nearly cried. "Especially when it's taken such a long time. It's your memory. It latches on to random moments. Gradually your brain'll process everything and file it all away. Don't concern yourself, it'll get put in the right place soon enough."

But it didn't. That was weeks ago and there's been no sign of Dad shifting.

"Yer'll not get rid of me," he said that last night once Mark and Jase had gone. "I won't be givin' up the ghost." And then he yawned. A great hole opened in his head and I just couldn't bear to look at him. Quite frankly I was scared to death of all those teeth.

*

All sorts of demons haunt this world. You never know who's been tormented by an incubus or succubus, or who's been swept away by aliens. It only takes a synapse to send out stray signals and a whole host of phenomena get conjured up from nothing. The truth is everyone is scrambling to make some sense out of chaos, but once Obic sees that he believes in the impossible, I don't think Daniel will remain attractive very long. She's not the sort to hook up with a man who's spooked so easily.

It's odd to think that at this very moment Daniel's one floor up from us. There might be a slight time-lag – just a second, maybe – but to all intents and purposes his world's an instant duplicate appearing on our screen. His life is simultaneously here and there. No wonder that he finds it hard to tell what's real and what's imagined. The camera scans the hall upstairs and all the contents of the workhouse, flattened into two dimensions, transform from the things we know quite well into new versions of themselves, and in so doing become a little unfamiliar.

The lens dips down to document the moment when he turns his key and walks into a meta-room. He crosses over, stands beside its vacant window underneath our noses, at the same time in the room above our heads. How weird. Although we recognise enough to know that what we see on screen is real, it's easy to forget he's also structuring this version of the truth to meet our need for entertainment.

*

I was at work when I got the call. I'd just opened a radiator bleed valve when my mobile phone vibrated in my pocket.

"Adrian here," a voice began.

"I'm sorry, who?" I said. I couldn't think of any customer called Adrian.

"It's Adrian Kelly, from the Club," he said, and told me Dad had lost his voice whilst chairing a committee meeting. "I took him home, but then he said he couldn't swallow, so I've dropped him at the hospital. Just to be on the safe side, you understand. Best get there quickly, son. If possible."

"Yer in the dog 'ouse," Dad mouthed when he saw me. They'd laid him on a trolley and he was green as the sheet. "What took yer so long?"

The hospital sent him home with a bunch of painkillers and a few weeks to live. He lasted nine days before a doctor shook his head and told me that he needed to go back.

"You'll be more comfortable there," I pleaded, did my best to persuade him to be reasonable. "They know what they're doing and they'll have everything to hand."

"Nah, too noisy," he said, "too much messin' me about when all I want's a bit of peace."

Well, that's a laugh, 'cos when could he claim ever to be peaceful?

"I'll come and see you every night," I promised, and I did, though he was never grateful, never pleased to see me. I'd sit beside his bed and wait for him to say something.

"It's out of order to me way of thinkin'," he'd say.

"What is, Dad?" I'd ask, although I knew.

"Them keepin' me in 'ere. An 'ospital is for the sick."

"Well, you are sick."

"Rubbish. No point tryin' to be better, is there? They should send me 'ome. And I want yer to tell 'em. Me last wish, it is. I'll go 'ome and 'ave me things around me. I want to die in me own chair. Yer should grant me that and bring me last wish to fulfilment."

I tried to argue with him, tried to tell him that it wasn't such a good idea, but he wasn't having any of it. "What does stuff matter?" I said.

"Yer sound just like yer mother," he said bitterly. "'Yer can't take it with yer when yer go,' that's what she said, but I'm not goin' anywhere, I tell yer."

"What is it that you want so badly?" I asked. "I can bring it in, you'll have it here." I even tried me hand at blackmail. "You'll not want me to be thinking only of your death each time I'm home now, will you?"

But he didn't give a monkeys. He was set on dying in his home where I could see him.

"There's better parkin' at the 'ouse," he said, "so no restrictions or expense for visitors." And that was that as far as he was concerned.

No one visited, of course, not even Mr Kelly from the Club. Dad wasn't liked enough in life for people to put themselves out for him in death. He'd spent too long behind his gates thinking he was better than the next man, so they didn't bother. Still, home he came, whether I liked it or not. The *paramedics put him in an ambulance and stretchered him indoors, where he was propped up in his chair. They left me with a lockbox for his medicines.*

"There we are. You're back where you belong," they said.

Then twice a week a nurse would come to check on us. She'd bathe me dad and sit me in the kitchen, treat me to a bit of sympathy. "So how you doing?" she'd ask, and she'd tilt her head a little to one side.

"I'm all right," I'd say, lying.

"There's no need to be so scared," she said. "This happens to us all, sooner or later." She'd tell me what an honour I'd been granted 'cos I could be there for him in his last days, but it never felt that way to me. Even if you didn't hate someone and loved them very much, I reckon it'd be a dreadful strain to care for them at home.

And death is slow. Well, his was, anyway. The weeks passed and he just slept more and more. Sixteen, eighteen, twenty hours a day towards the end. And when he was awake he spoke up less and less. He'd always been a noisy person, had me dad. He'd shout and bang a door and throw his weight about and make a fuss. But now he sat there in his chair, a shrivelled blanket on his knees, and got so quiet, short of breath, you had to get up close to check he was still there. I started to believe he'd keep his word and never leave at all. I'd watch him, hope to see the moment when his life would end and all his threats would perish.

*

I notice Specky lifting up an eyebrow. He's leaning forward, drinking in his every word. Experience suggests it's far too much to ask that Daniel might confess to a murder live-streamed on the internet, but then again, you never know. It happens rarely, but it does. Even I can't quite escape a quiver of excitement. We've lived too long within the sphere of ordinary celebrity to shun the promise of a cliff-hanger. It sharpens up the senses and reminds us that we haven't hit his all-time low. At least our lives aren't crap enough to leave us watching someone fade out on an old recliner.

*

One night he crooked his finger, curled his claw and called me over, made me put me ear against his mouth. Oh, here we go, I thought, this must be it. He's gonna tell me that he's sorry he was such a nasty bugger. So I crouched down low and tried me best not to reveal how glad I was if he was going. "Now I'm here, Dad, what d'you want?" I said. I half expected him to tell me some great secret, maybe something about what had really happened to me mum, but no, he didn't. I could tell it took an effort to croak anything. His voice was dry and crusty – what was left of it – but he enjoyed himself and I would find out that he still had tricks tucked up his sleeve.

"I'll not leave yer an orphan, Dan." That's what he said.

"What's that supposed to mean?" I asked, and couldn't make a head or tail of it.

"I'll not go anywhere," he rasped, and chuckled, "even though I saw yer mother just a moment since." It's the drugs, I thought. They've made him go doo-lally. "She's come to get me," he said. "Waitin' for me down the bottom of the garden, so she is."

"You've just been dreaming, Dad," I said, and swabbed his lips with a sponge of water, sat meself back on the couch to wait for him to die.

*

"Ghosts in the genome," Specky says. "His dad bequeathed him that if nothing else."

"Do you really think that seeing spirits is inherited?" I ask, but Specky only shrugs.

"*I don't know what the time was when I woke up,*" says the voice of Daniel and my eyes jerk back towards the screen, "*but I knew straight off that he was dead.*" He's looking from the upstairs window out across the street towards Connection House. In the daytime no lights are illuminated so you can't tell if the souls in there have any reason to be up. "*It's funny, in the end there isn't any need to touch a body to know that someone's gone,*" he says. "*It was as though he'd had his likeness captured and they'd got his character exactly, right down to the top lip that always curled back in disgust, but I could tell he wasn't in there anymore. Well, that's that then, I thought to meself. That's the last of him, thank God. I let meself think how the worms would eat him, how they'd whittle him right back to bone, and then me shoulders settled for the first time in an age.*"

When Daniel looks directly into camera, I could easily believe he looks at me, that there is only me and him, and that I'm whirling in the darkness of his eye and spun with every bit of his confusion. It's just a trick. He holds my gaze much longer than he should, until the closeness starts to get a little awkward and it almost tinges on aggressive. Cheap magic, I admit, but it's effective. I'm pleased when Janet comes in in her dressing gown and Specky quickly shuts the screen. Together we three gaze towards the boxy windows of Connection House.

"She's such a treasure, that creature," mutters Janet. "D'you know, I wouldn't be without her now. I just woke up and my first thought was wondering how she's been doing. And when I'm out I count the hours until I'm home and I can see how she's got on."

We're not surprised and understand the fascination. This girl's our private soap opera. Our problems all evaporate when we are watching hers.

"Have you noticed that she's lost some weight?" asks Janet.

Yes, we think, it's true. She has.

"She doesn't do that much between his visits," Janet speaks as though she is the leader of a vigil who must whisper supplications for the girl, "though I'm pleased to say he hasn't hurt her yet for all he waves his arms about. Of course that might be down to us. Our watchful eye might keep her safe." She likes to think that wishes or a prayer won't ever go to waste.

I'm rather proud that Janet has included us. She thinks that we too hold this girl's best interests at heart, is so adapted to our presence that she thinks we're only useful and benevolent. We have to make sure her dependency grows stronger, I decide. We ought to hang out in a dressing gown and buy her some more Battenburg. I make a mental note to give a prompt to Kevin, who'll be happy humming arias.

The days run by and now a row of apples almost fills the windowsill.

Anger flares across the street.

We watch Janet watch the man slam doors and corner that poor girl. "The brute!" she cries, and starts to add a little brandy to our cups of tea to calm our quaking nerves.

"You must prepare yourself for what you might now see," I say, and rest the comfort of a hand upon her arm. "This man won't be the type to act more altruistically because he knows he's being watched. I bet he doesn't give a damn about the judgement of a group of strangers."

Janet nods. "He'd think his reputation is enhanced because we're witness to his cruelty," she says. "I don't think he's averse to strong-arm tactics." She shares a worry about bruises which are blooming on the girl's arm from repeated jabs. "Heaven knows what he'll do next," she says, and promises that – with our help – she'll make sure that he doesn't get away with it.

Next time she's out, she buys a notebook, starts to make a diary of everything she sees.

By March the girl no longer lifts a hand or looks across at us, and as the month rolls on she thinks each day is less important than the last. She shrinks and slumps and then, one evening when the man has worn her out, we see her give a little nod. It's clear he's pleased as punch. He grins and tosses something at her feet. Janet is perplexed to note the girl picks up a stub of candle and a spoon, a screw of paper.

"That's her reward," says Obic. "It'll take the edge off when she's on her own."

We notice Janet's starting to cut corners. She no longer stays away all day but hurries home, is always back by three o'clock. She's anxious not to miss a single episode, has sworn an oath that she'll do something – *anything* – and in no circumstances will she let us all stand by. "Once I've collected enough evidence I'll hand it over to the authorities," she confides to Kevin. "I've found out there's a local women's refuge round the corner, or I could take the things I know to the police? I might provide some evidence that's incontrovertible."

Kev nods and tells her this idea is good and praises her for borrowing binoculars.

"Oh yes, they're Daniel's. Well, his father's anyway," she says. "He said he's got no use for them and they should help us pick up all the little details."

"Important not to make mistakes," nods Kev. "Best if we avoid false allegations."

At twilight we observe the man. He leaves the building, walks a little way along the pavement. Specky's made a tripod so that Janet doesn't need to hold up the binoculars, can concentrate on rotating the focusing ring. The man looms large and crisp in both the lenses. We trail him to the corner of the street and see him greet a younger man. We recognise the man as Mark, whom we've seen hanging out with Daniel.

"He's hardly more than a boy!" cries Janet as a package swaps from pocket into palm.

She monitors the transaction and Obic makes a note of date and time.

We turn the eyeglass back towards the window and we wait.

The girl is waiting too. She's draped the bed with patterned cloths and stands before a mirror dabbing perfume on her wrists.

"I imagine she would smell of cinnamon," breathes Janet to herself.

By the time the men have climbed the stairs the girl is lying on the bed. She's chosen all her clothes with utmost care, has made sure that she wears long sleeves to hide her scabs.

When Mark is shown into the room he neither hesitates nor asks permission. She doesn't try to stop him and she's confident he won't take very long. The worst is when he hangs around and paws at her as though he wants to get to know her better. She might be skinny but she's beautiful. He doesn't get the chance to graft a girl like that too often here in Combfoot Chase. He simply can't believe his luck.

Janet tuts but knows the way it goes because she's seen it all before. The only difference tonight is that this man helps himself and takes an apple. We observe his greedy fingers reach for it and draw in a collective breath before he bites. The outside still looks green enough and so Mark doesn't realise that the apple's very old. He sinks his teeth into the desiccated flesh and then he grimaces and spits and drops the apple in disgust.

The girl says nothing.

She waits until he leaves and then she puts the apple back in place beside the others on the windowsill. Where his teeth have punctured it the apple will react, turn acid brown and pull its injured flesh back from the skin.

"Oh dear," says Janet.

Alone again, the girl veers back and forth between being limp and being restless.

She rolls a cigarette and smokes it.

Although we watch her late into the night, she hardly sleeps. She sometimes scratches at her skin as though she'd like to peel her layers off and throw herself away.

*

The problems really started when Mr Kelly said the Club wanted to plant a tree for Dad. They asked me if I'd go there for a ceremony, a short memorial, or so he said. All I'd have to do is hold a watering can while someone else there lowered down the root-ball in a hole they'd previously dug. I wouldn't have to worry 'cos I wouldn't have to say a thing.

"All right," I said, although I didn't want to.

They chose a yew which Mr Kelly said would represent Dad's great longevity. I stood there with the can while he went through his little speech, just a few words on the theme of long life – as if that is enough if not well-lived – and then I had to water in the tree. But all the time I kept on thinking about poison. I don't know why that yew might be the thing that made a difference, but it did. It was right after that me dad came back.

If truth be told I'd been enjoying being in the house all on me own. I'd shut up almost all the rooms and in the general run of things I only went from bedroom to the kitchen and then back again. Then for some reason one evening I took it into me head that I might like to watch the big-screen television in the lounge. The light switch is across the room. It doesn't make much sense but when they built the house they put it opposite the door. It's always been a pain and I'd always meant to fix it, but I'd never got around to it, and so I had to cross the room in total dark and fumble till I found it.

It was quite a shock I tell you when I turned around and I found him back there in his chair, laughing his head off like he always had.

"I told yer so," he said.

*

A pyramid of fruit has burgeoned on the windowsill. The apples at the top are green and bright, but those beneath are shrivelled. Their surfaces are wrinkled and degraded where the moulds and yeasts have taken hold and gorged themselves, have broken cells and structures down. Janet doesn't count how many apples there now are. She's just appalled by all the mess of flesh, outraged and grateful that the man has never put a curtain up and that the girl has never thought to turn the lightbulb off. She keeps a watchful eye on her, hopes for the best and worries endlessly, this makeshift guardian of the girl.

"Stay safe," she whispers to the bare cube of the room.

*

I didn't know what to do with meself. I tried to bury meself in work, barely ever went home and never in the lounge unless I had to. "Don't look round," I'd mutter like a mantra, "and whatever else you do, don't ever look at that recliner."

Even without looking I could feel his eyes dig holes into me back.

Needless to say I've not told Mark or Jase about this. Well, they'd think I was a proper nutjob, wouldn't they? They thought that I could plan on having parties in that house, but I'd got no desire to spend another night there. Never. Then it happened Janet mentioned that this flat was coming up and I jumped at the chance. I don't know quite what kind of hole it would've had to be for me to have rejected it, but I knew one thing for sure, I wasn't ever going back to Dad's.

"Are you quite sure about this?" Janet asked. "It's something of a comedown from what you've been used to, isn't it?" She was looking out across this street and watching all the lights come on in other windows. I remember thinking, that's another person safely home. I bet they're glad as me that this day's over and I walked over to this window and stood next to her. Then Janet put an arm around me shoulders which was nice. "Won't it be strange to live somewhere like this after being in the same place all your life?" she asked.

"No," I said, and shook me head. "I think I'll like it. I'll like being by meself for once."

Janet shot a look at me as though I'd uttered something very strange, but she didn't challenge me again. "All right," was all she said after a bit. "Remember, I'll be downstairs if you need me."

*

Janet balances the binoculars on the tripod, trains them in between the slats of blind. The picture is in every way familiar, every corner of the room much like it has been every other day, as though the hours connect in sequence, as though the girl does not experience each minute independent of the others.

*

I s'pose you can't tell yet that I've moved in. I've only brought a small case, the bits and bobs I need for work, a sleeping bag. That's it rolled out there on the floor beside the window, look. Although it looks uncomfortable, or rudimentary, as me English teacher would've said, I've had a few nights' better sleep in that than I've had in the past two years.

Mark and Jase came round last night but said they weren't impressed.

"There's nowhere we can sit, mate," Jason said, then he and Mark both raised their eyebrows higher than you'd think they'd go.

"I'll sort it out eventually," I told them, and at least the previous tenant left a mug or two in cupboards so I had the things to give them both a drink.

"Why not go back, grab some furniture?" suggested Mark. "It wouldn't hurt to make yerself more comfortable."

"Yeah, I will do, when I'm ready," I said, handed him a glug of cider in a mug. I won't, though, 'cos I like the emptiness. The last thing I would want is Dad's stuff crowding me again.

Mark sighed. "It's like a monk's cell, this," he said, and sat cross-legged on the floor. He kept on looking out the window.

*

She's on the bed, her arms and legs sprawled out.

"Oh, bless her, she's asleep," says Janet, but we know that isn't true. She looks too heavy and unnatural. And she's lying very, very still.

Janet's taught herself to use the diopter adjustment which makes allowances for the difference in the vision of each eye. She fiddles with it, pauses, can't compute what she has seen and tries to tell herself her sight is playing tricks. The girl's skin is quite ashen and her face is looking really clammy. Although her eyes are open, the pupils are now far too small and too contracted. We don't know how to break the news to Janet that those eyes see nothing anymore, and there's no one there to see.

*

These weeks have been the happiest of me life, I reckon. I know it's been a while since last I posted, but there's not been anything to say. As you can see, there's not much change. Just as predicted, I didn't bother with the furniture. After a day at work, I'd roll meself up in me sleeping bag and watch a video or summat else on YouTube. It felt like freedom having nothing else around me.

Even memories of Dad and all his anger, all his envy had begun to fade, and I'd got to the point where I believed he'd gone into his grave and would never come again. I've never had so little and so much.

And when tonight I put the key into the lock, well, I was whistling. Actually whistling! I can't remember when I last did that, nor when I was so happy and relaxed. I'd been down to the shop and treated meself to a can of beer, a microwave lasagne. And I had nothing, not an inkling in me head until I got in and I flicked the light on.

It took a mo before it registered. At first I couldn't think why I'd been brought up quite so short, or why me heart was hammering so hard and in me gullet. And then I realised…

*

He turns the camera from a greying face to swing around the room and then it settles. We have to blink a few times so that we can grasp the facts of what he's seen.

"You're kidding me," I say. "I wouldn't have believed it."

Obic stares with narrowed eyes.

113

In the middle of the floor, where it's no right to be, stands an old, enormous cream leather recliner.

*

Janet swallows, rests her forehead on the meeting rail. "Should we call someone?" she asks. We don't reply. "We must have obligations as her neighbours?"

"Technically *we* don't live here…" I point out.

Obic's sharper. "On what grounds?" she says. "What would you say?"

Janet thinks of all the questions to which she doesn't have an answer. She doesn't have a name and Janet's never met this girl, has never even passed the time of day with her. "No, I suppose you're right," she says at last.

"You can't lay claim to any real relationship," says Obic.

Janet lifts the binoculars from off the tripod, replaces the two plastic caps meant to protect the lenses. "I'd better take these back to Daniel," she says. "He'll be missing them, no doubt." A pause, then, "Best not interfere, you say? Best to make sure that we mind our business?"

We say nothing.

Specky stretches out a hand and pulls the cord to shut the blind.

I turn around to look at Kevin.

He is crying.

Away from the Body and at Home

Another day.

A Saturday? Or maybe it's a Sunday. The weekend anyway. Beyond that no one knows and no one cares. I'm leafing through a copy of *The Chronicle* which Kev has left. I've spread its supplements across the floor and idle through the minutes in consideration of potential purchases of clocks, a globe that opens up to show a hidden drinks collection and a lamp. It's not your standard sort of lamp. Compact and portable, this lamp boasts a dimmer switch, the perfect quantity of balanced light – as close to natural as anyone can get – delivered at exactly the right angle when you're reading. Too good a promise to be true, you think? But if like me your work is creepy, and it tends to reach its peak at night when mouths hang open and your clients are asleep, a lamp like that could be invaluable. The beamwidth is adjustable, the whole thing is upgraded with the newest LED technology. Extortionately priced, of course, but quality like this can't be acquired off-the-shelf and must be sent for. It might be worth investing several hundred pounds and perhaps once we've got used to parting with that much, we won't care that they've added extra for the postage. In the timed-out boredom of a Saturday – a Sunday? – I'll admit that I'm quite tempted, am about to take a punt, to be persuaded I'm in dire need of lamps, but then I get distracted by another supplement.

Another leaflet for a moment leads the race for my attention. This one advertises sweaters for the chronically unstylish. It features pictures of a woman who might as well be Janet if she lost some weight and grew her hair and airbrushed all the wrinkles out. A Janet as she wishes she were twenty years ago. The company which flogs these sweaters claims they'll fool the most perceptive of your neighbours into thinking that you're flush enough to dress yourself in real cashmere. Although it's not, they snigger, a confession from behind a notional raised hand in such a tiny print the implication is a whisper. This is nylon. But they pledge it's just as soft and delicate as cashmere and at a fraction of the price. It also comes in thirty colours. Thirty colours! Did you know you wanted this much choice before you saw it laid out on a page? Swatches line both edges, show the colours in their not-quite-infinite variety. Take your pick from shades of daffodil or cyclamen or bluebell. Shipped in under fourteen days, or seven if you choose express delivery, though for an extra fee, of course.

I'm pleased to say I'm not susceptible to this particular advertisement. It's far too brash and don't forget I'm not a woman. I see exactly how it works. The names they've chosen are evocative of nature when in fact they aim to kit you out in thermoplastic. The references to flowers are an invitation to forget that every time you wash such items microfibres sweep far out to sea and gather in the stomach of a fish. Only idiots would order luxuries like these and for the bargain price of fifty quid, or ninety-eight should you be shrewd and order two at once.

"D'you think that Janet might like some of these?" I ask. They're clingier than anything we've seen her wear to date but do come with a vast, disguising cardigan to match. You spend a hundred pounds or more, the company will even send the products in a special ventilated pouch, a little freebie for their trusting customers. They're meant to give the sweaters some protection, to keep the jumpers guarded from imaginary plastic moths which patrons are encouraged to believe are loitering in wardrobes, waiting for the chance to munch on artificial fibres. "Don't you think that Janet might like one of these?" I say again, and wave the leaflet, rattle it to shake the air. It suddenly occurs to me that we should buy her something as a thank-you present because we've been here in her flat far longer than we'd ever planned.

There's no reply from Obic, nor from Specky. They've pulled the duvet up across the sofa and the mound they've made begins to stir. I see that all their feet are intertwined and stick out at one end. I can't help thinking that although we're meant to be in this together, we weren't supposed to be as much together as they're being now. We're meant to be one team, a whole, and not supposed to split up into pairs. Specks and Obic shut me out and leave me more and more with Kevin, or entirely to my own devices. Even when I'm with them, I still feel completely on my own.

We've spent too long already in not doing very much, I think. We ought to leave, to go outside to make some further progress in our shadowing. We're wasting time on Janet now we've not seen her for days. Not since she hid inside her bedroom after witnessing the death of that young girl across the road.

Obic said it wasn't possible to feel so much for someone you don't know. She claims that Janet had exaggerated her reaction, that she made too big a meal of it, that most of what she claims as pity for the girl is really sorrow for herself. To engage your parasympathetic nervous system is a selfish act – so Obic says – and Janet only sought a rush of oxytocin in a bid to make herself feel good.

I don't know if that is true.

Credit where it's due, Kev did his best. He hugged the woman, tried to calm her down when she gave in to strong outbursts of indignation, waved her fists in anger and frustration at the world beyond her blind. "We have *a duty* to inform someone," she sobbed into his collar, and then stamped a slippered foot and caught his toe. Kev – bless him – didn't even wince but nodded kindly when she said, "That man's just *murdered* her as near as makes no difference. Someone ought to flag it, make him pay for everything he's done."

"You could say that," said Obic as she took a knife and sliced a piece of cake. "I can see why that occurred to you and why you'd argue it's a valid point of view. But don't you think a man like that would thrive on the attention? Publicity would only stoke his ego. Just imagine if he got his picture in the paper with his palm put up to block the lens, the headlines calling him notorious. He'd get a kick from that."

"I don't think we should let him have the satisfaction," Specky said, then added, "I'm about to clean my glasses, by the way. Would it help if I did yours too while I'm at it? It'd get rid of the smears across your lenses, help you see things far more clearly."

"'Cos if you really think about it," Obic carried on, "all anybody's got is what they've done and what they choose to do in future." She put the slice of cake on Janet's favourite plate and held it out as an inducement. "We all die in the end however we decide to spend our time, and as you're knocking on a bit there's not much left for you. It would be such a shame for you to waste the few years that you've still got left. Why don't you focus on the things that really matter?" She spoke in circles, waved the plate so sugared scents hung in the air. "Can you really say you care enough about that girl to give up chunks of your remaining time to help identify her killer?"

"The best way with a narcissist is to make sure you ignore them," Specks agreed. I watched him unwrap sticks of chewing gum and start to soften them between his teeth. "Ignoring them eradicates their sense of worth," he said, "so worse for him, in fact, if you do nothing."

"I hadn't thought of that… Perhaps you're right," sniffed Janet. She shot a look towards me, then returned her gaze to Kev, then settled on the cake. She wanted it, but didn't know if she should take it. Maybe she was too distressed to eat? Certainly she wasn't able to commit herself. She gave a little laugh, a strangled squeal, then tried to cover it by fussing with her handkerchief. I thought we'd lost her then, that she was starting to be cagey. Perhaps she made her mind up then and there to hide from us, because she said, "I don't know what's come over me," and disappeared into her bedroom.

Specks and Obic raised a toast to closed doors and uncertainty, but Kev and I would not join in.

We all agreed it would be most appropriate for Kev to check on Janet. She likes him best and he's the oldest, so if he goes in her bedroom then there's never any hint of how's-your-father. No one thinks the elderly get turned on by a counterpane.

We followed him into the corridor and waited as he crouched outside her door. He tapped and paused and tapped again, and cooed something innocuous. I don't remember what exactly. Janet didn't answer, so he pottered off and got a tray of tea and custard creams.

"I'll close my eyes or come in blindfolded if you like," he offered.

The rest of us can testify that she said no, it was all right, she was quite decent in her nightie and her dressing gown.

She let him in.

He got to stay all night.

I don't know what they talked about. I'm always first to fess up to mistakes and I'll admit it was another slip-up when I thought that we didn't have to listen. All our conversations are encrypted end-to-end and so I can't just open up those files. I thought we could rely on Kev. I thought he'd give a blow-by-blow account of everything that happened. We never dreamed someone as bland as Janet could have such a huge effect on him, that he'd come out so moody and dissatisfied.

"God... look at you..." I said. It was apparent that he'd hardly slept. His skin was pale and dappled – though that might have been the early morning light. He stared at me with bloodshot eyes. "But what on earth has happened, mate?" I asked, and even Obic would've put an arm round him if he'd not been so quick and ducked away.

"I don't... especially... want to talk about... it." He spaced his words out, like he had to think hard which was next and what the order was, and how to make some sense out of the muddle in his head.

A quick hack into Janet's ancient laptop and we saw they'd spent the night researching stats about the dead and dying. Thirteen people every day are killed from poisoning by drugs, it's claimed, and though the town of Combfoot Chase is not high on the table – a little too far south to be amongst the very badly hit – it still has its fair share of the appalling stories. Janet's copied documents from websites, stored them in a separate file and saved it on her home screen. The file contains a string of data, all the latest news, the breaking stories, plus a range of articles of comment and opinion. We read through all the arguments, the words of bourgeois columnists who say we should be sorry for the victims, that we should own the guilt and make ourselves responsible for other people's outcomes, in contrast with another point of view which seeks to pin the blame on those who occupy the upper middle classes. According to this version then a death by drugs is all the fault of neoliberal elites. Their metropolitan habits – although casual and recreational – cause misery for others further down the economic chain, they say.

We've also seen an entry written into Janet's diary. We snatched a peek when she went to the loo and quite forgot she'd left her journal open on the bedspread. She's not the type to keep religious records of each day. In fact this is the first time in the year she's noted anything substantial and other entries are just lists of scheduled appointments and reminders, notes to meet a friend for coffee, or a date to get a cut and set, a memo of a mammogram. She's unaccustomed to the diarist's form of self-reflection, so her thoughts are pretty garbled, but we got the general gist. As you'd expect, the style is stream-of-consciousness. She hasn't written anything original, but no one's managed that for years, though we were quite impressed by how she made her feelings seem authentic. There's skill in that; not everyone achieves it. In her diary she expresses sorrow at the waste of life. If someone with a gun had mowed down thirteen people, she maintains, there'd be an uproar, so why overlook a death when it's by drugs? She speculates on how to bring due pressure to bear on the town's police. Although we've told her she should leave it, *someone* has to stand up for the vulnerable, she writes.

We only got to read as far as that and then the toilet flushed and we all had to rush back to the living room, pretend to twiddle thumbs. The one of us who's good at whistling whistled and the rest of us made out that we'd seen nothing.

Obic's desperate to read the rest, but Kev's first time in Janet's bedroom was his one-and-only last. No one goes in anymore and Janet asks for trays of tea and biscuits to be left outside the door.

The first few days she picked at biscuits. We took photos of discarded halves where teeth had scraped off buttercream and put them in a file as evidence. It's harder to find proof she drank some tea. Today it's clear the tray's been left untouched. It seems that this late on in life she's raised a guard against her gluttony, begun a fast to purify her thoughts.

Obic scoffs and says her actions are misplaced, that Janet cannot hope to make amends for what she's seen. "It won't do any good," she mocks. "She'll starve herself to death and it won't make the slightest difference." She says we ought to barge in and force-feed her, through a tube if necessary. "And while we're at it, Kev can grab her diary." She says if someone's broken down or ill, they've no entitlement to privacy.

This statement makes me feel uneasy and I'd like to chat it through with Kevin. Someone who's as old as him can take the longer view, I think, but when I look for him, he's nowhere to be seen. Without his back-up will I dare stand up to Obic's strengthening opinions? Specky's hardly helpful at the best of times and recently he's too preoccupied with trying to look like Daniel. He's bought himself the same design of T-shirt, though without the pecs to stretch it out it doesn't have the same effect.

"Do either of you know where Kev has gone?" I ask.

The mounded duvet undulates, the only answer muffled moans from Obic.

I dare say they were not intended in reply to me.

*

I walk away from Janet's flat and from Connection House. Vacated streets unfurl as though they shrug me off. The sound of footsteps bounces back and forth between the walls of silent buildings. Is it still so early? I'd have thought the town would be awake by now.

If you should ever think to make a film of this, I'd recommend you use a long shot, chase that plastic bag which whirls around the lamppost, track the rustle of the litter in the gutter. Only long enough to emphasise the emptiness, you understand, to stir the audience to question what has caused the citizens to hunker down and hide. Perhaps a rumour has gone round, a tweet about a prowler has gone viral and a mob has loosed the metaphorical dogs. The buzz is that a paedophile is stalking Combfoot Chase. He's turned up in the suburbs, somewhere nice, where deviants are neither welcome nor expected. The twist is that in truth he's just a paediatrician, but people find it hard to spot the difference and will muddle up desire to heal with a presumption of an ugly love.

The next scene will be in the school where teachers call the kids into an emergency assembly. "We've got to talk to them again," they say in huddled staffroom voices, "and remind them of the principles of stranger-danger." For everybody needs to know about the hazards which we let in when we open up our doors and our computers.

Fade to Mr Tombleson, who's reading something that his daughter's posted on her newsfeed. Cut to a close-up of a letter sent by Mr Locke describing how a group of unknown figures have been spotted lingering around the school gates looking shifty. Mr Tombleson again, but in a state of utter outrage. He decides he'd better dust off all the hoes and rakes and spades he keeps on neat racks in his garden shed, because you never know he might be called upon to wield one. He will telephone his daughter, tell her she must stay indoors and keep her kiddies off the streets. "If push does come to shove," he'll say, "you can rely on me to keep the family safe from all the freaks and predators out there." He'll do his bit to drive out the unsavoury types – there's no room for the likes of them in pleasant middle-class communities – because you can't trust the authorities to do what's right these days. If jobs need doing, then it takes the likes of him to take the matter in his own two hands. It's part and parcel of his civic duty. The music swells as he asserts that if he must resort to violence, then so be it. His desire for law and order will be at the very root of any rioting.

Of course it's far more probable Combfootians have decided that they'd simply rather stay at home. The likelihood is nothing's happening at all; it's just that nothing in these streets can tempt the people of the town out into the chill spring weather. Admittedly there's no engaging drama in this version, but real life hardly ever brings the frisson of excitement that we crave, and fear of unknown threats will always make a more sensational story. If there ever was a ruckus here in placid Combfoot Chase, no word has got as far as me, and ignorance is harder to achieve these days when every citizen's a journalist and news will never sleep.

The team that fronts *The Chronicle* will say its mission is to document the first version of history. To that end it reports even the most trivial of events because, it thinks, what will become important tends to hide behind what comes across as unassuming, and truth is more banal than any tale that truly captures our attention.

At the junction of two roads I turn towards the part of town in which we launched our observations several weeks ago – remember Ruth and her ill-judged rejection of the idylls of Victoriana? Here every house is like a little library or a university made miniature. The tiled paths flanked by painted railings lead towards the sturdy doorways studded with bright panels of stained glass. The steep-pitched roofs sport ornate gables, make a feature of a churchlike finial. These are the homes of doctors, lawyers, teachers, even the odd council official. Of all those Mr Tombleson despises, the anybodies who aspire to leadership or government. Of those who think advanced degrees engender a distinct advantage. Of those who – though they'd never say it where it might be caught on tape or overheard – believe they've earnt the right to think themselves a cut above the rest. Of those who think because they've been successful they are also right. Of those who are quite certain that they'll never be the thoughtless and impulsive scum like you and me.

I don't know why I've come this way. I can't imagine Kev would choose a place like this to take time out and put his feet up. These are streets for intellectuals – or those who like to pass as such – and that would not appeal to him. He harbours a romantic vision of the working man and of the past because he can't remember how it really was, and thinks that people used to live in simpler times. Still, as I have to start my search and start it somewhere, I cross the road and duck inside a café.

"Have you seen this chap?" I ask the man behind the counter.

His look to me is one of sheer astonishment. No lost or missing souls have ever passed this way, he thinks. Perhaps his café's too far off the beaten track, or those who seek obscurity would rather not hang out at long communal tables? They'd favour grubby mugs of instant, would prefer to save their last few pennies, not to spend them on a choice of seventeen varieties of the world's most banging roasts, he thinks. Most probably they don't care if their vegan fakon is made out of aubergine or old banana skins. Whatever be the reason, no one's ever made enquiries for a missing person here. His regulars know who they are and what they want, and that their coffee's at its very best once shat out of a civet.

The man wipes coffee grounds from off his hands onto the tea towel, which is tucked in coolly in the pocket of his jeans. The towel is linen, ethically sourced, of course. He takes my phone and studies Kevin's photo, then he shakes his head. "Nah, 'aven't seen 'im. Not in 'ere, mate. Not the last few days at any rate."

"You sure?" I say. "Could you just take a closer look?"

"I don't think I could miss 'im, mate. 'E's not the usual for in 'ere, is 'e?"

And he's right. Kev would stand out and like the sorest sort of thumb. He's old, he trims his beard and doesn't wear a pair of braces with a bright plaid shirt.

Nor are there flocks of customers in here. He'd have no hope of taking cover in a crowd. Only one long table has been occupied. At one end two men bow their heads and mutter over what is written on a piece of paper. The paper looks official, a report of sorts. It's taken from its envelope, brown paper, lying on the stripped-back wood between them, and the older of the two is asking questions. He follows every word with an underlining finger, is alert to every detail, reads each line that's written like his life depends on it. It's easy to deduce he's concentrating hard, because his lips form all the words to help his brain soak up the information. The paper doesn't tell familiar stories. You can see he's reading something alien or difficult. The younger man who's with him looks on and waits patiently. He sips a coffee, seems relaxed and confident of a beneficial outcome.

At the far end of the same table, a figure in an anorak. Its coat is padded and its hood pulled up against the cold, although a log fire roars in a stove not more than two metres away. From the dark interior of the hood, the white wires of a set of earphones wind and snake their way around the body, disappear into a pocket. Private sound to blot the choice of cool, ironic music which is ground out of an ancient record player from the corner of the café. The occupier of the coat has one hand visible. It clasps a book – a play to judge from how the print's laid out. A finger hovers, is occasionally lifted to a hidden tongue for dampening, is used to leaf a page before a pause and a repeat. A sharpened pencil idles on the table, kept at hand in case it's called upon to underscore a line or mark the rise of an inflection. Should the need crop up. The pencil's squeaky sharp. No lines have yet been chosen. None it seems are deemed significant enough to stand above the rest.

There's something in that cushioned body that's familiar. I'm certain that we've met before and that I know that posture.

"Ava?" I presume to slide onto an empty bench. Best not ask for permission if there's any chance you'll be refused. "How nice to see a friendly face," I say. The look she gives me isn't friendly. She snaps the book shut, turns it face down on the table. "What you reading?" She lays a palm across the cover, ducks her thumb in vain attempt to hide the spine. "*A Doll's House*? Only like the classics, do you?" A pursed lip signals her displeasure in case I hadn't noticed that my interruption is unwelcome. "I can see you playing Nora…" A fluttered lash. It's good to see that even with defences up she's still prone to the dash of flattery. "I'm not entirely ignorant of literature," I say. "You're not still working on *Medea* then?" A little shaking of the head. She slides a white bud from each ear and winds the wires into a tight, neat coil. "Why not?"

"Run's ended." Whispered through a stiffened lip.

"Oh… Ah." She drums three fingers on the book, taps out a hollow and repeated pattern, as if to say, *I'm rather busy, must you go so soon?* "Hey, nice to have the chance to catch up, though," I say, deliberately oblivious. Oh no, don't think that I'll be going anywhere. The thin end's in and now, you see, I only have to shove the wedge. "You must remember me. I'm Mr Arak… You remember? We have met up before."

Ava casts a hooded glance towards the men, who pass another page of text across the table. "Just there, where I've put a cross, down at the bottom there," the younger one is saying. The older one picks up a pen and signs.

To what?

To something.

I wonder if she knows the men and if I've gate-crashed an appointment. No one in their right mind would believe in the connection. The parties are positioned far too far apart, for one thing, but I might suggest it in the hope of jolting a reaction, of nudging her into a conversation that she doesn't want to have. Any information she reveals could count as useful. Nothing is so slight it can't be added to the pile. You never know when you'll turn up a key piece of the jigsaw, find that one small precious link that makes full sense of everything once slotted into place.

The younger man looks pleased. He nods and folds the papers, slides them back into the envelope. "Thanks so much, Paul. I can't say it enough. You're such a help," he says.

The two men shake hands over the expanse of table.

Ava fiddles with a wristband stuffed beneath her cuff.

"What you got there?" I ask curiously. "That's new…"

"It's nothing. Just something a friend passed on to me."

"What, Grace? How is she by the way? Say hi when you next see her, won't you?"

The features of the band are simple, one blue button and a yellow. Ava's fingers seem uncertain which she ought to press. And then she sighs. "It's meant to track my mood," she says. "You press the yellow if you feel okay, the blue if something makes you sad." She shows me, albeit reluctantly. "Grace thinks I've been a little down of late. She says I need to figure out what's bugging me and need to do a bit more of what makes me happier…" And then she tails off, thinks already that she's said too much. She snaps her mouth shut, followed by a swift and shallow frown. She stands up and attempts to stuff her book into her pocket. The book is obstinate and doesn't want to go. When the designer made a coat for women, he spent longer paring back the hips into a pleasing shape than pandering to the demands of function. If Ava wants to squeeze that book into that pocket, she'll have to make the effort to make room. She takes her phone out, lays it on the table, makes a sharp cluck of despair when even after this manoeuvre she's not done enough to be successful. The book refuses to cooperate – oh, fuck a duck, I'm stuck here – and she slumps back down and sighs again.

I wait. I know she'll have been trained to be uncomfortable with a long gap in a conversation. All I have to do is stay and her surrender will be guaranteed.

"So, Mr Arak, is it?" she submits. Hah, good, I knew it. Lovely to be right occasionally. "I don't believe I ever knew your name."

"Oh, really? No, well, maybe not. But there we are. You do remember me, though?"

The tiniest of nods. A little folding of the hands. To help keep her fear under control. When she speaks she says, "But then again, I don't know *who* you are."

"I'm no one special—"

"But you're following me."

"No. Not at all… A lucky chance. I happened to look over, and ta-dah, you're here. You happen to be sitting here all by yourself. Though actually I'm glad I've managed to catch up with you."

"Because? What d'you want from me? I don't think I've got anything you need. Are you a journalist? Are you about to run an article? You want an interview and think you've got a lead on something, want to get a scoop?"

"No, no…" Someone ought to advise Ava not to get ideas above her station. We mustn't think we're individually important. The fact is, most of us are quite dispensable especially at work, though no one likes to hear that no one cares.

"Oh, so not a talent scout?" she says. The disappointment twitches round her mouth. "That would've made a sort of sense," she broods. "You know, of all the sneaking round behind the scenes. I thought there was a chance you'd come on the behalf of big producers."

"No, not that. I'm sorry."

"Grace said she thought you might have plans to whisk me off, to give me an audition for a West End show. She said it as a joke, but I still thought about it and I got a bit excited." When Ava laughs it's full of both regret and longing.

"What a great imagination," I say.

"No, it's not." A scowl. "It happens. It's been known. You read about someone who got a lucky break in all the magazines. And lots of them are far less talented than me, Grace says."

"I s'pose she would." It might have happened. Once. In dreams. Or in a play. A film. It might make life pass easier if you can kid yourself there's something wonderful just waiting round the corner.

"So if you're not a scout, who are you and why me?" Ava chews her lip and concentrates.

"Why not?" I say, and watch her thoughts go dark.

It's times like this that she's supposed to press the blue button, she thinks. "I reckon that you're here for something sinister …" she says at last, still unconvinced success and happiness are built on little things. She signals to the man behind the counter. "It's not exactly hard to see you're shady," she says, and she gives an order for another Costa Rican Tarrazu. She pauses, but she can't resist a courtesy. "I suppose you'd better make it two," she says. She doesn't have to tell him that she wants it white, because he knows her and he knows. "So let me see… You're in the military?" she asks. The café fills with scents of citrus mingled with dark chocolate. "Or a member of a thinktank? Or the civil service? No, too far-fetched. I can't believe that anyone would think that *I'd* be useful to the state… But something deep, I think, for sure, something clandestine… Perhaps the freemasons, or the papists? Not a communist?"

"No, no, I'm none of those…" Or all of them, depending how you want to look at it. "But when did *you* get so suspicious?" I try to laugh her questions off. At least, I think, she knows that someone's watching her. For these few moments, when she makes a new world out of nothing, dreams of something so improbable it's almost possible to think it might come true, she's lit up, not a matter of complete indifference.

"It's your behaviour," she says. "Smacks of con-man or of rogue."

That hits a spot. "We're none of us as competent as we let our colleagues think," I say.

The man behind the counter has made fancy leaf-shapes in the crema. He's practised for a long time, got the technique down to a fine art. He tries hard not to take offence when customers pick up a spoon and stir the crema to a sludge before his skill is noticed or appreciated.

Ava scoops the froth into her mouth and sucks the teaspoon thoughtfully. "So tell me then. What is it that you want? What brings you here, to me?"

The truth is far too boring to pique anybody's interest. An old man wandered off is commonplace and no one's shocked by stories of the absent elderly these days. In Combfoot Chase a doddery soul is packed off pronto. No one thinks they should be made accountable for their forebears. Once the number of departed is sufficiently enormous, it's impossible to treat the disappearances with anything but nonchalance. Example. Grace and Ava met when they decided to despatch their mothers to a nursing home and settled on the same place, a place where once-sharp shrivelled minds are rendered absolutely useless. The two girls face the chairs where mothers used to sit each day without regret, and tell each other what they did was simply to be kind. In the face of such alarming level-headedness, my tale of losing Kev will not be good enough for jazz, because Ava – like the rest of us – prefers her stories more exciting. She likes a fairy tale or anything with the promise of adventure. She reads crime fiction so she's sure a villain always gets what's coming. There must be risks, but mysteries must be possible to solve if the narratives are to be kept appealing.

I fit my pitch to all her preconceptions. "I think that something *really bad* has happened," I begin. I drop my voice and throw a furtive glance along the table for good measure. "Kev has *vanished* recently, d'you see? He's… *disappeared.*" Yeah, that should do it. That should be enough, I think. Most people are a sucker for hyperbole. Ava frowns and lifts a hand to slide her hood from off her head. She turns an unplugged ear towards me. I take this as an invitation to continue. "I'm on a hunt for him," I whisper. Best stick close to the truth. Much harder to unpick it from the lies.

"Who's Kev?" she asks.

I hold my phone out, Kev's mug lit up on the screen. "There, that should jog your memory," I say.

Ava slides her coffee cup to one side, leans across the table, pays attention to his face. "Oh, him. The little one," she says.

"That's right."

"The one whose eyes droop. And whose mouth droops at the corners. And whose stomach droops and who wears the droopy clothes."

"The one whose everything has drooped," I say, "except his hair, which sticks up straight on end."

"And has he really… *disappeared*?" She's not convinced. I see the scepticism and the hesitation. She looks at me as though she's calculating how far she could throw me if she had to. "He's called Kev, you say?" she asks.

"That's it. He is."

"And you're out searching for him?" Ava says a search and thinks of quests, of stalking and of journeys.

I hear search and think of click-through quick-and-easy bait, solutions predetermined, all the answers ready, waiting, all you have to do is open them and read. "Yes. Yes, I'm very worried," I say. "*Seriously*." I take a sip of the delicious coffee, leave a line of crema all along my upper lip.

"I'm sorry, but I don't think I can help you," Ava says. She twiddles with her earphones. She wants to put them in again and block me out, but etiquette will not permit it. "I wish I could," she says, then offers me a napkin with a gesture that I need to wipe my mouth, "but I can't say that I've seen him."

"I'd not've thought such things could happen in a town as nice as Combfoot Chase…" I say. I'll be persistent if I'm nothing else.

She sighs. "All right," she says, "so when did you last see him?"

"Yesterday. The day before? I'm not exactly sure."

"So not *that* long ago…?"

"You'll help me look, though, won't you?" I grasp the padded sleeve of Ava's coat.

She eyes my clutching fingers narrowly and weighs up her choices. She lifts her pencil, toys with it. She rocks it in between her fingers like a see-saw or a scale, this way, that way, then with added complications. The pencil does not grasp it should be mastered, that like the truth it should be brought under control. It flicks high in the air and clatters back unruly on the table. The two men at the other end are startled and look up.

"Sorry," Ava mouths to them, and then returns her gaze to me. "I don't know why you think that you can turn up out of nowhere and assume I'll help to do your dirty work," she says.

"Kev isn't dirty!" I protest. He does look rather dirty in the photograph. "And I've not come out of nowhere..." I might be buried deeper than I was when she last saw me and so discrete I'd fit inside that pocket where her book won't go, but just because she hasn't noticed me, it doesn't mean I've not been here at all. "I thought it would be faster if you helped," I say. "I thought you'd *like* to, 'cos you know Kev personally. I thought you'd *want* to know what happened to him—"

"Oh, c'mon! You can't say that I know him—"

"But you've met him."

"Not the same thing."

"Still..."

A pause.

"So say again what makes you think he's disappeared. Why don't you think he's made his mind up to head off, to go, oh, I don't know... just, somewhere else?"

Most of us can be sucked in by signs, for all we claim to base our lives on science and on reason, so I'll titillate her actor's penchant for a prophecy. "Well, probably nothing, silly, really," I say, half an eye trained on her mood band. "It's just the other night he asked me if I'd look after his pocket watch."

"His pocket watch?"

"It's very old. I think he said his parents gave it to him." Yep, that's good. This detail builds a backstory and gives her hooks to hang imagination on.

"Go on…" Down the rabbit hole you go, sweet Ava.

"Yeah, you know the sort of thing, old-fashioned, made for waistcoats, on a chain… I think it was an heirloom, think his grandpa took it with him to the war. It's gold. Engraved. He said it was significant, for sure." All these morsels are important to the character. Impossible to ever have enough. And if you need some further bites of information, you've got my full permission to invent them for yourself.

"Oh, yes, I see. So have you brought it with you? Can I have a look?"

If only I could manage alchemy. "No… No, I haven't got it on me. Thought it better if I kept it safe, back at the ranch."

"But this inscription… what's it say?"

A silken line, a sticky thread to make the unreal real. "It's written on the casing, on the back, some sort of quote, I think, or aphorism, engraved in scrolly writing…"

"Copperplate?"

"That's it. Yeah, that exactly. It says that, *All we have is time well spent.*"

"That's interesting," she says, "and apt." She shuffles on the bench. Her body points towards me now, her hands, her feet, her torso and her face aligned, alive with interest. "So, if it's so precious, like you say, why'd he pass it on to you, not take it with him?"

"That's the point. That's why I'm worried. I've got no idea. He simply wandered over, asked me to look after it." It doesn't matter what I say, as long as I can say it with conviction. I could ramble, interrupt myself and leap from one thing to another, and she'd still think there was something real to understand, some truth to dig out of the nonsense. "It isn't like him. And he tried to give the watch to Obic first…" And bingo, now she pities me. It's easier to empathise with nobodies who know they're second best. She knows exactly how it feels to lose and knows that losers tend to lose it all.

"Oh, hang on, though, who's Obic?" Ava asks. She rests her elbows on the table, chin rests in her hands, is lost amongst my loops of yarn already.

"The woman on our team." Of all the details this one, I think, must be least important.

"Oh, I *do* remember her. And she was *gorgeous*."

"Was she? Is she?" Not the answer I predicted, not the way the story is supposed to go.

"Oh, yeah, she is. You can't pretend you haven't noticed."

"I don't think I'd rank her so high—"

"Oh, would you not? Matter of taste, perhaps?"

"I suppose. Depends what sort of thing you like."

"She turn you down then, did she?" Ava laughs. A sting. "So why did she not want it then?" She laughs again. "The pocket watch, I mean."

"She said she didn't need it as she's got a Fitbit."

"Right… And that's it? All we've got to indicate he's disappeared? You don't think that we've jumped the gun?"

The gun goes bang and earns us both a bonus. Game on. Story back on track. She's still in and she called us 'we'. "I know it doesn't seem like much," I plead, "but it's not normally how he is. The Kev I know is utterly reliable. I can't stress this enough: it's absolutely out of character." I close my eyes, can conjure up Kev's furrowed face when he is handing me his pocket watch. How funny, I think. Part of me believes this really happened, though with eyes wide open I know nothing really did. The pocket watch does not exist, is just a loot box I discovered as I made my way inside Ava's imagination.

"Okay, perhaps you're right to worry," Ava says, "but people can surprise you. They do all sorts of things you don't expect them to. The chances are he'll soon turn up…" She presses quit. The End. And they lived happily ever after. She's stuck on yellow-button happy, in a state of skilled obstruction.

I'm so disappointed I have to distract myself by reading through the list of specials that the man behind the counter has begun to scrawl up on the chalkboard. Would I rather have the sprouted artichoke toast with the grilled shishitos, or the whey brioche bun with a side of menemen? "What d'you mean by people are surprising?" It's an empty question asked to keep a conversation going, but I'm lucky. Ava wants to give me an example and sets off in a sing-song tone.

"I once knew this librarian when I was still at school…" she says.

I yawn and think, the menemen for preference because I like an egg.

"…Now *she* surprised me. I think I was the most surprised I've ever been by her. Though not when she was living. To be quite honest I don't remember giving her the time of day in the time she was alive. Although we used to bitch about the fact she wore her hair up in a bun and never got it in the middle. It always used to sit on one side of her neck or on the other, and we used to tell each other how we thought that that looked really stupid, although it didn't really, and no one really cared about the way she did her hair. The only time we took the slightest notice was when she told us to be quiet. She wanted us to use the library silently and read these deadly books by dead white men. She wouldn't have a graphic novel in the library, wouldn't give them houseroom, though a lot of us were desperate to read them. 'Oh, go on, Miss,' we all used to beg, 'it's still a sort of reading, in't it?' But though she always said she wanted us to read, she never let us have the books we wanted."

This librarian is dull enough to be believable, I think, though hardly someone I'd choose to remember. My mind stirs onions, peppers, chillis, cracks an egg inside a pocket of tomato.

"Then one lad, Mark, it was, decided he would start up a petition. He put a notice up with 'Give us Manga' printed at the top, and stuck it on the students' notice board. We signed it, whether we had any urge to read that sort of thing or not, because we wanted our revenge on the librarian, I think. I felt quite naughty when I wrote my name, then spent a whole day with my heart up in my mouth 'cos someone took the notice down and gave it in to Mr Locke. I was terrified to think my name was on a piece of paper in my own hand as proof that I believed in something that I wasn't absolutely sure that I believed in.

A few days later our English lesson was interrupted by the secretary. The head had called Mark in, she said. He wanted him to talk to the librarian about their disagreement over graphic novels, and had sent her with instructions they should meet him in his office. The dull librarian wouldn't give an inch, so Mark said afterwards. She'd simply said there were too many pictures in a book like that, and had insisted libraries were intended to house words. She'd told him if he wanted to acquire such things, he'd have to use the public library down in town. They stocked all sorts, she'd told him, and they seemed to think that anything in print had value. When Mark told us everything she'd said, we all agreed she was a cow and someone used a Frube to scribble 'Moo' across her car at lunchtime." Ava's story gathers pace and every detail shared begins to crack her world a little wider. "When I look back now, I know that the librarian held a view like that only because she was much older. She must've been, oh, sixty at the very least when I last saw her, and that *is* old from the viewpoint of a kid, don't you agree? Her attitude came from her generation, and it wasn't her fault she was out of touch. She thought that she was standing up for what was right and proper."

I give Ava a wordless thumbs-up signal of support and hope that she keeps talking.

"Okay, so now I'm getting to the bit where's she's surprising. She died and it was sudden. The caretaker was on his rounds, he said. He had to turn the lights off every night and lock the doors when all the students and the teachers had gone home, and that was when he'd found her. She was still sat on her library chair as if she were engrossed in reading. He'd only realised she was dead when he had tried to talk to her and didn't get replies. And then he said he'd touched her and he'd found that she was cold. Oh, we all shuddered when we heard that, I can tell you.

Anyway, they had to send the body for a post mortem. Not because there was reason for suspicion, but because she'd not been ill and no one saw her die and they were following procedure. You have to do it to rule out foul play, so everybody said. And when they got her body on the slab, they found that underneath her clothes she had a load of body piercings! No, no one *told* us, not officially, but I know absolutely cross-my-heart-and-hope-to-die it's true, because we had this service in the school hall to commemorate her, and I heard Mrs Kelly whispering about it. I'd ended up right at the far end of a row, so there I was, sat by her feet, and I remember everything verbatim. Mrs Kelly had to hold her hymn book up to hide her giggles. 'Would you credit it, though, Delia? In her clitoris and *everything*,' that's word for word precisely what she said. I think I nearly wet myself it was so funny. And I saw the teachers' bodies doubled up with laughter, so much so, another teacher sitting near to them gave little coughs and nods towards the stage where Mr Locke was standing, frowning down on them with obvious displeasure. Just as soon as he'd got everybody quiet, he made a signal to the head of music so we knew the time had come for him to plonk a dreary tune out on the school piano. That music was supposed to make us dutifully sad, I think, and as he played it really loud, I couldn't catch another word that Mrs Kelly said.

By the end of the assembly the school was full of it. Word had whipped along the rows of us cross-legged on the floor, and everyone believed that it was true, although there wasn't anything abnormal on the outside. Nobody had had a clue by looking at the dull librarian that her nipples and her clitoris were stapled full of silver. All we'd seen was the cocoon of tweed, a woman who'd spent every day in nagging us to read our Dickens, Hardy, Shakespeare, Trollope, even though we couldn't see how dead men could have anything to say to us.

I don't think I'd have fallen for it if I'd only heard it as a bit of idle chatter passed along by someone else, but as I'd got it from the horse's mouth, and heard it with my own two ears, that makes a difference, doesn't it? So there you have it. Like I said, most people are surprising." And Ava claps her hand across her mouth as if she's just confessed a dreadful crime.

A clock high on the café wall chimes out the hour, the turn of cogs half-visible beneath a cutwork skeleton.

"Oh, bloody hell, is that the time?" says Ava. "I'm so sorry, Mr Arak, but I've got to go. I've got auditions. Good luck finding Kev…" She stands and tucks her copy of *A Doll's House* underneath her arm.

"Well, don't forget your phone," I say.

"Oh… thanks," she says. "I don't know why I bother with it really. It's got so slow. The battery barely lasts the day. I shouldn't be surprised because I've had it years. Grace keeps on telling me I ought to get an upgrade…" She picks the phone up, displays a web of cracks across its screen.

"The chances are you'd find a cheaper contract if you did," I say, "and lots of apps won't run on a device as old as that."

"I know," she says, seems sad and adds, "They build in obsolescence, don't they, nowadays?"

I think about how short a lifetime is and how decline and degradation are inevitable.

"But I don't want a new one," Ava says. She holds her phone as if it were a loved and ugly friend. "I can't be bothered to start over."

No one does, but it's a fact of life that change will come, invited in or not.

"Right then, goodbye, good luck," she says, extends her hand for me to shake as though we've finished all our business and as though we part as friends. I see her nails are bitten to the quick. The padded sleeves of anorak are tugged down in a hurry. "No, don't read too much into that," she says. "I've just been worried. Nothing serious… No more than the usual, you know. The money worries… and some complications with… a man…" She grimaces. "I've only met Phil recently, and I'm not sure…" A pause and then an afterthought.

"Why don't you talk to those two over there?" she says, and tips a wink towards the far end of the table. "I dunno, they might know something which could help you. You could ask if they've seen Kevin, couldn't you?"

I watch her plug her earphones in and pull her hood up as she exits the café. I raise my hand to wave her off. She doesn't look back, doesn't see me or my wave, and so my gesture ends up meaning nothing, a friendly signal only to myself.

"Well, break a leg," I say, and turn to watch a tiny beetle. It's busy planning its attack upon a nut, a nut that's strayed and rolls loose on the floor.

*

"I'm not sure that I've got the time to help you..." Paul says. He's anxious, presses his palm flat against the middle of his chest. I notice that he blinks too much. The younger man has gone now and as no one else has come, we're left, the only customers remaining in the café.

The man behind the counter wets a corner of the tea towel and wipes the list of specials off the board. As far as I can see no one has bought them, but he checks the clock, decides that time is up and those particular specials aren't available anymore. The board won't stay blank very long. The man projects an image of invention. He likes people to think he is creative and will mix things up. He'll write up other dishes soon enough and make sure that his menu stays both fashionable and interesting.

"It won't take very long," I say. "Can we just walk and talk? You might've seen something and not have noticed, not have realised it's important."

The beetle has now gnawed a hole right through the side of the discarded nut. The hole is perfect, exact and round, and just three millimetres in diameter. The beetle's tunnelled no more than it has to, just enough to let it crawl inside and lay its grub-like larva. The larva will then gradually consume the nut over the course of several years, starting from the inside, working out.

*

We leave the café and we wend our way through town. Paul tells me that I'd better not expect too much. "It's not a big house," he regrets. "It's just a little terrace near the cliff. I've lived there with me wife for twenty-summat years. That is, me wife in theory, but I don't believe our marriage means that much these days." He takes great care to lower any expectations of his house and of his wife. A stranger is allowed to hear much more than he would ever tell his friends, he says. He's not got many friends. Oh no, the young man he'd met up with in the café is no friend, just someone he does business with from time to time. He sometimes chats to neighbours, though. He'll pass a bit of rhubarb or a few courgettes across the garden fence, so yes, he'd say he's got a friend in Tom next door, but they're too similar to ever compare secrets. They daren't get too much further than a quick discussion of their vegetables and topiary, so Tom has no idea of the troubles Paul is facing. He finds it quite impossible to confide in someone that he's used to seeing every day. "I thought I'd married me best mate," he says, "but it seems I was mistaken." He tells me how that morning he'd been in the bathroom, had squeezed the paste onto his brush and was about to clean his teeth when Andrea had interrupted him. "I had to suck me paunch in, pray to God she didn't notice how me nipples sat on mounds of flesh," he says, and laughs, although there isn't any humour in it. "It in't the growin' old that bothers me," he says, "it's *lookin'* old that does it. I've got moobs!" He slaps his hands onto his chest and lets his fingers fret the fat. "And when she looks at me, I realise I'm decayin'."

I don't attempt to convince Paul that old is gold, that youth can also be a burden, or to tell him he'll find freedom in acceptance of the stage he's at. I'm not his friend and so I can be blunt. "It's true," I say, "we're on the downward slope," and then we mourn our loss of youth together and wallow in regrets about the march of time.

If only we could shed these bodies, we both say. I wonder if Kev ever felt like this.

"And in the past she never used to judge me," Paul continues. "She never used to think appearances were everythin'. She used to say it was what's underneath that counts. I wish I could go back and have her see me as I was, not as I am."

"You sure it's okay if I tag along?" I ask.

"Of course," says Paul. "I don't suppose she'll notice."

*

"You're back then?" Paul's wife stops her humming when she hears the front door clack. She reaches out and switches off the radio. She's sitting at the kitchen table, doesn't turn to face Paul when he comes into the room and so she doesn't see me standing just behind him, doesn't realise she should feign a warmer greeting.

Paul halts inside the doorway and he tugs hard on his earlobe. "Yep," he says, "I'm back."

I watch him hold a hand out at the level of her shoulder and understand he wishes he could touch her. He wants to draw her to him and embrace her, but he stops himself and lets his hand drop by his side. It's clear that there's been little welcome here for ages. No longer does he dare to ask for her affection, though he still believes a man deserves to come home to a kiss. The air between them bristles with a host of unheard accusations. Do life and love boil down to this, I think, this endless giving up? I cough and touch Paul's elbow, mutter that I ought to leave him to it. He didn't give consent to this, I think. He didn't think he'd have to play his awkward private scenes in front of me.

He shakes his head to tell me that it doesn't matter. I can stay or go; it won't make any difference. There's nothing here that can't be done in public.

The woman rises suddenly, as if she senses Paul's threat to expose her. She thrusts her chair back with a screech of legs. Her hands swoop on the crockery and cutlery that had been set for dinner, and she moves away from us towards the sink beneath the window, as far away as she can get whilst staying in the kitchen. The man and wife are stationed on opposing sides, are stranded with the table filling all the gaps between. "So," she says in brittle silence, "there's another one."

It's not a question, but I see Paul hesitate. He'd like to be a rogue, but when it comes to it he stops and doubts the wisdom of a lie. "Though truth won't do me any good," he thinks. He's always subject to her anger and her censure now, only ever gets a penalty and never a reward, so speaking truth is not a matter of expedience, is more a choice about the sort of person that he wants to be. "Of whether I can live with me, not whether I can live with her." He screws his courage up and says, "Yes, there *is* somebody else," and then he braces for the onslaught.

She clatters all the dishes that have held his dinner violently into the sink. She doesn't speak.

He wishes that she would.

In rocky silence I watch Paul's wife work the washing up. She swirls rough suds with toughened hands, although I notice that she's not surprised by his behaviour. It's a consequence of age, and ageing doesn't only come to someone else, I think. She's older too and must be plumper than she was when she was young. There's evidence of back fat where her bra cuts in and apron cords are tied too tight and slice into a thickened waist. She's tied herself in knots to keep him out, I think, and nothing he can do or say will ever now unravel her. He wants her notice, but she lets him feel forgotten. I wonder when these two last saw each other naked. Long ago, I'm sure. At night, like Janet, she will probably change behind the locked door of the bathroom, only let him see her shrouded in a nightie or a dressing gown. It won't be long before she makes the proposition that he moves into the other room. It's hardly any wonder if he looks elsewhere for comfort.

"D'you know what sparked the change?" I'd asked him as we'd made our way through Combfoot Chase. We'd had some time to talk because Paul had suggested that we take the long way round, divert into the park and stop beside the pond.

"Let's feed the ducks," he'd said, and showed me how he kept a plastic bag for crusts in his coat pocket for this very purpose. We'd joined a cluster of small children who had reached the banks before us. Unlike them – who'd cast their bread at random on the waters and had quickly become bored, had had to be placated with ice cream – Paul had taken time, had made sure crumbs had fallen close to every opened beak.

While he'd been occupied with this, I'd looked around and spotted the young mum. She'd parked her pram nearby, was slumped down in exhaustion on a bench. She'd walked for ages while the baby howled, had traipsed for miles and miles before at last the damn thing stopped, had had to trudge through almost every street in town, though she'd been careful to avoid the fancy houses by the river. I'd quickly turned my head away from her, though I was pretty sure she hadn't seen me. She was busy pulling empty packs of cigarettes from out of pockets. In the end she'd found a fag, had lit it, sucked it hungrily. I was relieved to see she didn't blow her smoke in the direction of her child.

"You have to watch out for that duck there," Paul had said, had pointed to a snapping, quacking bird which was much bigger than the rest. "It snatches from the others' mouths and takes the lot if you allow it." Paul had yah-ed and shooed the duck away, determined that the weakest would be given every chance to feed. He'd said he likes the sense of being kind and since he has retired, he's tried to end each day with one thing done he thinks might have been useful.

I didn't tell him bread has little value for a duck. They fill their stomachs, then don't bother to find food that does them good. I shut my mouth and let him keep his few illusions. I'd only said the ducks reminded me of all those men lined up outside the kebab van. "It's how they're queuing up," I'd said. They'd waddled after Paul complacently, had known their turn would come, that all they had to do was quack and open up their beaks and somehow they'd be fed.

"Well, so they do!" Paul had said, and then he'd laughed out loud.

That laugh had drawn the attention of the young mum on the bench. She'd peered at me through screwed-up eyes. "Oh, bloody hell," she'd said, "you're everywhere." She'd stubbed her cigarette out on the path and scooted off, had pushed the pram in front of her at highest speed. She'd almost crashed straight into Jason, who at that moment was exactly two thirds through the standard circuit of his daily jog.

"Watch out there, will you?" he'd said, cheerfully enough.

"Fuck off," she'd yelled, and disappeared behind a bandstand and a laurel bush.

"Was there any trigger in particular," I'd asked, "for you and Andrea, I mean?"

Paul had thought a moment, unsure what to tell a friendly stranger, nor if he could trust others not to pass his secrets round. "The only thing was that I had a heart attack," he'd said. "I know it frightened her, though I can't remember much of it meself. Only a sense of levitation, like I was movin' up. And then I came back down and something had detached." He'd paused to watch the bobbing of the ducks. "I thought emergencies like that would bring us close together," he'd continued. "I thought that it might make us need each other more, but no, it didn't work that way for us. And when I tell her that I love her now, I don't think she believes me and she never says it back."

I was pleased that he'd decided to confide in an outsider. It's easier to talk to someone when they have no inkling of your past or reputation. I hoped he'd feel freed once he'd spoken everything aloud.

He'd realised, with a mild dose of surprise, he'd said, that he'd been feeling rather desperate. "And then a month or so ago I overheard her on the phone," he'd carried on. "I'd been out for a walk on doctor's orders. Nothing strenuous, not enough to make me chest pump, just a stroll, but still important for recovery, so they'd said. I'd got back, taken off me coat and shoes and left 'em in the porch, just like she asks me to, and then I heard her. I wasn't snoopin', but she'd raised her voice and so I couldn't help it…"

By this point we had left the park, were walking down the street which runs along beneath the cliff. I noticed Paul's pace getting slower, guessed we must be close to home.

"…She was talkin' to a friend of hers. 'Just tell me what to do, *please*, Janet,' I heard her say. 'We've spent our lives together, not accomplished *anythin'*. I can't help thinkin' he's too young to be this ill, and I can't stand it. Now I've no choice but be *nice* to him.' When I opened up the door she had the courtesy to redden. And I did me best to talk about it reasonably," he'd said, "'cos we're both adults, aren't we, so it's okay if we sometimes have unpleasant feelin's? 'Tell me what I've done,' I begged, but she could only say I'd changed. I don't know what she really meant by that." Paul had admitted to some differences. He'd seen them too, he'd said, just hadn't thought of them as interruptions to his marriage. "If anythin' I think I've made improvements to me character," he'd stressed. "I'd like to think I'm more compassionate and less concerned with things like wealth and status. I try to make a difference in the world. You'd think she'd like that, wouldn't you?"

To see her now it's clear that Andrea's tolerance of Paul is quite diminished. Her jaw is set; a pulse pounds in her neck as she ploughs through the soapy piles of dishes. She washes in a way that demonstrates her anger, because she's not allowed to shout at him now that his heart is weakened.

Paul speculates that she would rather he had died and that she's disappointed that he didn't. "At night when I'm beyond sleep," he'd told me, "I'll tiptoe from the bedroom in me slippers and sit downstairs like an old, old man. Sometimes I put the radio on. Not music – just in case it's loud and wakes her up – I try to find a station with a bit of chatter going on. It's company of sorts and I enjoy the drone of voices. It reminds me there's a whole world out there, in't there?

"Well, there's this one show late at night where people phone in and discuss things. I've not called in meself, but it was on that show I heard about it, sittin' on me own one night and in the dark. They mentioned it, and I thought, oh, that sounds so good. That might give me a proper sense of purpose, so to speak. I only wanted to be less lonely. So I started with a simple email, nothin' much, just sayin' I'd quite like to meet 'em. When I didn't get replies I sent another and another. I don't know why I didn't give up, but I s'pose I wore 'em down because after a bit I gained a sort of entry and arranged to meet 'em in the café. No, I didn't say a thing to Andrea. I thought it mightn't come to anythin', I mightn't manage to *do* anythin', but I can see why she'd think I was hidin' it and why she'd call it a deception.

"The first time it was strange. That chap you saw, the younger bloke, he showed me photographs and told me a few facts about a young girl in her twenties. An immigrant, he said, and that he thought her name was Lillith, but as she'd not got any papers he couldn't be entirely sure. I took the pictures, looked at her and was surprised because her body was so ordinary. I'd expected to be shocked, but in point of fact I wasn't horrified at all.

"The chap described how she'd been used as a container. Dozens and dozens of tiny balloons, she'd swallowed. 'She went for the big payoff, got unlucky,' he said. 'Only takes the one to rupture, then you know… lights out.' I got distressed because he seemed so casual about it and he must've noticed 'cos he coughed and changed his tune. 'On the plus side death came pretty quick,' he said. 'With that amount ingested, heart failure, you know, yeah, pretty quick.'

"I sat and stared for ages at a nut that lay unnoticed on the floor. I couldn't help imaginin' the moment of her death. Was it when she first stopped breathin', I kept askin', or much earlier, when someone thought so little of her as to stuff her full of latex? Or don't they say that death comes when your name slips off the last tongue to have known you and you pass out of all memory? Who knows. But anyway, before I knew what I was doin', I'd said, 'Let me organise a funeral. A proper one in church, with flowers, music, poems even.'

"The chap sat there and scratched his head. 'I'm sorry, Paul, but I can't sanction that,' he said. 'The council hasn't got the funds, we only do the basic. Coffin, crem, no fanfare, I'm afraid.'

"'No, I mean, let *me* do it, pay for it an' all,' I said. I made the promise before I'd had the chance to talk it through with Andrea. Inside I knew she'd have a fit if she had any notion what I planned to do with all our savin's, but I reckoned everyone deserves a send-off. Someone ought to stand beside your coffin and pretend that you meant summat. It's about respect."

I hadn't said his kindness would've served Lillith much better while alive. No point when it's too late to bring her back, I'd thought.

"The chap took me to see the room where Lillith had been found," Paul had said. "I hadn't realised that I lived so near a place so grotty and so bare. I'd passed that block a thousand times and never knew the people in there lived like that. I tried to look for clues around the room, a hint of who she really was, but all I found was a CD beneath the mattress. I didn't recognise the singer, a youngish girl who wears a lot of make-up, but as there wasn't summat else I thought I might as well give it a listen, and I hoped that that CD had once been Lillith's. The lyrics struck me as appropriate and so I chose a song and used it at the funeral. I bought some flowers to top her coffin and I even thought about a headstone, but decided in the end I'd best not go as far as that. Even so the funeral cost a lot, much more than I'd expected, and it wasn't long before Andrea noticed how our bank account was shrinkin' and demanded I explained meself. 'Everyone should be the same in death,' I said, and then I asked her if she'd come with me to Lillith's funeral.

"'Let me get this straight,' she said, 'you want me to go to the funeral of a girl I never knew, and what's more was a drug mule?' Any more revulsion, she'd have spat.

"'It's not like that,' I said. I wanted her to understand that I was thinkin' of *our* circumstances, that I'd realised that you can't predict what's comin' at you round the corner. 'The right thing is to help,' I said, but she just didn't get it, didn't think there was a link, couldn't credit the connection. In her opinion the decent thing to do was turn your back, approach mortality in silence.

"'We are *clean* people,' she said. I remember thinkin' how she seemed repulsed and fascinated more or less in equal measure. 'We live in a *good* street and we're *not* responsible for what goes on in other people's houses.'

"So I went alone. I sat there in an empty pew and listened to the echoes. The only other people were the celebrant and the chap I'd met who represents the council. Halfway through the service the celebrant forgot her name and after that he only called her 'the deceased'. Ten minutes later it was over and the council chap was holdin' out his hand for me to shake. 'That's that,' he said. 'A job well done, Paul. Thank you very much.' It made me think, is this all that it comes to in the end? Will no one notice when I pop me clogs meself? I'd offered her so little – just a moment's honour – and though I told meself that that alone had been important and worthwhile, before I had a chance to stop meself, I'd said I'd do it all again.

"Word soon got round about a crazy man who'd pay to bury all the lonely dead, and what you saw today back in the café was me agreein' to another. Me seventh, as it happens. I've spent the last few months in thinkin' about people that I've never even met. I've travelled round the town and seen some godforsaken places in the hope that I can make a stranger for a moment summat more than humdrum. I keep comin' back to thinkin' about poetry. It seems fittin' somehow, so I tried to write one, but I never got beyond the phrase 'Remember me…'"

Andrea has finished with the washing up. Her fingers fiddle with her apron, free the knot behind her back. She takes it off and folds it over the edge of the sink. "When will all this end?" she whispers. I can see her shoulders heaving.

Paul looks at his feet. "It gives me summat to do, love," he wheedles, "since I haven't been able to go to work—"

"But why *this*?"

"Well, it's necessary…" he begins, then switches to belligerence, "and someone has to do it!"

"But why *you*?" Her voice is raw, demolishes his confidence.

He can't find words to tell her what he really thinks, can't clarify the notion that the least of us deserves a ritual, that a tribute can't be plucked out of the air, that something has to be invented. So instead of speaking he makes sure he's neat and tidy, even though she isn't looking. He checks his shirt is tucked into the waistband of his trousers, hopes his stomach doesn't bulge too much above his belt.

"But what about the *living*, Paul?" Andrea asks. She means herself, of course. Her husband lives already with the dead. She knows she only has to wait and death will come, though it's so tiring not to know which day will be his last. Perhaps his feeble heart will do the trick? Next time she prays he'll just let go, won't feel obliged to scrabble back inside his body. But she shouldn't have to wait that long to live, she thinks. She ought to pack her bags, collect the bits and bobs which are important to her, and go to stay with Janet. They could drink some wine and chat about him in the past tense.

Paul has tried to picture this too, his life without Andrea. "The house would be too large," he thinks, "and I don't know how best to clean it. I'd probably live in one room, let the papers stack up in the corners. Empty tins would pile up on the counter and the washin' up would go undone." He imagines he'd sit out his life in just one chair and hear no voices but the ones on phone-ins on the radio. If he's lucky when he dies someone will come and have a root around the house. They'll find a record and deduce he liked that sort of music.

They'll pick a song and play it at a makeshift ceremony, a kind of proof he'd once had an opinion or a preference. That song will be the only evidence he's ever been alive.

Paul turns and ushers me out of the kitchen, along the hall towards the front door. "Sorry, I can't come with you to look for Kev," he says apologetically. "As it turns out, this in't the right time after all."

And so I step again onto the street. The clouds above the cliff seem steely, weighty and absorbed with every promise of a downpour. They stretch from edge to edge of sky, so all encompassing it's hard to notice them, as though they never want us to remember that there can be different kinds of weather and it's possible to hope for something more than rain. But wait, look closer, here and there are tiny glimpses in between the clouds, occasional bright fragments of a scattered short-wave blue, reminders that behind the grey is colour quite extraordinary.

Before I set off in pursuit of Kev, I wonder whether Paul will have the guts to take the time he has and spend it really well. The door is closing and I hear him say to Andrea, "I'm sorry, love, I know we can't go on like this. I promise you, I'm gonna to finish it."

The Dance of the Two Camps

Dawn comes with rosy fingers. Lucky Dawn, thinks Obic. She wishes Janet had installed a blackout blind. She hasn't slept too well, has struggled to digest a late-night heavy meal and isn't ready to accept the coming of the morning. She drags the duvet up above her head and hopes to thwart the glaring fingers which have probed their way in through the slats and prod between her eyelids.

The unrepentant sun mounts vehement assaults on Obic. This bright weather, she thinks through the rhythmic pounding of a thick head, comes too late to throw a light on anything. Their infiltration of the town is comprehensive and now people have grown used to having them around. Poor Janet, with her love of Battenburg and custard creams, has come to be dependent on her visitors for all her day-to-day supplies, has given up the right to choose her favourite seller because her guests have made the process of acquiring cake and biscuits so straightforward and reliable. It doesn't seem important now to go out to the bakery, and she's not had any recent thoughts to spare for Mrs Jasper or her business. Janet simply puts in a request, then trusts her guests to pick who wins the buy box. They do this based on lowest price, whose reputation has been ranked the highest, and the speed a seller says they can deliver. This way Janet's charged much less but gets much more, and is assured that the experience will be easy and enjoyable. She never has to step outside her door these days and recommends to friends like Andrea that they should also take in houseguests.

"I don't know what I'd do without them anymore," she's often heard to say.

It's morning and Combfootians will be waking up. Obic wonders if they're utterly delighted by a glimpse of pink and early sun, so cheered by birdsong and narcissi that they'll venture out to greet each other with polite exchange of mundane courtesies. How glad they'll be to see the back of all those bucketloads of rain, they'll say, and kid each other that the sunshine makes their town look better, that the winter darkness has now gone away for good.

Obic knows the darkness bides its time in corners.

The sun is out, but she does not feel sunny.

*

Some hours later, Obic groans, and with her eyes still tightly shut, she rolls onto her elegant back and extracts her nostrils from the tufted cushion that has acted as her pillow. Every muscle aches, reminding her of the previous night's vigorous activity. She's still not ready to begin another day but knows there's no chance she can rest again until she's fully up-to-date with Kev and Arak. She needs to know exactly where they are and what they're up to, and knows that who knows most will always win.

Every morning Obic makes a brief inspection of her body. Sometimes this is the best part of her day. She likes her shape, the feeling of her form. In contrast everybody else she's ever met has always been so very disappointing. Autonomy has taught her not to hope too much, nor to expect good things from other people. She lets her hands sweep over every feature, every mound and bone. She traces every segment of her flesh. Sometimes she'll give herself a moment to appreciate a touch which is both practised and efficient.

She prefers this to the unskilled fumblings of any other lover.

However this is not that sort of day. This is another kind, when motivation doesn't stem from pleasure but is driven by anxiety, the need to catalogue her parts and reassure herself that all her limbs are present and correct. This is a day when she must know herself to know she still exists, and such days come when she's been roused too early, or has stayed up far too late, or had a caffeinated drink before she went to bed.

She makes her checks, ticks through her register of parts.

Still here.

Relief brings her a rush of dopamine, though at the bottom of her brainstem lurks suspicion that her outer self may one day blow the whistle on what's going on within. She hasn't fully shaken off the notion that corruption rises to the surface, that given long enough it comes to taint what's visible, that evil must be evident for everyone to see. If you're determined to be wicked then it's likely you'll be plagued by fear. Depravity is obvious, you think, and simple facial profiles could betray your true intent. And so it is for Obic, who will wake up now and every day and wonder if her dissolution has begun. By now her crimes are surely bad enough to merit fulsome punishment, she thinks, but in spite of every effort at debauchery, she's pleased to note that nothing's happened yet. No boils or pustules have erupted, no limbs have dropped off in the night. She's still intact and big and beautiful, however much a prudish brain might think she should be taught a lesson. Perhaps she thinks she goes unnoticed not because she isn't vile but because the world at large is blind and bloody stupid.

Obic stretches out and lifts the covers, gazes down the whole length of her lovely naked shell. She's gratified by what she sees, is glad that Specky didn't get a chance to share this sofa with her overnight. She doesn't like to sleep with someone after sex and hates it when she's forced to share a space, or is compelled to stumble through the courtesies of conversation in the morning. Such talk is loose and meaningless, she thinks. You don't control the words you say and end up saying something you'll regret, or making promises that you don't want to keep. Relationships are sticky and exacting, and she doesn't have the stomach for idealism. Though that won't be a problem that she'll face this morning. Her mouth makes little twists, a tiny curve, as she remembers how she'd rid herself of Specks. The look of horror and of resignation on his face when he'd twigged she'd be shot of him. The satisfaction of the moment when at last he was despatched. She might not be at liberty to revel in her present solitude – and finds the quiet in the flat a trifle irritating – but last night's antics had generated genuine amusement.

She listens to the few sounds in the room. Janet's laptop humming softly on the kitchen counter, the periodic rush of tyres as cars pass by along the road outside the workhouse. Janet doesn't even have a ticking clock to shatter minutes into seconds. No instant is distinguished from another and unmarked time is hopeless, passes by unseen like transitory shadows. If she stay much longer disconnection will become an obstacle, will absolutely isolate her, will nudge her into insignificance.

Her stomach rumbles as it always does when she has eaten lots the night before. Perhaps, she thinks, she ought to have hung on to Specks. She could've given him another go before she did away with him. It might've helped alleviate the pangs of her voracious appetite. She wriggles one leg out from underneath the duvet. She likes her legs. They're long and supple, very strong. She loves to wrap them round a partner during copulation, to squeeze until he gasps his last between her thighs. She extends the leg and curls the toes into a claw so all the muscles of the calf become accentuated. A spring breeze stirs behind the blind and makes her hairs stand up on end. She's never shaved, not ever in her lifetime. She doesn't see the point and doesn't care what anybody else might think. No one's ever yet complained and certainly not Specky, who'd been so thrilled that he'd lost capacity to speak. Even those who manage intercourse with more than grunts don't dare suggest she might prefer to depilate. No one judges Obic's body because she doesn't let them.

Nor does she let on what she thinks about her partners. Specky, for example, was less than striking as a specimen. She'd been quite shocked when he'd hoicked off his T-shirt, shown how very small and skinny he was underneath. There'd been nothing to him once she'd got him naked, but she'd held her tongue, had not revealed how sickened she had been by all those veins which bulged close to the surface of his legs. An ugly twisted net of bluish purple lumps had spread beneath his skin, and later when he'd panted in delight, "Oh God, I think you're gonna kill me," she'd waited, fascinated, to see if clots would move or vessels grow engorged and burst their blood.

Sadly, he'd exaggerated. Nothing in real life is ever easy and the things you want to happen must be forced. Specky hadn't popped, had not fulfilled his offer to expire, had had no sacrificial tendencies at all. It turned out when he'd gasped for air and said he was about to die, he'd been susceptible to gallantry, the sucker-punch of hype which is a promise, though he'd almost said it like he meant it. Males tend to overstate their feelings, especially when they want something, she thinks. She yawns and stretches once again, will not allow her mind to linger on regrets. What's done is done and can't be taken back. It's time to get up, time to go, is too late now, whatever time it is.

Obic puts a foot down on the floor and promptly treads on something. Ouch, a shoe – more properly a trainer – the sole of which digs deep into her instep. She yelps, then stretches out another foot. Another trainer! What a bloody mess. She looks down, sees the floor is strewn with footwear. There must be seven or eight shoes dotted round the living room, and all of them are bright and white and new. Only Specks had favoured sportswear; only he had bothered to indulge in new clothes since they came to Combfoot Chase. She can't begin to guess why he would need so many. Who needs four pairs practically the same? It's such a waste, especially as he won't get to wear any of them now. She knows she ought to tidy up the shoes before she leaves but can't be bothered, so instead she kicks the trainers underneath the sofa. Out of sight, already out of mind. Let Janet find them later. Nothing matters once she's gone, and as you've probably noticed, Obic only pays attention to the parts of life that interest her.

Her hands root round the sofa, part the cushions with her fingers, make a systematic search to find her phone. It must be here, she thinks. She always keeps it close at hand beneath her pillow. She never sleeps without it and her phone's the first thing that she looks for when she wakes. She needs it now to figure out where she should head to next. She needs to check the app she's secretly installed on all the others' phones.

The app is represented by a harmless icon – the stylised image of a kite – and bears the name 'Days Out'. On the surface it looks innocent enough. You open it and it'll tell you what attractions lie in this vicinity, where – within a given radius which it's possible to specify – to go for cultural enrichment. Visitors have left reviews, have given stars to what they'd recommend. Obic's rightly dubious about these ratings. Someone gave the town museum four stars out of five, for fuck's sake. Someone else waxed lyrical about the path that lets you wander round the reservoir. There's nothing here in Combfoot Chase that she would score so high. But Obic isn't looking for excursions. She's modified the app so it'll monitor her colleagues' GPS locations. She only has to click on it to know exactly where they are at any given time. If any of them ever notice, she'll just tell them it's a safety measure. It helps her know they're safe and sound, she'll say, the implication being that she worries and she cares. In fact she only wants to keep them under strict surveillance. She wants to know precisely where they are and everywhere they've been. Obic has no qualms at all in breaking someone's trust but thinks it's probably better if she keeps her methods cloak-and-dagger, keeps her secrets to herself.

A map of Combfoot Chase emerges on her screen. She looks for pins which signal the positions of both Arak and of Kevin. What luck, she thinks. They're both located in one neighbourhood, among the streets close to the cliff, the one not very distant from the other. Two birds, she thinks, only one stone needed.

How convenient.

*

At the end of a busy and demanding day, Obic finds herself in a part of town she doesn't like. The streets are narrow, seedy, and she hates these mediocre houses, how they scramble up against each other, share their walls and roofs and even chimneys. And the cliff is very dark and very menacing. She doesn't need a geotechnical engineer to tell her that the land's unstable, could slip and slide at any moment. Above her rows of daffodils bob in amongst the grass grown long around the fence which barricades the cliff. The cheerful yellow of their heads bely the danger to their bulbs and roots which are exposed beneath, made visible where rain has rubbed away the earth. Great fissures run deep through the cliff and open up the rock. Despite the obvious risks, the people who live in its shadow continue to build summer houses, wendy houses, gazebos or a potting shed. They don't look up, pretend the cliff is just a wall and tend their primrose-ed garden paths beneath. They must know all their efforts could be wiped out in an instant, in a rockfall, but they persevere and blindly hope the worst won't come to pass.

A quick search through the archives of *The Chronicle* brings up numerous stories of retaining walls collapsed and houses duly cordoned off. Look closely and you'll see that someone has installed a mesh in an attempt to hold the boulders back, whilst other portions of the cliff are laced with concrete. The council can't decide who's the true owner of the land, whether the cliff is rightfully the property of the private operators of the car park at the top, or if unfortunates who live beneath will have to take responsibility. Once they've made their minds up, whoever's named as owner will begin to live in fear of heavy rain, because they'll have to pay for all the subsequent evacuations and meet the costs of having future piles of debris shovelled up.

Another expert's looking into whether they can also send them all the bills for tidying up the suicides.

The pins on the location app are red and ready. Obic knows that Kev is outside and not very far away, but Arak is still closer. She sees he's found his way into a house somewhere along this street and so she now begins to work out how she too can make her entrance. Unlike him she'll need a good excuse to knock on doors, because it takes some balls for someone beautiful to talk to normal people.

So far no one's noticed that she's here except perhaps a ginger cat. It's just come back from sniffing round a body which has tumbled and is sprawled out underneath the cliff. No one's found the body yet, so there are no forlorn handwritten messages, no teddy bears or bunches of fresh flowers. The cat is glad because those blooms distract his delicate olfactory system and overpower the pleasant scent of flesh.

The cat is doing very well considering it only has three legs. It hops along the road quite easily, meanders past the lamp posts feeling good. In younger, lovelier days it did have four but was the victim of an incident outside its house some seven years ago. The incident involved a van and a mistimed mad dash across the road. In his defence, Mr Tombleson was late for dinner and it was getting very dark and it was raining. He did know that he'd hit something, but when he'd looked around he'd realised that this road was not covered by CCTV. The houses here were modest and the residents not rich enough to make demands for cameras. They could leave their doors unlocked without the fear of crime, he'd thought, because everyone in town knew there was nothing here to steal.

Mr Tombleson had told himself it must have been a rabbit that had crept out from the roughage at the bottom of the cliff. If he had realised he'd hit someone's pet, he'd certainly have hung around, he reassured himself, and would've done his very best to hunt the owner down. But a rabbit could be left for dead and no one even cared. He'd got back in his van – was glad he'd borrowed it from work so anybody could've been the driver – and had sped away. He hasn't thought about the incident again so hasn't had to think about how injured cats might have to drag themselves back home. The cat had looked so weak and mournful Andrea had cancelled all her plans for her next summer holiday and had spent the several hundred pounds she'd saved on vet's bills for an amputation.

The incident's too long ago for the cat to have a recollection of it. He can't remember why one eye is higher than the other, and why one ear is wrinkled and his coat is very shabby. Even if he could remember it would hardly matter because Andrea still tells him he's a beauty. He slinks between her legs under the kitchen table and she scoops him up and plonks him in her lap. She feeds him titbits from Paul's plate. She runs her hands along his back and purrs to him how much she loves him. He prefers the house when Paul's not there because when Paul's at home she gets so starchy. Alone she never notices the ridges in his spine, nor that his fur is not as soft and thick as it once was. The cat has no idea he's old and ugly, not until he happens to encounter Obic.

He makes an effort to be charming, marches straight across the road – more carefully than he was wont to do in youth – and twists his body in a figure eight around her ankles. He has no reason to doubt the wisdom of this action, nor to reassess his high opinion of himself, because Obic crouches down and chucks her lovely fingers underneath his chin. The cat on instinct is attracted to her and doesn't notice anything at all is wrong until it's far too late.

"Well, hello," Obic says, and sweetly, as she greets the cat and picks him up. "It's nice to meet you. What fine whiskers you have there! Oh yes, I do believe you'll do."

*

Pick a door. Any door. Knock knock.

Who's there? This is where he's meant to use the spy hole. Maureen had it fitted so they'd know who'd knocked before they answered, so they could make conscious choices who to keep out and who to grant permission to come in. Outside there is a woman. She's very tall, is carrying a bag. To be more accurate, a sack.

Knock knock.

And what a lovely woman. Tom has rarely seen a face so beautiful. She sure as hell does not come from round here. He can't imagine what her business is because it's fair to say that stunning people don't have any truck with him and might as well be quite another species. And she can't be a cold caller because Maureen put a sticker on the door to make it clear they don't buy anything from strangers. Tom fumbles with the chain and slides the bolt.

Who's there?

The door creaks just a little as he opens it. "Hello?" he says. "How can I help you?"

The woman holds the sack up and he notices her other hand is carrying a spade. Tom doesn't know what he's supposed to do. No one's ever landed on his doorstep with a spade before. It's not the usual, not for Combfoot Chase. You might expect it in the country, but he's always lived here in the town. He looks down at the spade and wonders if she means to clock him on the head and bury him in the back garden. Then he chuckles. That's ridiculous, he thinks. He's being daft because a lovely woman wouldn't do a thing like that.

"This yours?" she says, and signals to the sack.

"The sack? No, no it's not," he says.

"No, what I mean is, what's inside," she says.

He shrugs. "No, I would doubt it," he replies. He can't imagine anything he has that might have turned up in a sack.

"Oh, right," she says, and moves to walk away.

"Hang on a sec," he says, vaguely surprised to find he doesn't want her heading off just yet. He doesn't want this moment to be over, because interesting and unusual encounters rarely come his way. He's careful not to gaze at the extraordinary length of leg that stretches out of her incredibly short skirt. He coughs. "What's in it?" he enquires.

"Not your business if it's not yours," says the woman.

He doesn't know if she intends to be so rude. "But if you show me what it is, then I could help you, p'rhaps?" he says. He hopes this offer doesn't come across as though he's desperate for attention.

She pauses, seems unable to decide if what he's said would be a good idea.

"So, what is it then?" he asks again.

"A cat," she shrugs.

"A cat?"

"Yes. A dead cat."

"Oh…" Tom hasn't got a cat but looks around to see if he can spot the ginger one his neighbour's had for years. It had been tucked beneath the hedge a little earlier, was safe and sound and curled up in a favoured spot. He'd watched it yawn and show a pink mouth and its spikes of tiny teeth. It usually waited there for Andrea to call it in to dinner. The cat's not there, but that does not imply that something's happened to it, he thinks. It's much more likely that his neighbour's let it in already, though he can't help but feel a little queasy and he hopes the cat has not met with another accident. It makes it better if the cat that's dead is not one that he knows. "Um… did you kill it?" he asks, before he realises how hostile this might sound and that a lovely lady hardly goes round bumping off a cat. "I don't mean purposely," he clarifies. "I thought that p'rhaps you'd had an accident, had run it over." How awful to have killed somebody's pet. That must be why she's turned up here, he thinks. An honest person would be riddled with remorse and would go door to door.

"Oh… no…" she says.

Tom looks at her and can't see any trace of guilt.

"I only found it," she says, "on the pavement over there."

"Ah," he says. "Somebody else has run it over, hasn't had the decency to stop."

"Yeah, that's as may be," she says. "So, your house was closest and I thought it might be yours?"

"No, no, it's not. I haven't got a cat." He pauses. "Should I have a look at it," he offers, "see if I can recognise it?"

"I wouldn't. It's been quite messed up." She screws her lovely face into a grimace. Tom's not looking at the spade, so doesn't see a trace of cat blood and a clump of ginger hair. "I didn't want to touch it," she continues as she slides the spade behind her back. "And I want to bury it if I can't find the owner."

Well, that's kind of her, Tom thinks. If it had been his cat, he'd rather someone else would do the honours, that he'd not be forced to know the details of what happened. Better to believe it simply wandered off, had not come back. Better to remember it as it had been before. Tom knows that if you don't see and you don't know, you can hang on to your hope. A stranger standing on your doorstep with a shovel and your precious pet lugged round like lumps of coal gives you no option but to know the truth. And truth is often awful.

"And no one's mentioned that they've lost their cat?"

"No, I don't think so," he says slowly. "Hold on, we can double-check, though, with my wife…"

And thus, for all their stickers and their spyholes, and despite the locks and bolts that fortify their doors, Obic gains an entry into Tom and Maureen's home. They've got no means to guard against incursions so unprecedented.

But, you ask, could it be possible that Arak too is in that house? Could Obic have knocked first time on the right door by pure chance? We don't know yet for certain, but we'll soon find out. And anyway, there's nowhere he can hide. Now Obic's found a way in, she won't give up until she tracks him down.

*

162

Maureen makes the announcement just as they're about to finish tea. "I saw him today," she says.

They seem innocuous, those little words, but Obic knows it's not what people say that counts, but how they speak, how much they say and whether they prefer to use a simple sentence or a complex one.

Tom catches Obic's eye. His head is tilted back, the last dregs tipped in silence from his mug onto his tongue.

"Well, here we go," thinks Obic.

She's watched this couple through a meal she's forced herself to eat, has had to swallow every trace of disappointment and to stop herself from kicking at the table leg. It hadn't taken very long to realise Arak wasn't in the house. She'd sneaked her phone out underneath the tablecloth and checked the app. It still claimed he was here at ///plot.sinks.deeper, though sometimes he had moved across to ///shaky.turning.finish. He must be in the house next door, the only barrier a thin partition wall. Every time she hears a neighbour's footstep or the shadow of a voice next door she shakes with irritation and with rage. She cannot kick the table leg, but she can surely kick herself.

Just pick a door. Oh, any door.

No, not that one, the other one.

The app's been known to get it wrong before. Embedded in the Ts&Cs is an admission of a slight margin of error. Obic remembers glancing at the document. She'd given it a standard fourteen seconds before she'd clicked accept. It isn't fair to think someone would read the text in full, she thinks. It would've taken hours and no one has that sort of time to spare these days. But now the app has let her down she's visibly pissed off. She's come too far and done too much to think that close is ever close enough. She's very close, is resolute she'll get to Arak in the end.

She'd tried to make excuses, tried to skip this chapter full of petty details of these people's little lives, but Maureen had insisted that she'd stayed. It was an obligation, she'd explained. It wasn't possible to let a caller leave before they'd been well fed. You're judged on hospitality – both in this life and the next – and will be damned if you forget the rules of kindness to a stranger. The table was already laid but it would be the work of seconds to set out another place. Obic – who can happily kill cats and tread on spiders – hadn't managed to escape benevolence, had been condemned to stay and share their tea, to listen to the chinking of convention and of cutlery on china.

Throughout the meal, Maureen had been on tenterhooks. Obic saw her almost bite her tongue off in a bid to keep up the illusion everything was normal, though it was bloody obvious that something was afoot. Maureen had strained with the effort to procure an opening, a moment she could speak her truth, her patience shredded by the wait for Tom to gnaw through piles of sandwiches and cake. And the impact of a cake on Tom had been substantial. As soon as he had seen it on the table, his eyebrows shot up and he'd turned and mouthed to Obic, "But it's Wednesday, and we never have a cake on Wednesday." If Maureen really wants to make out everything is normal, she shouldn't lay out tea with cake. Only very great distraction makes a cautious wife cut quarters of Victoria sponge, all thick and rich with cream and jam, and pass it off as nothing more than normal. Tom had feigned he didn't know that this was more than just a midweek treat, of course, but Obic knew he knew, and more importantly, she thinks, so did his wife.

Another object of suspicion is the little bud vase full of flowers which stands full centre on the table and surrounded by the now-demolished tea. Only cafés bother with a prissy bunch of daffodils and snowdrops, Obic thinks, believing that it gives their tables more appeal, that customers will hang around a little longer, will be nudged into an order of a second coffee or dessert if the environment is pretty, that the separation of a patron from their cash will be a little easier if the setting is made more desirable. But why would Maureen gather flowers from the garden, tie them round with threads of blue? She's really tried to bring a whiff of spring into the house. Perhaps she hopes that Tom will scent the promise of a better future. Obic wonders what he'll have to give up in return.

"I knew that something was about to happen," Maureen says, "as soon as I noticed that moth this morning."

Now that she's at last begun to speak, Tom behaves as though he's caught red-handed, frozen in a searchlight with the crumbs that prove he's guilty of a crime still on his lips and on his fingers. He coughs. He follows her gaze through the window to the garden, tries not to linger on the fact her voice has taken on a dreamlike quality, one he's learnt to link with her less rational moments. "Bit early in the season for a moth, me love," he says.

"I know!" she says, face clear as the moon. "But it was there, I swear it was."

Obic listens to descriptions of a pure white moth with just a thin line, blackish brown, around the edges of its wings.

"And it was... *iridescent.*" Maureen's waited long to use this choice of word and is unduly proud of it. She savours it before she carries on. "It looked like *them*, you know, though obviously much smaller." Her mug is empty, but she mimes another sip. "That's how I knew it was a sign and something *always* happens after I get signs," she says.

Tom knows the moth she means. It's one he's come to hate. "We had a plague of 'em last summer," he explains to Obic. "Its caterpillars ate me box and ruined me entire hedge." He shakes his head. There isn't any omen here, he thinks, and as soon as he can get his hands on an appropriate pesticide, he'll let the little bastards have it. "It took me hours to pick off every chrysalis by hand," he says. "I wanted not to have to spray, because I didn't want to harm the bees, you know, but now I'm done with softly-softly. All guns blazing, it'll be, from now on." He brushes one palm swish, swish, swish against the other, and specks and scraps of cake spray out across the tablecloth.

Maureen tuts, stands up and holds her hand out for his mug. "I spoke to him, you know," she says.

"What, the moth?" Tom cracks, and winks at Obic.

"Don't be daft," says Maureen, and her cheeks grow red. It isn't proper that he teases her when they have company. "You know exactly who I mean. I saw Gil, and I spoke to Gil."

"Who's Gil?" asks Obic.

"Dead," mouths Tom.

"I knew that it was him," says Maureen, "'cos it looked exactly like him. I'd had to pop down into town to get some bits and bobs and there he was, as bold as brass, as though he never went away."

Tom shakes his head again and drops his gaze. He lets a finger scratch a loop around the tablecloth in patterns that he's traced for years. "She just reads into things a little differently," he mutters underneath his breath to Obic, wishes Maureen hadn't thought today would be a good day to make a spectacle of herself.

Maureen huffs and sniffs. "I don't suppose that you'll believe me," she says, hands on hips, "because you never do."

Obic waits to see if Tom will try to cut her visions off. A part of him still thinks he should confront her, that he should chip away at her conviction, that if he makes her face up to the bare-faced facts, he might begin to make a difference and bring about a change in her beliefs. He hopes she knows she only makes these stories up to ease her grief. "Why don't you show me where you saw the moth?" he says at last. He pushes back his chair and stands, holds out his hand to her. He likes to think that he'll be gentle when he demonstrates – though very kindly – that there can't be any grain of truth in anything she says.

Maureen smiles and grasps his hand. "You mean the angel," she corrects.

"Oh… right," he says, and feels his stomach cave as though he's just about to plummet off the cliff.

They step outside, all three of them, and Maureen leads them up the garden path.

"Tom laid this path when Gil was still a toddler," she tells Obic proudly. The timelines in her mind are often muddled. She sees the images and echoes of the years gone by as clearly as the present. "He can't ride on his bike, though, Tom," her past self says again. "I won't allow him on the street, it just in't safe, but back here in the garden all the ground's too bumpy. When it's wet his stabilisers get bogged down."

Tom too is picturing his wife as she once was, a flashback to another day when she was younger, flushed and clasping the infant Gil in careful arms. "I did," he says. "I slaved the whole weekend to build this path, although I'd done a week on site and I was knackered."

"He made sure it was wide enough so Gil could turn his little bike round at the top," says Maureen, gives a short, sharp laugh. "D'you remember, Tom, how bright it was at first? I said I thought we'd have to put our shades on, but you said not to worry, that the path wouldn't stay bright and orange very long. 'Bricks always settle,' you said, and it happened you were right."

"It's just the moss and lichen growing," Tom says, happy to make sense of what has changed. "That, plus in time we just got used to it."

What once had seemed extraordinary had soon become familiar, and Gil had pottered up and down that path so often that the mud had spattered over it, so it'd not been long before they couldn't see the colour of the bricks at all. They'd quite forgotten what their garden looked like prior to the building of the path, just as they struggled to remember what their life had been before they'd thought of Gil.

Maureen wanders further up the path towards a low hedge which is meant to mark a boundary. It separates the lawn from Tom's small plot of vegetables. She plants her feet on one particular spot and turns her face back to the house. She speaks as if to Obic, but her longing is all trained on Tom. "I was standing here," she says. "I'd noticed from the kitchen window that the snowdrops had come out under that tree, so I came up to see 'em. I know, I thought, I'll cut a little bunch of 'em for teatime, was about to head indoors to fetch a pair of scissors, when the angel fluttered past me face." Her fingers find their way to flit against her cheek, dislodge a tear which wells up, raw and antisocial. "Oh, Tom, it touched me, brushed across me cheek…" To Maureen past and present only start to make sense filtered through imagination. "I thought at first it might've settled, but it didn't. It went up and flew high over the fence just there and disappeared away across Paul's garden."

Tom frowns. It's too early in the year for a cocoon to hatch, he thinks, let alone for full-grown moths to fly. There's no doubt that she's dreamed this, but someone who sees angels can concoct them out of anything. He makes a mental note to pop next door and give the neighbours a heads-up about the problems he's had with his box last summer. They've got a bit of topiary out the back. He wouldn't want to see that also stripped to twigs.

"It looked exactly like 'em," Maureen says. Her voice adopts a dogged edge.

Tom isn't really listening now, is too diverted by the ruination of his hedge. "Who did, me love?" he asks.

"The *angels*." Maureen stamps her foot and turns to Obic. "Oh, yes, I've known about 'em for a decade," she declares. "I saw 'em first around me boy, although it took a while to realise what they were because the church has got 'em wrong, you know." She crouches down and makes a show of sandwiching the head of one white snowdrop in between her fingers. She cradles tender petals, tries to recapture the feeling of a moth's fleet wing. "Those pictures in the stained-glass windows are all wrong," she says again. "Though angels do have wings, they're not like birds'. They're much more like a butterfly's or moth's. All that nonsense folk say about finding feathers doesn't mean an angel's watching over 'em. That feather's off a pigeon, or a dove or summat, and it's not the angels' job to guard us humans."

Tom shifts his weight from foot to foot and shuffles closer to his hedge. He clears his throat and stoops to peer between the twigs. He beckons Obic, signals her to follow, wants her to look deep into the plant. She sees the greenish cobwebs of the box moth pupae. In this one hedge alone there must be hundreds of them, far too many for Tom to defeat them on his own.

"When I saw 'em, they looked thin and harsh..." Maureen doesn't care that both the others have just turned their backs. She's used to no one listening and frequently forgets when someone does. Once she starts to speak unguardedly, she shares as if with no one but herself. "And they all wore the same clothes as the paramedics. Of course they did. They had to blend in, didn't they? I only recognised 'em 'cos they glowed and 'cos they had those wings..."

Tom sighs. He can't do anything to save this hedge. He must admit defeat. It's well and truly done for. "Please don't dwell on things, me love," he begs half-heartedly. "We both know it don't do you any good."

"It does," she says. "It means that God's involved. The angels came and took our Gil and so it means he in't quite gone, he's only waiting for us somewhere else."

As though Gil were on top of the cliff, thinks Obic, just beyond her rim of vision. She watches Tom work at a white web shrouding the skeleton of a leaf.

"I wouldn't mind," he grumbles softly, "but it's not an honour that she gives our other child." It's been a million years since anybody heard his side, he thinks. He'd tried to talk to someone on a phone line – one of those you call and someone offers you a little comfort in your grief – but disembodied voices hadn't been enough. He'd done it once or twice and given up. "We were expecting twins," he whispers, "but we lost one. I was devastated, but Maureen only seemed relieved. 'Oh, in't it marvellous?' that's what she said. 'In't it lucky that we didn't lose 'em both?' I tried to go along with it, forget the one because we had the other, but I couldn't make that work for me. And Maureen never let me talk about our girl, decided that she wasn't really real. 'You can't mourn what you've never had,' was her philosophy. 'I'm glad we haven't got to deal with two,' she said. I know she only said it to be practical, but I could barely bear to look at her. She wouldn't let me name our daughter either, so I grew to think of her just as me Beloved. About that time I planted up this hedge.

And now I think about her every time I come up here but try to leave her in amongst the cabbages and sprouts and know it's better not to bring her back into the house."

Maureen's wandered further off, has plucked that snowdrop which she twiddles now between her fingers, makes a map of petalled circles in the air. "The angels can't waste time in sending pools of light to cheer you up," she chants, "nor finding your umbrella, nor suggesting you should eat bananas if you know what's good for you…"

"And then when Gil went too, she still forgot to think about Beloved, though she'll never sacrifice her version of our boy…"

"…the stuff of life and death is what they're here for, nothing less than life or death…"

"…and Gil was not a cherub," Tom insists, "but flesh and bone like any other boy." He tells Obic how his son had been a lad who'd got himself in trouble, how he'd stolen vodka with his mates and downed it by the duck pond in the park. "He had the fortune to have sicked it up," Tom says, "to have collapsed in public and to land face-down in flowerbeds. They had to pump his stomach out," he mutters, "though I haven't told our Maureen that. She wasn't home, had gone off for a weekend out of town with Andrea and Janet, but it meant she didn't have to watch 'em wipe the vomit off his face. I've let her think our son's an angel, but if either of our children are, it must be me Beloved, I'd have thought."

"…he was at the bus stop," Maureen says. Her hand has crushed the snowdrop's head against her body so its petals droop against the fabric of her skirt.

"Who was, me love?" asks Tom. He straightens up and looks back down the path towards his wife.

"You know… our Gil," she says. "I knew they'd sent him straight away because he had his skateboard with him. 'Oh, hello,' I said, I couldn't stop meself, though I don't think the lad was used to adults talking to him 'cos his head jerked up and he looked like I'd caught him doing summat that he shouldn't. 'Do I know you?' he asked me, and when I said, 'No,' he seemed comforted by that. 'At least not in this lifetime,' I went on—"

"Oh, Maureen!" Tom cries out. "You should be far more careful, love. You can't go round saying things like that to random lads—"

"Why not? I wasn't doing any harm. And it was Gil, I *knew* it was. He had the same hair and those rosy cheeks. And you can't say it wasn't 'cos you weren't there and you didn't see him."

"But it couldn't be—"

"Why not? You tell me that."

"Well… how old was this lad, for starters?"

"Fourteen, maybe fifteen—"

"There you see, it can't be Gil. He'd have been in his twenties now," he pleads.

"It doesn't work like that. You're far too literal." Maureen's adamant and obstinate. "'Off skateboarding then, are you?' I said to him. 'Summat like that,' he said." She talks faster, faster. Her tale must needs be told at any cost. "'Oh yeah, there's a nice park, in't there?' I said. 'Lots of ramps and that.' It was my idea to give Gil his first skateboard," Maureen adds, a brief and proud aside to Obic.

"I didn't think it such a good idea," mutters Tom. "I was worried what he might get up to, who he might hang out with, tattooed thugs and that who might lead him astray. I thought he might get into drugs."

Maureen's laugh is stiff and brittle. "Then he picked his rucksack up. He'd had it at his feet and I'd not noticed it till then. 'You going somewhere nice?' I asked him 'cos his rucksack was stuffed to the gills so I could tell he must be off somewhere. 'To me mum's,' he said, and then his bus arrived and he got on. I waved him off but I don't think he'd have noticed. He was looking at his phone, I think, and didn't see me."

Tom is lost for words. He works the web of the cocoon until it's worn away, until it releases what is left of the leaf, only for Tom to find the skeleton crumbles to nothing in his fingers. His shoulders slump. "Why don't you head inside, me love?" he murmurs. "It's too chilly to stay out."

He watches her retreat back down the path towards the house.

"She pestered that poor lad," he says to Obic, awkward and apologetic. "I don't know, we'll have police round here one of these days."

It isn't comfortable to think his wife has hunted a young boy, has hounded him with clumsy intimacy. Gil might be fresh in his wife's mind, but when Tom thinks about his son he only sees a body lying on the ground, a host of paramedics round it in a circle. They each take turns at CPR and do their best to keep the body going while another pumps it with adrenaline. It seems impossible that any face could go so white, or lips so swollen, or a chest so flushed with hives. A skateboard is still lying at its side.

Each time this picture comes it's always followed by another. Gil's friend bursts into Tom's remembrance, a sallow lad who'd had the energy of a goat. "You must come quick," he always says. "Gil's on the ground and says that he can't breathe." Then Tom is raging down the streets of his imagination just as he did all those years ago. "What the bloody hell have you lot done to him?" he shouts again, and rounds on all the frightened boys who crowd forever in the skatepark, who've tried to hide from this disaster in the shadow of the halfpipe. "Tell me truthfully, you lot, what drugs have you taken?"

"We never took no drugs," they bleat. "We shared a bit of cake, that's all." And then the memory is swamped again by ambulances and paramedics, by the scramble and the chaos of the vain attempt to save his son which always comes too late and never brings him back. It makes no difference where Tom stands and how he views his recollection of these scenes; they always stay the same and never change, no matter how much he might wish it.

"No one's an angel, really, are they?" Tom asks Obic. "We're all just human, doing what we can against the odds."

Obic doesn't answer. She doesn't say that it's much worse than that, that the very best that anyone can hope for is to know we're animals and believe we're free.

The cliff looms darker as the sun sinks down, becomes a jagged shadow cutting up the sky. The day has crept and stretches into night and evening falls too heavy and too fast.

"Our Maureen's giving up on me," Tom says into the dusk because the darkness always prompts confession. "She thinks I don't try hard enough to remember what was good in Gil, although I do. I try. It's just I can't hold on to him. I think I've got him, conjured him the way she wants me to. I can even make him hover for a second, but I can't quite get his feet to touch the ground if you can catch me meaning. So it's never any good." He sniffs and pauses, pulls a tissue from a pocket, wipes his nose. "I always end up thinking that the reason I can't picture him the way she does, is 'cos it must've been my fault. I know she thinks that I'm the one to blame, although we neither of us knew. If I'd known Gil had had an allergy to nuts I would've drummed it into him to not eat cake." Tom bows his head and walks back down the path towards the house, his wife and all the wrongs they've done each other. With one foot on the threshold he hesitates and looks back up the garden. "Oh, Beloved…" he breathes, a lament to everything that still lives underneath the darkening sky.

He steps inside and shuts the door and shoots the bolts that keep them locked up safe and sound. He must live life without the hope that Maureen's attitudes will soften. They won't, he realises. It's far too late for that.

Obic stands forgotten in the garden. She watches through the last hours of the evening as the residents of this small row of houses try to fend the darkness off. One by one they switch their lights on, try to buy themselves a bit more time, but soon enough they give in and head up to bed. She waits until the night has fully settled and then, when there's no longer anything to see and nothing more to know because she's bagged it all already, she makes a move to go.

And look, here's Arak, bang on cue. As if he knows that Obic has been waiting to catch up with him, he also makes his exit from the neighbours' house.

Before she goes Obic leans over the fence and dumps the cat-in-bag and spade into the next door garden. She leaves it in the darkest pool of shadow so that Paul won't find the precious pet till morning. When he does he'll wonder how it came to be there, wrapped up in a bag and ready with a spade and everything. He'll think it over for a while and not make any sense of it, will just assume the cat was found by friends who were too kind to break bad news themselves, who couldn't stand the thought of being witnesses to Andrea's anguish.

One quick glance inside the bag will be enough to spring him into action. He'll dig a hasty grave and bury the cat before he mentions anything to Andrea. He won't want her to see the cat like that, would rather she could keep her memories intact. And when his dirty duty's done, he'll trudge back to the house and think about how best to tell her.

There he'll find a note propped up against the teapot on the kitchen table.

Gone to Janet's, it'll say. Just that.

And Paul will sit and stare around the four walls of his empty kitchen, and finally admit he's scared to death.

Of the Fragments That Remained

The face is red. Its eyes bulge and the mouth is slightly open as though surprised, as though whatever the head had expected, it had not been this. Jem turns his eyes away and does his best not to remember how a thick dark circle has already spread, coagulates beneath the skull. He wishes that he'd not come here, had not had the misfortune to have seen the aftermath of this disaster. The universe has thrown enough at him today and he's got no desire to mop up a catastrophe belonging to somebody else.

Several minutes have already passed and Jem has found himself unable to decide what he should do. He's come to a complete halt, is stuck behind the gorse bush which conceals the body from the road. The street's not very far away. He's passed its rows and rows of little doors before he took this detour onto scrubland, but he doesn't think that he can go back and knock on one of them. What should be very simple – an act to make somebody come and take the weight of this from off his shoulders – now seems utterly impossible. He'd only have to say, "I've found a body," and to look a little bashful. He could hand on the calamity as though it were no more than an unwanted gift, although Jem knows that gifts come hand-in-hand with obligation and often with a liberal bout of bitterness.

His train of thought chugs on towards the sweet and sticky parcels of dark butterscotch wrapped up in tartan paper which are sent to him by distant Scottish aunts each Easter. Jem's never met these aunts who send him gifts like clockwork, though he knows what's in the packages as soon as he receives them. He never opens them, has learnt to hate the unknown women who endow him with detested presents just as much as he hates all their claggy, loathsome treats. Their offerings have taught him that a boy like him is never given what he wants. The gifts just nudge him one more step along the road to disappointment, and if a relative won't grant a wish, he thinks, then why on earth would any stranger?

Jem is filled with vague familiar terror when he thinks about the individuals he knows. He can't talk to the people in his family, so it's too much to assume that he could strike up conversation with a person he's not met. If he could send an email that'd be all right, he thinks, because he's sure he could write down the necessary facts about the body. He's certain he could list them in some useful form or other. It's different when you have to get your lips and tongue to shape coherent words, or come up with an answer off the cuff if you are asked a question. And strangers would be bound to ask him questions. They'd come over all concerned and query why a boy like him is not at home, is out and all alone at night. In no time they'd have weaselled out of him the details of his name and where he lives, and then they'd guide him gently to a car and take him back and hand him over to his father. Jem doesn't blame imagined good Samaritans for being good. He knows that all their actions would be done with misplaced kindness, but also knows it wouldn't matter how much he protested that he didn't want to go. A good Samaritan would still suppose he was obliged to do it, would insist on doing The Right Thing even if Jem got the guts up and could say why he could not bear one more second in his father's house.

Outwardly the house he lives in hasn't changed, but Jem can't shake the thought that something fundamental has still shifted. In recent weeks he's started to become unsettled by the costly furniture, the upholstery and the paintings in the place that Father calls his home. These assets have been gathered through his father's years of endless labour. They make Jem feel that life will promise nothing more than mortgages and bondage. All the windows threaten him with murky curtains. Each is hatted with a heavy pelmet, rich with fringes, dressed with sets of drapes made up elaborately of flounces. His house is like the town museum, he thinks. Every time he enters it, it's just the same, each item in its proper place with no attempt to engineer a new surprise or a discovery. He's walked from room to room and felt as though he's part of a display, as though the things around him are arranged to demonstrate that this is how a proper life is lived.

Only recently have voids begun to open up. Once Mum had left each object in the house he's lived in his whole life had begun to stand too far away from all the others. Vast gaps loomed in every room and waited to belittle him, and now he's noticed them they're only growing bigger and more menacing. Nothing feels connected anymore. The house has turned into a great *lacuna*. That's the word his father would've used, because he's very fond of saying things he thinks that other people are too dumb to understand. He likes to trick them into the belief that he's extremely clever, when in fact he's just a pompous twat.

"My power carries great responsibility, remember, Jeremy…" his father always lectures as he folds his napkin into a habitual and self-important square.

Jem doesn't only hate his aunts; he also hates his father. This afternoon he'd hoped not just to flee a house but to be free of all the things his father likes to say. He'd hoped the words would not catch up with him because he thinks a life that must be lived along his father's lines would not be worth the living. For one deep, dark and dismal second, Jem can understand the urge to climb the cliff and hurl yourself from off the top.

To stop himself from looking at the broken face again Jem focuses deliberately on the hands. The man wears gloves which have no fingers. Jem can see his nails are cracked and split and very grubby. One hand curves around the shattered fragments of a liquor bottle from which another dark patch spreads. The final dregs of whisky have already bled into the earth, have left behind a yeasty trail of cereal and malt. These smells are quite familiar and remind Jem of his father's study, though the memory brings no comfort with it. He'd caught a whiff of whisky earlier this afternoon, although there'd been a fierce attempt to mask it with another smell and Jem had used the strategy of focusing on the hands then too, as he'd endured another of his father's tellings-off. How clean they'd been with clipped and pampered nails when he compares them with these hands before him now. These hands look like they've made and mended many things, Jem thinks. He's fascinated by the thorny mesh of hairs which sprout up from the backs of every finger. Noticing such details helps him curb the urge to look again at what was once a face. He's glad that night has fallen and it's harder to make out the bleak and stunned expression. In the growing darkness even dreadful things resolve themselves into a purer abstract shape. When loveliness and ugliness turn into silhouettes, it's trickier to make out any difference between them.

Resigned that he can't bring himself to cry for help, Jem sits down, takes the weight off, puts his back against the cliff. He chooses his position so he only sees the black shape of the back of the man's head. The hair is ruffled, tufts on end so it cuts zigzag lines around the skull. He squints and tries to kid himself the body's just a tramp who's gone to sleep. Through webs of lashes he can make-believe the rise and fall of breath, can not-quite conjure up a snore. Though come to think of it, the posture's too unnatural. The body's sprawled and twisted with its palms held upwards and exposed, as though this man had tried to make a desperate final gesture, an exaggeration of his honesty.

The overstatement calls to mind a dreadful actor in that Greek play that his mum had taken him to see some weeks ago. The character had cursed his lot while the actor strode around the puppet bodies of his murdered children and struck a million poses which were staged to demonstrate an attitude of desolation. To Jem they'd had no truth in them at all. Even he – a boy of small experience – could tell the actor had no real understanding of the pain he meant to show. Afterwards he'd mentioned this to Mum, who'd said she thought the actor far too beautiful and lucky to be truly very talented. She'd guessed he'd only ever lived an easy life, had not met with obstructions and had never had a proper opportunity to build his character. Jem had thought his mum was being generous, too kind in her assessment of the actor's gifts. To him the man was simply fucking useless.

The actor hadn't risen in Jem's estimation when he'd seen him strutting round the foyer greeting fans and signing programmes after the performance. Jem had watched him roll his sleeves up, show off the tattoos of a dragon and a flaming sun that he'd had outlined on his biceps. The tattoos must have been done recently because his skin still looked a little raw where needles had dragged ink down deep below the dermis. The actor had been talking endless mumbo jumbo about Helios and other gods, and a gang of female fans who'd gathered round him hung on every word. They'd cooed and drooled, but Jem had not been fooled. Instead he'd felt a tide of fury at the recognition that to act was no more than to wear a mask for the duration of a show. In Jem's opinion actors took the wreckage off too easily. They hid behind the dark of velvet curtains, safe and certain that the lights would rise again. They laughed and flirted, swigged back pints as soon as all the lines were done, as though a play bore no relation to real life and they were quite entitled to feel nothing.

"He's a fake," he'd moaned to Mother, and she'd laughed.

"You don't want parents really to go round killing off their children, do you?" she'd said, and she'd punched him gently on the arm to tell him he should lighten up.

Jem had thought – but hadn't said – that actually they did, if only metaphorically. Mother was too nice to open up that conversation and it wasn't her fault Father was an ogre.

It strikes Jem that the position of this body by the cliff smacks of the self-same deceptions that he'd witnessed in the actor. Perhaps, he thinks, he's stumbled on another sham, another scene that's been constructed to resemble real life even in the moment when it seeks to show a death. You can't trust anything. You can't be certain what has happened here at all. All anyone can say for certain is a body's landed with its arms flung wide. They must have flapped and flailed like useless wings during the fall, he thinks, and wonders what might cross your mind in such a situation. Perhaps the man had spent his final second on regret. Or perhaps if he'd just tripped and tumbled by mistake he might have spent that moment in reproach, had wondered how he'd come to do a thing so very, very stupid. Or if in truth he had been pushed, he might have blustered, raged against a terrible injustice.

Jem – like so many adolescents – is consumed by this, the last, most lurid version. His principal emotion is a sense of irritation that he'll never know for sure. The corpse can't tell him what went on today. What brought a man to stand behind an old kebab van in a car park? Why was the fence not high enough to stop him falling over? Jem will have to learn to live with this uncertainty just like everybody else. He'll read the story in the paper once it's been investigated, though he doesn't know if he can trust the version as it will be written in *The Combfoot Chronicle*. He has a hunch that they don't always tell the truth. He's heard Mum call *The Chronicle* a rag and only fit for wrapping fish and chips. The folk who run it pedal rumours and stir up discontent in town, she'd said, though Father says she spoke a lot of nonsense and still reads the paper every week. He says it's best to keep one ear down to the ground and stay informed of popular opinion. Jem isn't sure what side he should be on, but leans towards the idea that the world's simply macabre and poor standards of reporting at *The Chronicle* are most probably to blame.

To keep a distance from an ugly truth, Jem often turns uneasy scenes into the panel of a graphic novel in his head. He starts to sketch a mental picture of the pointed edges of the cliff, the dark shape of a man scrawled briefly in the air. He's seen all sorts of violence in a cartoon strip and knows exactly how to show it. He'd use a spike of red or yellow energy and the jagged letters of *Kapow!* to represent the force that flung the man from off the edge. To draw such pictures makes Jem feel hot ripples of excitement. He thrills to know that he can choose a life or death for any character, has often moaned about resultant dullness in his actual existence when he compares it to the things he can imagine.

"There's only school and home, and worst of all the holidays," he's grumbled to the other boys who hang out in the growing folio section of the local library. They nodded so he thought they shared his grievance that nobody's life can live up to a story in a comic book, but now – when Jem has landed in a real-life quantifiable adventure – he realises he doesn't want to deal with anything so tangible. His stomach churns. He thinks he might be sick. He fears that dwelling too long on what's happened to this man might make him delve into the filthy layers of his character.

No one in their right mind would decide to end up here. For here is partial scrub and waste, a threshold just a step beyond the edge of town but not yet into country. His teachers give him frequent cautions, warn him off the liminal cliff and all its shiftiness. They hint at dangers and at dodgy dealings, have told him openly that anyone who puts a value on their future ought to stay in school and stay away. Jem knows he has no business here but doesn't want to concede that his only other option is to turn and go straight back.

The outline of the sports pitch of his school is visible on the edge of town. A high-wire fence surrounds it. The pupils joke that no one's sure if it was built to stop them getting out or to prevent the outside getting in. As darkness gathers over all of Combfoot Chase, the floodlights come on bright white, light the fake grass green. The boys who – unlike Jem – have made the football team, are running back and forth in the pretence that it's a preparation for a great career in sport. They shriek and slide towards their goals on raw knees with their shirts tugged up above their heads. Jem doesn't want to go back and to join in with their phoney shouts of optimism. For all they plan and plot and make a map of their supposed futures in their heads, at some point they will have to face the fact they haven't got a thing they wanted, much less any of the things they thought they might deserve. The truth is, Jem thinks, no one gets to shape their own existence.

He had woken up that morning and had thought that this was just another day, that everything would be entirely ordinary. And events had seemed to roll out as they always did except the sun had come out; that'd been the only difference. He'd gone to school as usual, had walked around all day within the chilliness of Father's shadow. He'd done his level best to disappear whilst waiting for the customary pounce as he'd proceeded down a corridor. At some point after lunch his father's secretary had duly been despatched to catch Jem in between two lessons, had marched him back towards the office and – just as he'd expected – had sat Jem on a hard chair by the door.

"Mr Locke has said he wants to see you," she'd announced, as though she didn't know that Mr Locke the head was also Father and had no idea that Jem had also seen him on the toilet and whilst picking bits of green out of his teeth.

Jem hadn't had a clue, nor had he cared that much what accusations would be levelled at him today. Such summons happened often, almost every day, because Jem tried to be unpopular with teachers. He made sure he was bad enough so other students didn't taunt him openly with nicknames and insulting labels kept tucked up their sleeves, reserved to goad the children of the teachers.

"It's not my fault that he's my dad," he'd said when he'd first started at the school. He'd thought the spotless logic of this statement must win everybody over but had given up his protest when he'd realised that it didn't make the slightest bit of difference. No one will forgive his ancestry, so now he just calls Dad a wanker and he makes sure that he says it loudly so it hammers home the point.

The other boys will sometimes laugh, though Jem can't tell if they think it's amusing or they're signalling contempt. The girls look on with much the same expression of disgust as when they find some dog shit on their shoes. Jem hates their unfair airbrushed cheeks, their swaying brushed-out hair, their pouting fluffed-up selfie faces. He bunches all the girls together with the boys, believes they're student peas popped out of one school pod, in the same way that they think that he's a potted version of his father.

Jem tries to demonstrate with every action that he's not a duplicate of anyone, although he's careful to be only bad enough to earn the reputation of a minor miscreant. For Mum's sake he's not crossed the line into the sorts of crime that would've caused her real anxiety and he's kept his head down recently. He's had no taste for trouble in these past few weeks since she has left, so when the secretary collared him today, he'd wracked his brains and really couldn't pinpoint what it was his father thought he'd done. Other than a crafty fag behind the bike sheds every breaktime and a row with snotty Charlotte, he'd done nothing that he'd count as a fair charge.

He'd missed almost the whole of French before his father had arrived. The man had blown into the office on a waft of whisky that was swamped by sudden pungent smells of onion. Ugh. Jem had pulled a face and had regretted it immediately. His father's head had zoomed towards him and his hand had grabbed a sleeve and dragged his son right past the silent secretary, on into the inner sanctum of the study. Behind closed doors he'd lost all inhibition and had thrust Jem up against the wall. His father always stood too close, intimidated him with gusts of onion breath. Jem found it hard to say if this had happened more, or if he'd only felt it more, now Mum was not around to save him.

"*You shouldn't snack on onions in the office...*" If he listens very hard, Jem can still make out the gentle bubbles of Mum's voice. "*It's bad enough at home, but you've no business taking onions into work. The smell is downright antisocial and you ought to think about the poor sods working with you…"* Mum had stood between them, had made Father seem less squalid and less cruel. But now she's gone the tear-inducing bite of onion hangs around them all the time, has sunk into the very fibres of his life.

Jem lifts an arm and sniffs the hoodie that he's wearing. Yes, it's there, the scallion taint of Father which he carries with him in his clothes. For once he might be glad of it, he thinks. He'll hide his nose deep in his elbow if the corpse begins to stink, conceal the smell of putrefaction with his father's stench instead. If someone had asked yesterday, Jem would have said he thought that death would smell a little stronger. Even when he concentrates he catches only faintest hints of copper. Perhaps the truth is that it takes a while for things to really start to reek and even death is not enough to drive away the strong pong of his father's onions.

Now the sun has set it's noticeably colder. Jem zips his coat up, wonders what it might be like to stay all night beside a body. Does he dare? It might be awful, ticking off the minutes through the dead of night, but when he tries to think of heading somewhere else, he can't think where he ought to go. He'd done his best to get away today. He'd thought he might find Mum, had packed a bag and caught a bus, but nothing panned out as he'd planned it and he'd wound up back in Combfoot Chase. The bag is with his skateboard hidden underneath the gorse. "There must be someone I can tell," he thinks, "someone who knows what you ought to do with bodies."

Of course Jem's seen the signs that list the number of the helpline you can phone for free. They make it free so anyone can call. The only stipulation is you must be desperate. No one who's queued for a burger can escape the knowledge of the helpline, though most people ignore it, labour under the misapprehension that they'll never sink so low they'll need to ring. Jem notices that no one's had the bright idea of pegging up a sign down here. The implication is that any help they're authorised to give would come too late for those already at the bottom of the cliff. No one spares a thought for hapless passers-by who are unfortunate and come across a body.

On top of that, most mobile phones are useless here. This part of town's a dead zone where – despite the installation of some complex and expensive infrastructure – it's hit and miss if you can get a signal. The microwaves bounce back and forth between the surface of the cliff and all the houses, are scattered in a pattern which is unpredictable. And even if by chance Jem happened on a spot where he could pick up signal, he knows it wouldn't be of help because he didn't charge his phone last night.

"Ahhh, shit," he'd muttered as he'd grabbed a few things from the shelves and cupboards in his bedroom. He'd stopped to check his phone, had looked for longed-for messages from Mum, had lost the little hope he'd had when the screen had blackened into low-power mode. "It's not my fault," he'd thought, "I didn't know that I was leaving home today and there were still two bars last night. That would've been enough to get through any normal day." He'd stuffed the phone into his pocket, had thought that he would charge it when he'd got to Nana's house. It's strange to think how disconnected he now is, and that his phone lies dead as any dodo in his bag.

And so the only courses of action available to Jem are stay and wait, or walk away and leave the body. He's weighing up the consequence of each, and thinking that it's hard to say which option would be better, when Obic and Arak happen to emerge out of the darkness at the very end of the very last street in Combfoot Chase.

The terraced houses peter out completely here and even the road stops abruptly, ends in the tight loop of a turning circle. The cliff has proved too difficult – by which read too expensive – for the engineers to get around because the land is too unsteady. Some years ago there was a plan to finish off this street and build a few more houses. Developers had hoped to market them as somewhat more exclusive, a cul-de-sac of homes for on-the-up executives, a bid to raise the general tenor of the area. They'd even dug a trench and laid a pipe and dropped a curb, so access would be good-to-go once it was called for, but a sudden rockfall in the region had undermined their confidence in this location. No one wants to take the risk of underwriting properties constructed here, so the site is long-abandoned and the road still makes its way towards the edge of nothing. If anyone should end up here, decide they want to leave the town, their only option is to turn back round and go along the roads already travelled, find another way to join the stream of traffic on the motorway.

When Jem first sees them, he thinks Arak and Obic make up one black shape. The shape moves into the triangle of light cast by the final street lamp and occupies the pallid void between opposing rows of houses. It halts and goes no further as though it doesn't care to venture into darkness, doesn't dare to trespass on the ground where shade's already won. He watches as the shape resolves itself into two separate bodies, clearer once they've stepped apart, each distinctly drawn beneath the pale glow of the lamp. His first thought is that these two must be lovers who have had a tiff. The woman grasps the man's sleeve, seems keen not to let him go. Her figure stands much taller than the other, but Jem's sure that it's a woman because she's side-on; he can see the tempting profile of her breasts. The man, held firm, must tilt his chin to look at her. She towers over him. He tugs his arm and tries to get away, to quit her grip, to no avail.

The woman leans down, puts her mouth close to his upturned face. Jem thinks she seeks a kiss and wishes that she wouldn't because he doesn't like that soppy shit. He's glad his mum had had the decency never to kiss his father – or not where he could see at any rate. When Jem knows that a man and woman are not mouth-to-mouth he always feels relieved. Their speech is urgent. Quarrelling? Jem tries to work out whether they'll be likely to resolve an argument, decides from studying their body language that he doesn't think so. The man persists in his attempts to twist away, but she won't let him and his head jerks back and beats time with his every failure.

However unappealing they may be, these strangers offer Jem his one and only chance to walk away from death. If he tells these two about the body he can slide off into the dark, once they're busy doing everything you have to do to clear disasters up. The body won't be left to rot, but he won't have to deal with it. It's not much of a plan, he thinks, but it's the best he's got. He stands up, shouts out, "Oi! Over here. I need a bit of help," and feels the satisfying surge of influence as both heads snap in his direction.

Obic strides ahead of Arak.

She covers all the ground in what to Jem looks like a step or two. He's never seen a woman like her. She's nothing like his mother, who was soft and round and shapeless in a comfy sort of way and who could pacify him just by calling him a silly goose. Nor is she pert like girls are at his school, like Charlotte, who will only look at him with wrinkles of disgust drawn on the bridge of her repugnant nose. Charlotte is the sort of girl who flaunts herself on purpose. Her fingers toy along the string of beads she always wears, a ploy which makes you pay attention to her throat. It's not his fault he can't help noticing the smoothness of her skin.

This woman is another sort, is made of power and bone and sinew. Jem wishes now that he had paused and thought a little harder before he'd made her look. It's not that he despises every woman. He likes his nan – his mother's mother – who's crabby but can make tremendous pies. He'd hoped for pie today when he had caught the bus out to her house beside the reservoir, had thought that if he were in luck she might have let him sit up on a stool and watch her make the pastry. He'd passed the journey looking at familiar townscapes passing by the window and all the while imagining her cutting fat into the flour, working quickly as she always does. Before you know it Nan has made a lump of dough! Remarkable, he thinks, how she can conjure something tasty out of almost nothing.

Jem respects his nan because she has no truck with any of his claptrap. She brushes off his grievances as the inevitable complaints of a fish which finds itself out of the water. "You're like your mum in that respect," she says. Her judgements might be tough, but they're elastic, and he thinks she means that one day he'll be bound to find the pond where he belongs.

He loves to watch his nan roll dough. She works and practised swells of muscle ripple through her shoulders, down her arms, as she makes sure the pastry submits to the pin. She lifts and drapes the new-made sheet over an oblong tin and presses with her knuckles till it looks as though she's made a tiny coffin. Jem can love a woman who prioritises the preparation of a decent supper over everything. It's only simperers like Charlotte that he hates.

"I've told you time and time again to stay out of her way, though, Jeremy," Father had commanded him again today. He'd said it in a tone meant to be clear and undisputed, had betrayed a sheer frustration that his son had let him down. "Instead I hear you called her, and I quote, 'a frigid bitch' again."

"She is, though," Jem had muttered.

"What d'you say?"

"No, nothing… Sorry, Sir," he'd sighed, and sunk his chin into his collar.

It's not as though he hasn't tried to follow Father's orders, though he believes it's unfair that he has to take the rap for simply stating what is true. Nor has his father been successful following his own advice. He's never managed to shake off the women he finds troublesome, is only prone to lose the ones like Mother who are tender and are kind.

"I've had that wretched woman on the phone again," he'll shout and slam around the office. He'll lift up papers, thunder over to his desk and dump the pile down on the top of several others. *Bam! Boom! Bash!* The stack will wobble, hold its shape a second, then will slide, subside, strew papers all across the desk. By the time he's finished the whole lot's been jumbled up and Father can't lay hands on what he needs.

"And that's my fault as well," Jem knows.

When Father says 'that wretched woman' it's in reference to Charlotte's mother. He's also heard his father call her spiteful and a bully. He complains of frequent phone calls, says she always threatens him with one thing or another. He does his best to palm her off and gets his secretary to send her toady messages, but Charlotte's mother hasn't gone away no matter how much Father tries to dodge her.

Although he's never met her, Jem imagines Charlotte's mother as an amplification of the daughter, a hefty figure with a wide stance and a pushed-in puggish nose. She'd probably wear too many bracelets, he decides, and jangle them to underline that she's pissed off. In his mind he frames her with a box and writes the caption *That Wretched Woman* underneath. With a border and a title he can keep her under his control, but try hard as he might he's never managed to put Charlotte in her place. She's always breaking out to rile him, never lets him have a moment's peace. It's not fair that he has to take the blame for everything that happens when she pushes him until he will react.

Last week when they'd been arguing, he'd made a point of asking her to please stop talking, but she frankly wouldn't. She'd refused point blank, had carried on and on, had touched those wretched beads of hers which poked out from her collar and they'd trembled to the tune of every word she spoke. He's not sure what it is about those beads that makes him so demented. They're like a speck of dust that gets lodged in his eye when all he wants is to get far away from her and all her madness. "You're a frigid bitch," he'd said, and had reached out and ripped the beads from off her neck. One tug was all it took. The thread had broken and he'd had one brief rewarding moment when he'd watched the wooden beads dance their way across the classroom floor. He'd even heard them bouncing on the tiles once girlish shrieks and chatter died away and utter silence fell.

And then he'd realised everyone was looking at him. He'd cringed and known that he'd be for it because he'd let so many people see exactly what he'd done. He'd happened to catch Charlotte's eye and had been shocked to see her grinning.

"Oh, you little fucker," was the only thing she'd said.

Of course she'd told on him and straight away. She'd shown the school nurse and her mother faint red marks around her neck, and had accused Jem of assault. Father made him crawl around the floor until he'd gathered every single dratted bead. "Apologise," he'd snarled, and he'd let Charlotte watch Jem on his hands and knees, humiliated.

"You don't let anybody else wear jewellery," Jem had argued as he'd faced his father down a long expanse of empty dinner table that evening. "Why should different pupils follow different rules? Girls get away with everything. You only let her 'cos you fancy her…" He'd shut up when his father growled and slammed his hand down on the table so that all the china jumped.

Charlotte's mother got the beads restrung, this time with the addition of a silver crucifix, which dangled teasingly between the clavicles. Charlotte showed it off in class, leant over Jem so he could not escape the hot smell of her skin, nor fail to see the shadow of the dip between her breasts under her blouse. "I got the one which has a little man on it," she'd boasted, "as a token of my faith. So you can't stop me, *Onion-Boy*."

Charlotte's taunts hang over Jem in a balloon as Obic strides towards him. He imagines Charlotte grown into a woman such as this and shivers, hopes she'll meet someone one day who'll take her confidence and smash it. He's scared of her, of Obic, of the thought that any second she'll come close to him and sniff the air. "What's that disgusting smell?" she'll say, and he'll be too debased to answer her. You mustn't trust a woman who knows she's got some clout, he thinks. You can't trust anyone who bleeds for days and still won't die.

Obic looks down on the hunched-up boy and smirks. "What's up?" she asks. "You lost?"

Jem shakes his head and nods towards the body.

Obic tracks his gesture, says, "Oh, right. Oh, shit."

Jem's shocked because the word is muddled with a chortle. "It isn't funny," he protests. He watches as she takes her phone out of her pocket and flicks on the torch. The white beam picks out every crumpled droop and fallen detail of the luckless man. Jem shuts his eyes. It's what his mum had said he ought to do when he was still a little boy and still allowed to say that he was frightened. "Don't look," she'd always said when Father geared up for a row. "There's no point tackling him head on." Her palms had blocked his eyes and he had screwed his mouth tight so he couldn't accidentally let a sound come out. Mum had always let him shove his fingers in his ears. He remembers how it felt to lean against her, how she'd been so firm and reassuring, one continuous curve uninterrupted by the jutting out of breasts or hips. He leans against the cliff but finds it cold and unforgiving. A ridge of rock digs right into his spine.

Obic makes a brief examination of the body. She whistles through her teeth. "Well, what a way to go…" she says. She squints up through the night to judge the length of fall. "Yeah, that'd do it," she confirms.

Jem doesn't want to think about the drop. He keeps his thoughts on Mum and concentrates as hard as possible, remembers how he'd liked to wind his fingers round her neck when she'd leant down to kiss him every night. "Sweet dreams," she'd whispered because she said she always loved to dream. She'd said it came as a release, was like a sort of swimming. He imagines her suspended in the water of the reservoir. She's dipping, diving just beyond his reach, her neck a gentle and dynamic arc between her head and shoulders. Jem had always loved the fact that it was hard to tell where one part of her body stopped before another started.

One night, about a year or two ago, when he'd just found the first coarse hairs grown out around the bottom of his penis, she'd come to tuck him up in bed and he had plucked up all his courage, told her that he thought that she was beautiful. She'd smiled the sort of smile that made her lips go absolutely flat. "Oh, don't be such a silly," she had said. "It's sweet of you, but I've completely lost my figure." He'd been shattered that she'd tried to make a joke of it. "Too much of Nana's cooking, I expect," she'd said, had stood and put her hands around her middle where her waist was meant to be. She'd waggled all her fingers so it emphasised how far they were apart. "You see!" she'd said. "I'm fusiform, like all those fish your nan puts in her pies." Though Jem had laughed along, he'd thought it wasn't possible that Mum could really find this funny. "Night-night, my Jem," was all she'd said, and he'd not twigged until much later she was scared.

"How could I be so stupid?" he thinks now. "I thought that she'd be always here and life could not get worse."

Breakfast, just a day or two before she'd left. He'd poured himself a cup of juice and noticed Mum had left her toast and egg uneaten on her plate. "Are you okay?" he'd whispered once he'd ascertained that Father's nose was buried in *The Chronicle*.

"Hmmm? Yes, I'm fine," she'd said.

"You look so tired," he'd worried, "and your eyes are really puffy. They're all pink around the edges."

Father made a show of folding up the paper. Then he'd picked his knife up, held it poised above a slab of haddock smoking on his plate.

"Shush now. I didn't sleep too well, that's all," his mum had said. "Too many dreams."

His father's knife had sunk into the yellow body of the fish which steamed and cooled as it was opened. One by one he'd separated off the flakes of flesh and forked them into pink.

Jem had watched the whole dissection in an awful silence.

Mum had kept her eyes well hidden in between the toast and eggs.

They both knew better than to interrupt a meal.

At last his father had put down his knife and fork, had wiped his mouth and folded up his napkin, followed all the ironed lines that made it smaller, kept it square. "I've made a dinner reservation for next week," he'd said. "You'll wear your green dress, won't you."

Not a question.

"All right," Mum had said.

Jem had seethed because she always let his father get away with an assumption, never thought she might deserve an invitation. "Why d'you allow it?" he'd hissed when they'd passed each other later on the landing.

Mum had turned her face away towards the wall. "He says I have to wear his mother's pearls," she'd whispered, "and I can't quite get them on. I tried them yesterday and no amount of tugging gets the two halves of the clasp to meet."

Jem knows the pearls she means. They're grey and form a three-strand choker, which is curled like eels inside a silk-lined chest, a trophy which his father likes her to display beside the mirror on her dressing table. Father likes to see reflections of possessions everywhere he looks. "I had to wear them on my wedding day," Mum had told him once, "although they were too tight and felt like a garotte."

"I don't know why you married such a cunt," Jem had said. She must have known that there was no chance of a happy home with someone so despicable.

"Oh, Jem…" she'd said, although it wasn't the first time that she'd heard him use such language.

Jem knows the story of his parents' meeting and their marriage, or at least he knows what Mum has told him, knows enough to know her life is nothing like her dreams. There'd been a ball to end the summer term at university and Mum had promised Father she would dance with him: "Because he'd asked and 'cos I thought it wouldn't be polite if I said no… Though actually I was surprised that he remembered. I thought he'd only asked me out of courtesy because I thought he had a preference for my best friend, Grace," she'd said. A pause and then, "In point of fact I think she'd have been better suited to him because she's clever and high-powered, far more interesting than I am. But he came back and he told me that I had to keep my promise. I dunno, I think there's something in him that reminds me of my mother because I feel as though with him I'm going back towards my place of birth…"

Jem understands that Mum believes she can't live up to Father's expectations but doesn't understand this urge towards return. He vows that when he's old enough he'll quit the places of his youth, will go elsewhere, will find a better place, select it more for what it's not than what it actually is.

"So when he stuck around, I married him and let him string his pearls around my neck." Mum had paused again as though she'd dropped a stitch of story which now threatened to unravel all the fabric if she didn't hurry back and pick it up. "Your nan said I was lucky," she'd said sadly. "'No one gets real pearls these days,' she said, and told me I'd done well against the odds."

Jem knows that Mum has left those pearls behind with lots of other precious things. He's seen the casket standing open in his parents' bedroom.

Arak catches up at last. "I'm not as fit as I once was, eh?" he pants, and he makes a clownish show of clutching at his sides. "So, lad, what seems to be the problem?"

"Just another suicide," says Obic.

The man squats next to Jem. "Are you all right?" he says. "You found the body, did you? Tough luck, that, though why you're out here on your own at night I can't imagine."

"I was on my way to meet my mum," Jem lies. "I'm going to live with her, you see." He puts his wishes into words and in an instant is excluded from them.

"That right? How come you've not got any stuff?"

"I do." Jem nods in the direction of the bush. "I've got a bag. My board and things are over there."

This afternoon he'd struggled over whether he should take his skateboard with him. When he'd broken free of school and crashed back home he'd wasted precious minutes in considering that very question. The board was cumbersome to carry, but could he truly be himself without it? Jem knows it's always possible to buy another board – to use a deck at all is to destroy it – but it wouldn't be the same. This board had been a gift from Mum. They'd chosen it together. He'd told himself it shouldn't be a thing left in the past without a part to play in any of his future.

The minutes he had lost had meant he'd missed a bus, had had to wait an hour for the next to come along. There'd been a stupid woman at the stop who'd talked to him as though she knew him and had freaked him out. He'd scowled and wished she would fuck off, but he couldn't bring himself to say rude things, not to a stranger. The orange wheels which so appealed when Mum had taken him to choose the board, had made him feel conspicuous. It hadn't helped that he has painted bright green images of Onion-Man along the deck.

The character of Onion-Man is one that Jem devised in an attempt to regulate his hateful feelings for his father. Reinvented as a cartoon he'd based the role on classic baddies. Onion-Man has got a long and tube-like cape and rooty fronds of hair which sprout out of a bulbous head. Jem has tried to make sure anyone can recognise him as a caricature of Father, was proud enough to take the board to school last Mufti day. He'd wanted to show off, had thought that if the other students saw him poking fun at Father, then they'd know that he was on their side and not a teacher's spy.

His plan had not been a success. Charlotte simply commandeered the board and had mistaken Onion-Man for Jem. "It's not me, it's supposed to be my dad," he'd said, although he knew to protest would betray the fact that he felt powerless.

"It *looks* like you," she'd tittered, which had drawn attention from the other girls. "And you *are* a stinking idiot."

In spite of setbacks Jem still wants to work on Onion-Man. He hasn't got him quite right yet. Although he's captured other faces easily his father's still eludes him. Today, whilst Father reeled through all the usual tactics of a telling-off, Jem had passed the time in the attempt to figure out where Onion-Man was going wrong and had thought he'd had a breakthrough. "Yeah, that's it!" he'd thought. "I need to stretch the head a bit and shrink the nose, and then I need to make more of those wisps of hair that cling around the ears."

Arak has retrieved the bag and board from underneath the gorse. The luminous green colour Jem has used pops in the dark and Arak holds the board up at an angle so it catches slanted shafts of light from one of the lamps on the street. "Hey, this is pretty good, you know," he says. "You do this, did you?"

Jem nods. "Yeah. I based it on my dad," he says, and is relieved when Arak only laughs.

"I bet you haven't told him that," he says, and comes back, sits down next to Jem. He sets the board across his knees and runs a finger round the outline of the character. "I like the way you've kept it simple, captured in a few lines," he says, almost to himself and then, "You got some more that I can see?"

Jem blinks. He hasn't thought that anyone he doesn't know could be so interested. "Yeah, in my bag, I think," he says. "I've got my sketch book with me."

Arak leafs through pages till he gets to all the pictures Jem has drawn of Mum. In some she is a rabbit or a doe. In most she ends up smooth and silver like a fish. He stops at one where Jem has drawn her as a haddock with a padlock on her head. "Oh, well now, that one's very interesting…" he says. "I think you love her, don't you?"

Jem nods, but can't – or won't – express himself in words. Too awkward to discuss his loves with unknown people, he's aware the rules of conversation mean he ought to offer something. "She was on my side," he says, although he doesn't realise that the phrase lets go of her. She slides into the past with a mere shift of tense. "She always tried to let me have a say, but Father would hear none of it," he adds.

A thousand times he'd pleaded, "Let me go to someone else's school. The comp might be the only one in town, but I could always catch a bus. It won't cause any trouble." He'd been convinced that if he could present his parents with a flawless plan they'd have no choice but to give in to him.

"What would the governors say if my child went elsewhere?" Father had roared on blasts of hot and pungent breath. "They'd say I don't trust my own school. I'd lose all credibility. They'd think that I'm a *failure*."

"D'you know where she is then?" Arak asks. "If you've got a number I could ring her for you and explain."

If only it could be so simple. On the one occasion he'd been brave enough to ask his father where his mum had gone, the man had flown into a rage and called her lurid names like whore and fucking harlot. Once Father had calmed down enough to fabricate a story, he'd told Jem that his mum had gone to sell a brand of pickle in a place called Oundle. Jem suspects this is an outright lie. No one disappears without a trace to do something so ordinary and Mum had vanished more or less at the exact same time that Father had brought diggers into school, had had them lay a brand new 5G pitch. It would be just his luck for Mum to have been buried there, Jem thinks, though he's too spineless to make unsubstantiated accusations of a murder, even to a stranger. "I'm a coward," he berates himself. It's the only explanation of why, when he'd got to Nana's house, he hadn't dared to ring the doorbell, had instead skulked round the garden like a burglar.

Behind the closed panes of the kitchen window he'd watched as Nan began to cook a meal. The shadows of her movements under glass had fought against the thin reflections of the sunlit waters of the reservoir. Nan had had no reason to suspect that she was under observation. She's of the generation which assumes that doors and windows maintain privacy and it never passes through her mind that she could choose to livestream cookery on Instagram, so she was easy and relaxed as she had taken a clean knife out of the rack and whetted it. Jem imagined every stiffened silence in between each sweep of blade along the honing rod. Her hand had reached for one of many pilchards in a dish. Chop-chop, the head was off. Nan had lopped up piles of fish until the mounds of heads and tails were left in heaps beside a row of neat and ordered fillets. These she'd seasoned with a grind of salt and pepper, spaced them on a tray, returned them underneath the grill. As she'd worked Nan's mouth had sometimes moved. The first time this had happened, Jem had jumped, had thought she must have company. It took him time to realise she was only talking to herself or to the radio. She's lived alone so long it has been easy to pick up a range of inward-looking habits. He'd tried to read the pattern of her lips, had seen her make a shape that looked like 'Jem', had felt the queasiness which comes when someone speaks about you when they don't know that you're there. Jem had crouched among the crocuses and wondered what she'd said. She'd disappeared into the pantry, gone to get the eggs which she would crack into cold water one by one. Then she'd re-emerged, had crossed the kitchen, flung a sudden casement open.

"In my day, when we'd made our bed, we had to lie in it," she'd told the garden.

Jem had had to duck behind a bush and hope she hadn't seen him. Who's bed, he'd thought, and who should lie? He'd looked up at the sky above the reservoir, had tried to seek out answers to the questions in the clouds. A few wisps scudded over blue, but all he'd spotted was one fragment with a forked tail almost like a fish, another blob resembling an onion. The minutes passed and these clouds too had lost themselves amongst the remnants of a mackerel sky.

In the distance Jem had seen a change was coming. A bank of dark grey cloud would soon condense along the line of the horizon. As sure as Charlotte's mouth could signify a change of face, then so, he knew, did dappled skies.

"She's got no notion what she'll lose…" The window wide and Nana's words had fluttered easily across the garden. "Not like me, 'cos I've lost everything."

This household tale is one that's been familiar since Jem was a boy, the little boy that Nana had to coax to play along the artificial banks that built the reservoir. She'd always pointed deep into the brackish dark and told him how when she'd been young enough to play, there'd been a meadow which was now submerged beneath that water. "There was a little stream down there," she used to say. "I used to pass the time in catching grasshoppers, then throw them to the trout. You'd see the fish dart in and out between the pebbles 'cos the water in the stream was very clear and very shallow. When they first announced the plans to build the reservoir we none of us believed that it was possible. We didn't think the stream was wet enough to fill it up."

Nana often told the tale of how the dam had risen, how the water had backed up and slowly swelled between the hills as if a ruination is a fact of any life. She's proud to say that she stood by and watched the waters creep over her house, over her school, and even over the tall spire of her church. "The bell still tolls," she'd told him just to spook him. "You can hear it when the pressure rises."

Jem had swallowed waves of horror. "Why not knock the village down before they built the dam?" he'd asked, although he was afraid he knew the answer.

"What for?" his nan had scoffed. "Don't be so sentimental. No point wasting time with Combfoot Chase in need of water."

The little boy in him still shivers. In the depths of his imagination Jem sees all the trout grow large. He'll close his eyes and watch them swim through sunken windows, swirl behind a sodden curtain, loll on soggy cushions left on waterlogged armchairs. He hates to think how water still flows through those cottages and streams towards the bell tower, where it stirs a clanger, rouses up a village from a drowning and encourages the ghosts to float. "But don't you miss your old house and the village?" he's asked before, and frequently, although her answers never vary.

"No, it was a worthless place," she says, "no loss to anyone. And this house is much nicer," and she'll tell him how she'd rather live beside the reservoir. "It's better than a measly stream because I've always loved the water. That's why I called your mum Marina."

Nana's stories – like her favourite recipes – are utterly inflexible. Nothing ever added or removed, so nothing ever changes. This is how Jem knew without the need to look that Nana would dot the pastry coffin with some tiny tender onions and would cover them in mustard. She would nestle pieces of the fillet in a saucy bed and tuck them up under their pastry lid. She'd make small slashes with a knife and poke the heads and tails into each slit.

The thought of finished pie had made Jem salivate. He'd realised he was hungry, that he'd not eaten anything since breakfast, had foolishly forgone his chance to have a lunchtime snack in favour of a fag.

He'd been about to sneak back to the front door, to pop up and present himself as if he'd just arrived, when he'd heard the swoop of tyres on the drive. A car door clunked and closed, was followed by the heel-toe strike of heavy footsteps on the path. The ding-dong chime of doorbell like the echo of a bell in church brought clack-clack-clack of mules along the parquet in the hall. A key had been inserted, had been twisted in a lock, accompanied by the loosening of chains.

"Oh, you." It had been Nana's voice. "I thought you mightn't be too far behind."

"And Jeremy is here as well?"

"No, can't say that I've seen him…"

The feet had made retreat, had carried voices off with them but on the back of vanishing, his father saying, "Well, it seems he's turned out slippery, just like his mother."

A latch had clicked and all Jem's chance of pie was up in smoke.

He'd hung around until the sound of Father stepping out into the garden had put a rocket up him and he'd made a mad dash back towards the bus stop. He'd kicked himself when he'd remembered that the last bus into town had left an hour ago. He knows the service ends at four o'clock. His nan has often said that only fools live by the reservoir in Combfoot Chase and trust the public transport system.

Last year the council slashed the number of bus routes by a half. They just weren't viable, they said, and excess unused seats were costing thousands. Mr Tombleson had read about it in *The Chronicle* and had told his wife that he agreed that it was right for councils to economise on services if no one wanted to make use of them. Besides, he'd said, most people who had anything about them bought their own cars nowadays. They made sure they were independent, like the Tomblesons had done as soon as they'd been told that Mr Tombleson was not allowed to use the work van anymore.

A few days later when their daughter brought her kids to tea, she'd told her parents how the children had to set off at ungodly hours to get to school these days. "There's no specific buses which run services for pupils anymore," she'd moaned. "They have to change bus twice to get from where we live" – down by the Cock and Bull – "to near the campus by eight-thirty in the morning."

At this point Mr Tombleson had changed his mind, had written strongly worded letters to *The Chronicle*, but it was too late to undo the cuts. Once something's lost and gone it's never possible to get it back.

So in the absence of a bus, Jem had no option but to use his skateboard for his getaway. His first idea was to camp out near the reservoir. He'd learn to fish, he thought. It might be fun and might be possible to stay there all the summer. Along the banks are lots of spots where you're allowed to pitch a tent, so no one would have questioned him. But Jem had been too cold for self-sufficiency. He'd thought about the submerged village and decided he'd no appetite for a life haunted by bells. Instead he'd headed back towards the town.

The journey – long enough when travelling by bus – had seemed interminable now he had had to skate it. The road to get to Nan's house runs for miles in parallel with the towpath and the river before it turns into the end of Treasury Row. Even then you have to dogleg past the library and museum, and only then do you approach the centre of the town. Jem had dug through all his pockets and had rooted out enough spare change to treat himself to a small pie from Jaspers' bakery. He knew that Jaspers' always opened late to catch the hungry crowds which headed home from work.

"I know, we'll grab a pie for tea," his mum had sometimes said if they'd spent too long doing something that they shouldn't. "They're so good Dad can't tell the difference. We'll just tell him that we made it. What d'you say then, Jem?"

He'd always lied for her and they had always got away with it.

He'd skated and decided he would choose either the beef and ale, or perhaps the ham and mushroom. He had thought about the pies so much he'd almost caught their flavours, felt the texture of the pastry flaking loose and fatty on his tongue. They'd tempted him and tantalised until he'd almost thought he couldn't bear it. Then he'd turned the final corner and discovered that the bakery had closed. *With thanks to all our loyal customers*, a notice said, *with great regret we have to shut up shop…* An ad for online pizza services was pasted over the bottom of the notice so he couldn't read the rest. The poster says the pizza company has a brand-new website. You click on everything you want and type in your delivery address and pay using their secure online services. They'll notify you when they've made the bases, when they've put your chosen toppings on, when they've put them in the oven, and when they're loaded in a box and ready to despatch. They send the pizzas out by bike so dodging traffic isn't any problem. In no time someone rings your bell and leaves the boxes on your doorstep. All this easily achieved without the need to speak to anyone.

Jem had had the money for a nine-inch margherita and didn't care they'd use a substitute for cheese and not shell out for genuine Italian mozzarella, but with no charged-up and internet-enabled phone the offer of the pizza company's services was useless.

"Well, you can't stay here all night." Arak gives Jem a slight nudge with his elbow. "Look, lad, I don't think there's a need for you to stick around and deal with this. Why don't you head off, leave it up to me and Obic, eh? We'll sort this out if you've got somewhere you can go?"

Jem knows his father will most likely be back home by now. He won't have notified police because he doesn't want a harmful story to come up if a prospective parent googles him by name. He's confident that given time his son will turn up once again because he knows there's nowhere else that Jem could ever go. He'll put the news on television and he'll fall asleep in front of it. Nothing bars Jem's father from a little nap. He's even nodded off in meetings like he did today when he'd let out a shudder and a snore bang in the middle of giving Jem a chiding. That's how Jem escaped, in fact. He'd slid the letter of complaint from Charlotte's mother out from underneath the snoozing fingers and had tiptoed out of Father's office. He'd read the letter later on the bus, had studied all its petty grievances, but a letter out of Father's hands had quickly lost authority. He'd screwed it up and chucked it in a bin near Nana's, though not before he'd drawn a picture on the back – his fist in a big red glove, smashing Charlotte's necklace into smithereens. "*Whoosh!*" he'd said. "I'll grab those beads and Christ will fall right off his cross."

Father's secretary had looked up only briefly as Jem had left the office. His exit wasn't extraordinary enough for her to stop the clatter of her stubby nails across the keyboard.

"Father said to tell you that he's very busy," Jem had said. He'd tried to use the sternest and most honest version of his voice. "He wants no further interruptions for an hour or two." He'd slid past Father's secretary and legged it straight across the sports field, where he'd scaled the wire fence on his way to freedom. "What a stupid woman," he had thought. "She's gullible and lets him train her not to ask him questions. She can only blame herself if she believes a single word I say."

Of course a tendency to sleep does not mean Father won't wake up when Jem attempts to creep into the house unnoticed. Since Mum has left, his father's primed to stir as soon as there is any movement near the door. Jem knows that he'll be hauled inside and slammed around until his father's let another bout of anger out. But then again, he thinks, perhaps an utter silence would be worse. He takes one last brief look towards the fallen corpse and thinks he'll run the risk of anger. Rather that, than face the hush of nothing left at all.

And after all, tomorrow's lessons include Art and Jem is not inclined to miss out on that. In drawing he escapes into the ease of pen and paper and likes to think – with some practice – he can make his ideas meaningful.

He nods to Arak. "Yes," he says, "I'm not that far from home."

"Good lad," says Arak, and watches as the boy scrambles away into the dark.

The little figure crosses the rough ground, bag slung over shoulder, skateboard tucked beneath an arm. He reaches the street and drops the board and in a few short scoots he's disappearing round a corner.

Obic's busy taking photos of the body. She snaps from every angle, plans to forward all the pictures to the features editor of *The Chronicle*. A recent campaign has attempted to raise general awareness of the silent crisis in Combfootians' mental health. The numbers are extremely worrying, the experts say. Too many people end up on the brink and no one is exactly sure what's causing it. Her one regret is that she wasn't down here with a camera, so couldn't film the actual fall. That sort of footage would've been a coup, and though they'd never dare to show it on the local news, she's pretty sure it would've made an impact on the internet. Outrageous scenes are usually the ones that have the best chance to go viral. But, she thinks, the sad truth is that even she can't be in two locations both at once. She'd had to choose between the top and bottom of the cliff, had reasoned it was more important just to make sure that the job was done. She rolls the body over so it flops onto its back and busies herself with the taking of some close-ups.

At this precise moment Arak loses sight of Jem and happens to turn round. For the first time he has the chance to see the broken face. Up till now the corpse has been anonymous and Arak's thought of it just as 'the body'. Now he's brought up short and has to take a few sharp conscious gulps of breath. "No... no," he stutters. "No, it can't be. No, there must be some mistake…" It must be just a trick played by the half-light of the street lamp?

But Arak isn't stupid and he can't delude himself for very long. He can't escape the fact that what is now a body was a person, and a person that he knew, and now that person is a body, they are – in Arak's personal opinion – absolutely and forever lost.

A Little Folding of the Hands

One way or another this will be Ava's final day in Combfoot Chase. It's not that she has made a firm decision – or not as yet at any rate – it's just a feeling in the air that things are coming to their end. This is one of those spring mornings which we recognise come with a promise of finality. Look, the birds and blossom seem to signal that the worst is over. Winter's over and at last you can relax.

Some kindly soul has stepped out early and has emptied pockets full of crusts and crumbs, has scattered them about the new-cut lawns around the park. A robin, one eye always open and alert to cats, darts down from off his twig and pecks between the severed blades of grass. How lovely to receive an easy breakfast, he would think if thinking were his thing. We can assume the robin's feeling optimistic. Today he greets the world as though it's kind, as though it's generous. And positivity makes him brave. Having eaten all the scraps which fall within his territory he decides today is just the day to take a risk and set off in pursuit of more.

A short flight lands him close to the young mum. She's brought her son out to the park in search of space and fresher air, has spread a jacket on the grass so Junior can sit in state. He clutches at a fragile wafer biscuit, thin and pink and grubby in his paw. The robin sees him and the biscuit and proceeds with caution but also with a sense of escalating hope. A chain of bashful hops and he rests no more than a metre from the young mum's hand. She'd only have to turn her head and she would see his broken white eye-ring, each separate feather as it's lifted by the breeze and how his chest vibrates with every trill of song. However because the young mum never looks about by habit and keeps her eyes trained on her handsome son, she doesn't see the robin, doesn't feel an unexpected thrill to be so intimate with nature, and thus the robin is allowed to eat his fill in peace, although it's true he is denied the sugared pink of biscuit. Nonetheless the robin comes to the conclusion that humanity can't be quite as bad as it's cracked up to be. He feels unusually bright and cheerful when he flies back to his twig and sings his heart out, hopes the invitation of his song will summon up a charming mate.

Indeed the air is full of birdsong on this loveliest of mornings, though the soundscape features only as a backdrop for the young mum, who to be quite frank has never learnt to love a bird, can't spot the difference between a sparrow and a wren. The tweeting of a bird is nice enough, she thinks, but she is young and still prefers the roar of traffic or the panic of a nightclub.

A cherry tree above the spot where she has spread her coat looks like it's just about to burst. The dark and vicious tips of brooding buds have here and there already given way to paler pink of full-blown blossom, and the sky behind them is the sort of limpid blue which no one's seen for months in Combfoot Chase. The young mum looks up through the branches, and is startled by how beautiful it is. We'd like to tell you that she has a lightbulb moment and thinks such contrasts must be purposely designed to set the blossom off, but please don't get your hopes up. She's not been trained to think about the metaphysical and the short-lived understated cherry blossom won't hold her notice very long. Quite soon she'll be distracted by a post on social, or if not that then by the bolder bulbs of spring which rise in brilliant circles at the bottom of the tree, poke gaudy flower-heads above the ground.

The council works on the assumption that a tulip or begonia will better anything. A year or two ago they started up a Facebook group which aimed to deck each lamppost in the town with hanging baskets. They've also asked the local businesses to please sponsor a roundabout. The sweetener – for the price of a small box of bulbs – is the promise of a plaque. It will be prominent enough to make sure that the generosity of each business that subscribes won't go unnoticed. Philanthropy will be rewarded and no good deed will go unpunished.

Mr Tombleson pointed out the Facebook page and told his wife she'd make a fine administrator of this group, so now she organises hordes of ageing female volunteers and makes sure that a host of vibrant colours are included in the geometric patterns that are favoured for municipal flowerbeds. Her approach is typified by zeal and makes no reference to consistent schemas.

From time to time a volunteer will dare to voice a doubt about the discord on display. Most often this is someone who has only just joined in and isn't yet familiar with the way we run such things round here. You'll notice someone cough politely, then they'll drop a hint the planting seems a little garish. Their scepticism doesn't bother Mrs Tombleson and older members of the group can be relied upon to shout a doubter down. "But kitsch is just the thing in spring," they call, "because it's jolly cheerful." A tasteless show is what the town expects and helps Combfootians to forget that winter was so drab. The sceptic quickly learns to toe the party line. Before they know it they've begun to plant out rigid rows of hyacinths and ring them round with dandy daffodils.

The young mum sits amongst the shouting flowers and gazes at her son. Junior has picked a daffodil and is proceeding to dissect it. He's tugged off all the petals and is showing fascination in its trumpet. He inserts the remnants of his soggy wafer into the corona, pumps it in and out, is only satisfied when he's mashed the filaments and stigmas. The pink tip of his biscuit drops off and this makes him laugh out loud. He lifts the ruined flower high, is proud to show his mother what he's done. She smiles a wreath of smiles and says, "Oh, yer a proper little man now, in't yer?" She hands him yet another wafer in reward.

Her boy has grown so much these past few weeks, and she's decided that the time has come to ditch the ugly and enormous pram. He's lain flat long enough, she thinks, it must be time to sit him up, and so she's bought herself a little buggy. It's lighter and much easier to lift when she's obliged to carry it up several flights of stairs. Moreover it takes up less space around her poky flat. She got it cheaply – second-hand – because she doesn't know how long she'll use it. Junior already promises to take his first few steps. He's into everything at home. She can't nip to the loo without him crawling everywhere and poking sticky fingers into something. The only thing that keeps him still is when she lets him have the iPad, then he'll spend an hour or two entranced by playing Starfall or on Fireworks Arcade. The young mum's brought him to the park so if he tries to walk and falls at least it will be on the grass and not as painful as it would be on the pavement. Although she thinks that real boys should have dirty knees, she'd rather clean up stains than scabs. She takes his hands and hauls him onto buckled legs. "C'mon then, mate," she says, "why don't we see what yer can do?"

He looks at her with total trust, disturbing from a face that daily looks more like his father's. During the most recent visit, she'd foolishly remarked on this resemblance. Father and son had been pointing at each other's faces in the mirror and the young mum had assumed a dad would be relieved to know his genes were winning through. There's no doubt of the boy's paternity. It's there in every curly strand of hair and in the blackness of his eyes. She'd been surprised when Junior's father had frowned and quickly put the boy down on the carpet. Only later had the thought occurred to her that he might not be happy with a mini version of himself parading round the same town as his wife and other children. The cat would be most definitely out of the proverbial bag if the young mum and the slightly older wife should ever end up in the same shop, or the same queue for an ice cream, or waiting in the park to take a turn on the same swings.

The young mum wonders if the father of her son is ever sorry for his extra-marital affair, or if he only curses her recessive genes and alleles. She tries hard not to think about the years ahead. She'll spend them bringing up the boy but knows her influence won't be enough to make him one thing in the world that's truly all her own. Although she'll give up everything for him, she can't eradicate half of his DNA and her only option is to find a way to come to terms with it.

In truth the young mum hasn't seen the father of her child for quite some time. She hasn't tracked the days but noticed when they spilled into a week and then a month. At first she'd called him now and then, only to be brushed off with a weak excuse. Work was very busy, he had said, and then he'd sighed and blamed his wife, who was unreasonably demanding. After that he'd had to take his boat out of the water and had had to scrub the bottom. These things were always very time-consuming. Give him credit where it's due, he had asked after Junior – although he always calls him Donald – and had seemed to be impressed when she'd revealed the boy was cruising.

"I know it's early but he's not far off from walking, I would think," she'd said. Her tongue had doubled up with pride.

"A son of mine is bound to be advanced," the father had proclaimed, had promised he would come to visit just as soon as he was able. "Just as soon as work and other things have levelled up," he'd said.

She'd asked when that would be.

The answer had been vague and he had hinted at the fact he might be travelling.

As absence lengthened she'd no longer felt obliged to call, nor yet to keep the flat as tidy as she had before. Junior had strewn his toys across the floor and she had stubbed her toe on His First Plastic

Tractor. She'd spilt her coffee and had grabbed whatever came to hand – a cloth-eared dog – had used the toy to mop the spillage up. A dark brown stain had quickly spread and soiled its artificial fibres so she'd stuffed the dog beneath the sofa. Nothing ruined matters just as long as it remains invisible. Nor does she now bother with the washing-up. If she needs cups or plates or bowls she rinses them beneath the tap and tells herself that's good enough. Of course if Junior's father were to say he's coming round she'd tidy up again, but till then there are better things to do. For life's too short to try to make impressions on a person that you never see.

Needless to say she's not heard hide nor hair of him for ages. She's not really surprised. The only shock is that she doesn't mind. She can't say that she misses him, has no desire for sex and thinks she only ever did it so he couldn't claim she didn't satisfy his urges. She's thankful if she's dressed in onesie or pyjamas all day long and can scrape her unwashed hair back with a scrunchie. The only wobble she'd experienced was when the calendar flipped over into April and she knew the rent would soon be due.

"Oh no, that's all been settled," said the landlord when she'd called under the pretext that the kitchen tap was dripping. "All paid, up front. Yer okay up till Christmas."

She'd tried to phone the father to say thank you, but the call had gone straight to his voicemail and she'd not troubled him with messages. As long as money's in the bank she won't object if he's inclined to bugger off.

The young mum's jacket is spread in the morning sun a little way away from a small group of people who have gathered round the duck pond. These folk have been invited as the witnesses to the unveiling of a fountain which Mr Kelly has donated to the town in memory of his wife and son. The council wouldn't usually condone this sort of thing. The risk is that they'll set a precedent and private monuments will sprout up everywhere, but Mr Kelly pointed out his family had been through extraordinary trauma. On this occasion they decided it was right to make a rare exception. It isn't often that a mother and a son are lost in quick succession and in such a set of tragic circumstances, so they've let him stage a quiet ceremony during which the fountain will turn on. It's helped that Mr Kelly was quite modest in his aspirations. If he'd wanted to install something gargantuan the council would have told him outright no, but as a patron he has proved to be entirely practical. He knows that Combfoot Chase can't tolerate a plan that's too ambitious and his chosen fountain is appropriately small. It stands two metres high and has three tiers, is topped off with a pineapple.

A recent council meeting spent some time considering if two metres high was high enough or far too high to complement the limited dimensions of the duck pond. Eventually one council member bravely stood and said she thought it could become a lovely focal point, would make a good impression on the visitors who came to town. She argued that a calm and peaceful flow of water ought to lend an air of elegance, of affluence, to an area which has formerly been overly neglected. Her points were noted and debate moved on to cover aspects of the fountain's weight and maintenance. The island where it stands has never borne a thing more hefty than a duck house. What would happen if the installation of the fountain triggered its collapse? Mr Kelly gently pointed out the fountain isn't carved from stone as it appears to be in photos but is cast in durable and lightweight polyresin. He also took the opportunity to emphasise it runs on solar power so the council mustn't worry they'll incur a further cost to stretch their tiny budgets. This point tipped the scales. The council voted to agree to his request for a memorial just as long as he would pay the bill associated with the relocation of the duck house.

The next week's *Combfoot Chronicle* had featured an artist's impression of the fountain on its front page. It would be transformative, they claimed. More people would be drawn to use the park. The ice-cream man had cautiously increased his orders in anticipation of a longer queue, but Mr Tombleson had phoned the council straight away and made it clear that he had serious objections. His protest was that when his aunt had died *his* family had been told no public space was made available for monuments. It isn't fair that Mrs Kelly and her son should be allowed the honour of a fountain. He'd lived here just as long as any Kelly, he'd insisted, why must he content himself with an engraved name on a bench inside the bandstand?

The Tomblesons make sure that Aunty's name is always shiny. Every Saturday the women in the family take a turn to use a chamois leather and polish up the plaque. This demonstrates how much they miss and are devoted to their long-dead aunt, though no one else round here remembers her.

A kindly representative of the council had explained the Kellys had been prominent about the town and Mrs Kelly had devoted all her working life to teaching generations of their children. She'd gently pointed out that Mrs Kelly even taught *his* daughter, but an argument like that can hold no sway with Mr Tombleson. He's in the park today and has a plan to mount a protest. He'd tried to bring a tin of paint, but Mrs Tombleson had had the great good sense to intervene. "You'll make more trouble than it's worth," she'd said, and warned him off an act of petty vandalism. "That fountain's just another useless object. And nothing in this town stays special very long, you wait and see." They'd both known what she'd meant was that within a week the fountain would be doused in duck shit just like Aunty's bench.

Denied a fully-fledged rebellion, Mr Tombleson made up his mind that the very least he was prepared to do was lift a banner. Someone has to make a stand and point out all the council's inconsistencies, he thinks. He's spent the previous evening in his garage making flags and placards out of broom handles and sheets. He's come up with some very nifty slogans, so he thinks, though won't say – especially to his wife – what he has written.

He insisted that they set off early so he could pick a suitable location. He sought a station some way from the duck pond so any onlooker can't mistake him for an ally of the ceremony. He chose a good position elevated on the steps that lead up to the bandstand, and now he gives his daughter one end of the banner and the other end he lifts himself. His wife is sandwiched in between. She doesn't like the fact her view is utterly obliterated by the sign once it's unfurled but thinks she'd better lump it. In secret she would like to see the ceremony, to have the opportunity to watch a fountain spring to life, but this is not the time to say so. Life is simpler when she doesn't make her husband angry. Instead she whiles away the minutes working out what he has written on the banner. It's back to front, although the lettering is clear enough where paint has seeped right through the sheeting. She deciphers that he's written *There Is No Collective History.*

When this phrase came to Mr Tombleson he'd been immensely proud. He likes to think he's struck a note of quiet intellectualism and believes the point is unassailable. Unfortunately neither his wife nor any of the other people in the park this morning grasp his meaning. They read the words and register they're intended as a protest – their brains being wired to pick up negative events more readily than positives – but are bewildered as to his exact objection. A few do scratch their heads and think about it for a second, but as thinking can be difficult and taxing they give up, and decide it's most straightforward to ignore him.

Mr Tombleson stands resolute throughout the half-hour ceremony.

At ten-thirty precisely Mr Kelly says a few words in remembrance of his wife and son. He aims for poignancy, is gratified when a woman takes a tissue out and dabs her eyes. He ends by reading the inscription on the fountain which reminds all those who've gathered here today that Ruth and Mattie have been lucky to be freed from all the perils of this mortal life. Everybody clasps their hands and hangs their heads and thanks God that such luck has gone to someone else instead of them. For now the members of the crowd remember

Ruth and Mattie's faces – though that's not so hard when photos have been hung around nearby. Right now they think that they'll remember always. They forget that people disappear, that soon these two will join the ranks of others in the graveyard, of those like Delia, for whom no one has bought a bench, whose names and souls may live in company with God but if they do are known to only Him.

Once Mr Kelly has completed his oration a spatter of polite applause is heard and the leader of the council does the honours by removing covers from the solar panel. An awkward pause before the fountain comes to life, before the spring begins, eternal just as long as there is sun enough to keep it going. At last a little joyous bulb of water pops up from the sacred opening of the pineapple. It swells and bursts, begins a cascade which will trickle down and wet the tiers below.

The curious robin hears the sound of running water. He's not heard that here before and though the duck pond stands outside the limits of his winter territory, he decides he will be brave and will investigate. He flies and perches boldly on the rim of the top tier from whence he starts his study of this new supply of water. The flow begins to make a pool and he delights the crowd by bathing in it, by a sudden shaking of his feathers which flings bright droplets high up into the air. The drops make prisms in the sunlight, a momentary micro-rainbow. The crowd is charmed, applauds. How lovely and uplifting nature is, they think. They tell each other that the robin is a sign of good luck coming back to Combfoot Chase, that everyone will soon be prosperous and happy.

Mr Tombleson does not join in with the clapping. Instead he's concentrating on an enormous duck who's waddled over to the bottom of the fountain. Thanks to an interesting feature of its eye, the duck can take in objects near and far and simultaneously, so it knows both that the fountain is a new and unsoiled surface, and that not too far way away a crowd is watching him. However as the duck has no control over its sphincter muscle and can't be potty trained – no matter how hard you might try – it promptly dumps its faecal matter on the polyresin-footing of the fountain. Mr Tombleson grunts a grunt of satisfaction. He'd like to say, "I told you so," to the leader of the council, though if we're honest it was Mrs Tombleson who really made that accurate prediction. Instead he rolls his banner up and herds his wife and daughter back towards the car. "That'll show 'em all," he says, and takes his family to The Cock and Bull, where they raise a toast to jobs well done.

The self-removal of the Tomblesons has opened up the view for Ava, who's been sitting all the while on a shadowed bench inside the bandstand. She selected this bench because it seemed a little cleaner than the others and she's wearing her best jeans. She read the plaque before she set her back against it. *In memory of Aunty Maud, much loved and missed by Harold, June and Sandra.* The names mean nothing and are easily forgotten.

Ava keeps her distance from the ceremony. Her mind is full of other things – we'll get to details later – and besides, she isn't sure if she'd be welcome. It's months since she's met anybody from the theatre company, was only driven here by niggling doubt she ought to pay respects to Mattie. She's often thought about what happened in the theatre, has relived every horror in her dreams more often than she dares admit even to a friend like Grace. She's come in hope that rituals are magical enough to put it all to bed. She scans the crowd, searches each and every gathered head for someone that she recognises, but realises there's no one. Jason is a no-show and Brogan disappeared a while ago, though Ava has no way of knowing this.

A few days after Mattie died, his sister's flat was on the market and solicitors were primed to say they had no knowledge of her whereabouts and held no forwarding address. At first the father worried and began to formulate a plan to search for his stray daughter. He'd lost a wife and son already, didn't think that Fate could be so cruel as to take Brogan too. However he'd soon given up when he'd been overcome by feelings of complete exhaustion. The forfeiture of family takes its tolls on even the most stoic souls.

Mr Kelly had been sitting in his living room one evening, a balloon of brandy warming in his hand, engrossed in contemplation of whether he should contact the police or whether he'd be better starting with the local paper, when suddenly he'd realised that he rather liked the silence. With first his wife then both his children gone, he was at last quite free to do exactly as he pleased. No one could stop him eating buttered eggs for breakfast, nor monitor his levels of cholesterol. He'd never have to gnaw his way through worthy plates of fruit and veg each day. He'd be allowed to have a brandy every evening if he wanted to and wouldn't have to sneak outdoors to have a cigarette. Such behaviour, he concedes, would be disgraceful – nay, completely irresponsible – if he'd still had to head a family, but as long as he's alone he figures anything can go and no one will be any more the wiser when he rocks up in his usual pew to join the congregation of the local Catholic church.

When Mr Kelly had first had this thought, he'd laughed out loud. He'd dosed his glass more generously with what was left in the decanter, had kicked off both his moccasins and put his feet up on the sofa, had decided then and there that he would no more hunt for Brogan. The ties of blood are thinner and much less rewarding than the ones we forge ourselves, he'd thought. He'd let himself lean back against the cushions, closed his eyes and conjured up the image of a saucy widow whom he'd happened to bump into quite by accident not long ago when he'd popped in to buy a latte from that trendy café round the corner. He'd let himself imagine what she looked like naked, hadn't shied away from all the shifting details of a slightly ageing body, had enjoyed a lengthy meditation on the shape she'd choose to trim her bush. Would she stick to bland and boring landing strips or would she dare to pluck a playful heart? In fact he'd got himself quite hot under the collar and had had to have a hasty wank before he could relax.

That self-same widow's here today, although discretely. Mr Kelly found out yesterday her pubic hair is shaped into a lightning bolt.

He's glad he'd shaved off his moustache in preparation for a new encounter, but doesn't think it's yet appropriate to have her at his elbow. He thinks it's best if she stays inconspicuous, so she lurks on the edges of the crowd and mingles with the other people who have no real memories of Ruth or Mattie. She thinks the fountain's very lovely, just the proper way to honour absent family and preferable to dealing with real people in real life. She's hit the jackpot, she believes, in having caught a man who comes with nothing but his money. He's the perfect prospect and she couldn't ask for more.

Ava's also thinking of relationships. She's had a proposition and is struggling to finalise her answer. The question had surprised her, had been sprung on her, had come completely out of empty blue. "I only said I'd go to supper, had no idea I might be faced with moving to Australia," she complains. Her phone is ready in her hand. Its screen displays a moody and persistent blank. There've been no texts from him today, no messages at all. At supper she had made a show of indecision because she'd wanted to be civil, but from the moment that he'd asked her if she'd go with him she'd understood herself to be conventional and square. Deep down her instinct is to say no to adventure. "I'm not the sort to take off on a whim," she thinks, "especially not to somewhere so far-flung."

She tries to ease the weight of her own limitations by following the passage of a wasp which makes its way into the bandstand. It dances circles in the darkened space as though it's dizzy, as though it's not sure where it ought to be. April is the crucial time to build its nest and it's survived for weeks on nothing but infrequent dandelions, but it's fuddled by the new array of flowers in the park and can't believe the glut is really real. Even if it only opts for flowers in its favourite colours – ignores the reds and sticks to white or yellow – there are still too many choices for decisions to be clear. Just this morning when it tried to feed on tubular flowers, it recognised its tongue was far too short to reach the stamen. Soon the wasp will figure out that if it bites a small hole at the base then it can rob this flower of nectar and a little innovation will release a world of possibility. For now it's still completely baffled. A few rounds of the bandstand and the wasp decides that this is not a place it wants to build a nest. It flies away to take its chance elsewhere.

Alas for Ava she can't bring herself to follow its example. Last week when sitting opposite at supper, Philip had exuded energy, had frightened her. A man on fire would burn her, surely? She'd tried to think of change as something to desire as he so obviously does. She'd stalled and played for time, had asked, "So when d'you imagine we would go?" She'd felt shocked when he'd said he'd made a plan to go next week.

"Only to check it out, you know…" He'd shrugged and left the offer hanging.

She'd laid her hands flat on the table, had straightened out the creases in the cloth, repeating the same action over and again. Philip had begun to throw her odd and anxious looks. She remembers a feeling of deflation, of all her hopes unfolding and flattening out, of an awareness that everything had been crumpled and spoilt. At the time she'd managed to say nothing more, had wanted to avoid a snare of worthless words, had tried to think of the suggestion without prejudice. As yet she's not convinced migration is the answer to her troubles, but the asking of the question made a cut and she has no idea what glue might fix what she had felt for Philip. Ava tracks the wasp as long as she is able. She keeps her eyes on it and watches as it flies above the crowd, then loses it when people start to separate, when shadows move and shift formation round the fountain.

"My relationship is over," she announces to the empty bandstand. She says the sentence out loud as a thought experiment, though she knows the words don't taste good in her mouth and make her feel immensely wretched. The decision may be prudent, but it doesn't make her happy.

"Sleep on it," Philip had said, and then he'd winked at her. She hadn't liked that. Not at all. He'd only meant it lightly, she was sure, but she believed the gesture smacked of trickery. It was a side of him she'd never seen before, as though someone had turned him over, shown her secret messages they'd written on his back.

A lying tongue had promised she would weigh his proposition and she'd duly slept on it, although a week of slumber hadn't made the answer any clearer. She worries that to cross the world with Philip would make him responsible for her and she can't contemplate existing under someone else's wing. "I've never had much luck with men," says Ava. Good fortune is a magic that she's never had and now does not expect.

She presses the power button on her phone and Philip's image is illuminated on the lock screen. That picture had been taken on the day they'd motored his boat out onto the reservoir. The wind is in his hair and all his teeth grin at the camera. Through every failure, Ava thinks, through all her days and nights alone, she's wished and wished for that one person around whom to build her rituals. She's yearned to make a pattern of repeated ceremonies, to mark off anniversaries and birthdays as she thinks most families – or at least their women – do. She's not known Philip very long, but had thought he might possibly become that fulcrum. All those dreams seem very silly now. She ought to know that wishes are not granted.

"Just think about the weather," he'd said as they'd sat by their uneaten suppers. He'd reached across the table, grabbed her hand and popped the fatal question. Then he'd topped up both their glasses with more wine – Australian Shiraz, she notes now, wryly. When she'd hesitated, he'd smiled, had tried to soothe away her doubts and to entice her with a vague hint at the possibility of marriage. "Though no pressure," he'd said casually, "but it might make coming with me easier."

She hopes the look she'd given him was proud. "If I should think of getting married, my only motivation would be love," she tells the lock screen picture, and then presses the power button once again, this time to make his picture disappear. There ought to be no mention of convenience where weddings are concerned. And yet, she thinks, she had been tempted. For a week she's flirted with the thought of being Mrs Turner but can't make up her mind to call him and to publicly admit a change of heart.

Australia is still too far and far too new.

So yesterday when they had met for morning coffee in the café, she'd told him that she couldn't go. She'd tried to stress how seriously she'd mulled the question over. "I didn't, though," she thinks now. "No, I didn't. Not at all."

He'd looked put out and ruffled, had sat back and crossed his arms in a defensive gesture which had not escaped her. Any hope that he might stay in Combfoot Chase, that his proposal was an early wrinkle they could iron out with time and effort, had evaporated when he'd told her he'd already said yes to a job and packed his bags. "I'll keep your ticket, just in case you change your mind," he'd said. But he would leave, accompanied or not.

Since then she's heard nothing from him. No text, no message. Nothing.

Perhaps, thinks Ava, Phil is right to cut things off. There's no point in a late-night phone call from across the world, or streams of messages if you can't touch each other. There's no point drawing out the agony, though renewed acquaintance with a lover's silence has been awful. She knows his flight takes off tomorrow and then he will be gone, and she'll go back to being absolutely on her own.

Last night she'd gone to Grace's house in search of company, had been distraught to find her friend was not at home. She'd used her key, had waited curled up on the sofa, but Grace had not come back.

Thoughts of the ending of her love affair had stopped her sleeping. She'd woken frequently, had had to while away the hours reading tweets. When bored of social media she'd checked her emails. Not a single one was personal, just streams of messages from shops and businesses she'd bought from in the past. She'd flicked through them, deleted them. One subject line had caught her eye. *Please Tell Us*

Where We've Gone Astray, it begged. She'd clicked on it and read the contents. *We've noticed that you haven't opened any of our emails lately. What did we do wrong?* The message had read rather like a love letter, had pleaded for an explanation why she'd gone away. *Why don't you need to buy another dozen pairs of socks, or trainers, headphones, bicycles, bananas? Why don't you want us, don't you need us, don't you love us anymore?* "It's scary that my phone is tailing me," she'd thought, had shuddered and had turned the damn thing off. "*Do* something," she'd insisted to herself. "Do *anything*, even if you only visit the museum."

Ava takes her comfort in familiarity and seeks a consolation in the past. She goes to the museum often – more and more in recent weeks – enjoys the atmosphere of custom and tradition ossified, though cases full of porcelain and marble aren't to everybody's taste. "Though I prefer it once my visit's over," she has realised. Only later when she's pottering around the park among the flowerbeds, or when she's breathing fresh air underneath the trees, does she appreciate a dip into her heritage. "It's not that I love claustrophobic cups in casements, but I feel relief once I can leave it all behind." The past is not somewhere she wants to live, but is a root which gives her space to grow.

Although today her visit had been bothered by surprises. She'd made her way from room to room without expecting novelty or innovation, had been a little startled when she'd come across a corner that she's never noticed on her visits there before. She must have passed it every other time she's been, though perhaps she'd been swept on by flocks of other visitors, or had her nose stuck very deep into the guidebook. It's easy to see only the historic highlights specified by experts and never pause to peer through the protective gloom all by yourself. And so she's never raised her eyes to see that there's a cupola – there's always been a cupola – which lets in light to spiral down a simple staircase and illuminates it from the very top right to the very bottom. She'd almost missed it once again today because although the niche was very brightly lit, it had been stuffed to bursting with a host of other people.

A teacher from the school had crowded in a group of children – too many to jam into the space – so some had spilled out, made themselves a nuisance in the corridor. The teacher had been pointing up. The children dutifully craned their necks and angled camera phones at something Ava couldn't see. She'd tried to look above the strange hubbub of heads but gave up, had decided it was better to be patient. All the children had oohed and ahhed on cue, then turned their backs on what they were supposed to notice. They'd wielded selfie-sticks, created Snaps, had occupied themselves by tagging all their friends in every photo.

"I didn't come for this," Ava had grumbled to herself, "I came to think, to find some peace and quiet."

The teacher had then spotted Ava and had herded all the kids away, revealing a discrete attendant who'd been hidden in a corner. She must have sat in silence with the gaggle all around her, head bowed, concentrating on a book and pleased to disregard the boisterous muddle. But when Ava had entered she'd looked up, had welcomed her and smiled. "Hello," she'd said. "If you hold on a mo, that lot will soon move off and you can have a look in peace."

"Oh, yes, I will. Yes, thank you," Ava had said, had done as she was told and waited, had then asked, "So what's the fuss about?"

"A Temporary Art Installation," the girl had said, the capitals embedded in her emphasis.

"Oh...?" Ava had registered the faintest trace of disappointment. It wasn't that she objected to the thought of modern art – in capitals or not – but she had hoped simply to look up and appreciate the natural light which poured in through the cupola. She'd hoped that with the pupils gone the space would become empty and correct. And now she'd have to feign an interest in some upstart of an artist and their complication of ideas. The very thought was tiring, but the room attendant had already spoken and with no polite way out she was condemned to take part in the conversation, and to listen to prescribed interpretations of the art. She'd closed her eyes, had waited till she'd heard the teacher's voice a long way off, had only then allowed herself to look.

She had been speechless.

In the alcove cantilevered stairs rose up and drew her eyes towards the light. Each step hovered out of the wall and a balustrade curved and twined its neat and ordered ovals in between the floor and ceiling. Everywhere, suspended on wires so thin and light as to be almost invisible, flew hundreds and hundreds of origami birds. They'd soared and spiralled round a lantern which hung down through the centre of the stairwell, as though it were the law to cut sharp circles in the air. At the bottom of the installation the birds had been pure white and crisp, but as they rose they'd faded into the lightest of light blues, and then had darkened steadily until they reached the top, where closest to the cupola they were so blue that the sky had paled to nothingness behind them through the glass. She'd looked and looked, had realised that each and every bird was unique in its size and in its shape. Some had been expertly folded, others frankly had been shabbily done, not that it had seemed to matter. Ava could see pencil marks or ends of words, a statement here, a question there, the tail end of a sentence, so many unknown messages penned onto paper before the creases had been made.

"Oh!" she'd said, feeling the inadequacy of thought, and once more, "Oh?" again.

"Breath-taking, isn't it?" the attendant had said, if somewhat smugly.

"I don't get it at all," Ava had said, had had the feeling that her mouth was flapping without forming any useful shapes.

The girl had sensed an opportunity, had been pleased to tell her all about it, spoke with all the confidence of the schooled. "This installation explores wishes," she'd set about her standard explanation. "In Japan there's a tradition called Senbazuru that says if someone folds a thousand origami birds their wishes will come true—"

"There are a *thousand*?" Ava's head had spun. Her eyes had tracked the lines of birds, the pairs of wings which carried all those cravings to the sky.

"...The artist sent a square of paper to a thousand people all over the world," the smug attendant had continued, "and asked them please to think of someone who'd died, or someone they'd lost touch with, and to write a wish for them on one side of the paper. Then they had to fold the square into a bird and send it back. The artist then installed them here."

"And did the artist read the wishes?"

"No. To read them would've ruined them. It's private. Just between the writer and the bird."

"So no one knows if they came true?"

The attendant had shrugged as though she didn't care or hadn't really thought about it.

Ava thinks about indifference and frowns. The sculpture had been beautiful, joyful even, but looking at the birds had left her restless. She'd not been able to prevent herself imagining the far-off people, all their thoughts and losses, all their reaching out to loved ones, all their flights of fancy, all their bids to flee the mundane, hopeful fingers teaching paper to take shape. "All that belief in possibility," she says out loud to no one in the bandstand.

And it makes her think of Philip.

"Will the sculpture stay here long?" she'd asked the smug attendant.

"Sadly not." The attendant had shaken her head. "The moisture content in the air's destroying all the paper. If you look," she'd pointed to a lower bird, "you'll see that they are wilting even now."

Ava had looked and had seen that they were.

"I'll miss it when it's gone," the girl had said, and Ava had felt sorry for her suddenly, for all the meaning and the pleasure which she'd poured into this sculpture, all the effort she must make to let it go.

"What'll happen to the birds?" she'd asked.

"They'll be sent back to the person who first made them." The girl had paused to give Ava the time to register this promise. "Actually it comes down tomorrow," she'd said almost as an afterthought, "so you're lucky to have caught it."

"*Am* I lucky?" Ava asks, and gazes out across the park. Luckier than some, she thinks as she spies the young mum on the other side of the duck pond. She watches as the woman struggles to release one fistful of long hair from her child's grasp only for him to grab and tug another. This process is repeated, on and on until the young mum shouts, "Shit, will yer stop it now, yer hurting me, yer little bastard," and she gives the boy a clip around the ear.

Other than these two, the park has emptied out. All those who came to see the fountain have already gone. They've paid their tributes to remembrance and have splintered off, have followed different paths to different gates, dispersed into the streets of Combfoot Chase. The unsuspecting park's returned to stillness, though Ava's more alert than she has been for weeks, as though she's been a sluggard, has only been aroused by a flight and flurry of birds.

"Yes, you're lucky," says a voice.

Ava blinks. She draws a breath. Did someone speak? Has she wished so hard she's summoned up a ghost?

The voice begins again. "More lucky than you know," it says.

The voice comes from behind the bandstand, from the darkness of a shrubbery beyond. Ava kneels up on the bench and leans over the railings, peers down, though there's nothing there to see but glossy evergreen. A laurel bush has made a canopy to hide the ground from view. She strains to listen for another sentence, another word, is on the cusp of giving up in the belief that yes, she really must be utterly delusional, when from the bush she hears the smothered snuffle of a sob. There's no doubt. Somebody *is* there. There must be.

Ava presses on her heart in recognition of a sudden palpitation. These are the symptoms of vicarious embarrassment, however – as she's programmed to assist a person in distress – she makes her way out of the bandstand, drops down on all fours and crawls between the twisted boughs of laurel. She ploughs through fag butts and through crisp packets and chocolate wrappers, breaks into the deeper damp of old and weathered leaves. A figure hunched beyond the undergrowth of litter turns a tear-stained face towards her. "Mr Arak!" she exclaims. "How long have *you* been here? Are you all right?" Without intending to – nor with an understanding of what she really does – she stretches out her hand.

Arak shakes his head and sniffs. He would be proud, he thinks, to accept a simple gesture of respect and friendship and to link himself to Ava. He could face the shocks to come more easily if he could do it hand-in-hand with her, he thinks, but the advantage would be only his. It isn't civil to be sinking and to drag another with you, so he doesn't take her hand. Instead he puts a finger to his lips and says, "Shhh, please don't speak so loud. I'm hiding."

"Whatever for?" says wide-eyed Ava, who is fighting off a sudden urge to laugh. These bushes are the daytime dens of school boys for their games of hide and seek. Their mothers try to warn them off, instil a fear of dirty needles and used cock socks in their sons, but no one really thinks that danger lies beneath this leafy bedding, even though it's here at night that all the cheaters and the rent boys come.

Ava waits, persists, her hand held out, though sagging now, weighed down by childish offers of a bond. She can't accept that anyone could see an outstretched hand and then be rude enough to disregard it. We're predetermined to appear polite, she thinks, the laws of courtesy won't allow for a rejection. And no one's hunted in real life. Perhaps this is a game, because she's only ever come across a drama quite so noir in films, or on TV, or in a play, or in some other a work of literary fiction. Arak must have invented the pursuit because a real life's always dull, is often dutiful, is never lived as though it is sensational.

He doesn't answer.

Ava's hand sinks lower.

Arak sighs and takes his glasses off. He uses thumb and forefinger to pinch hard at the bridge of his nose. The pads of his glasses have dug red marks into his skin, over which his fingers leave a smudge of leafy mulch. His breath, she notices, is audible as he struggles to coordinate his lungs and mouth and nose. "Obic's after me," he says at last, and then he looks at Ava with a slow and rueful smile.

"Really? Are you *sure* she's after you?" she doubts. Misgiving makes her pull her hand away and hide it in her pocket.

It's understandable that Ava hesitates. When faced with an emergency, the genuine necessity to keep a stronger grip, who doesn't have a slight crisis of confidence? She knows how to express what's wanted in the way of ordinary consternation and often leaves a sympathetic comment when she reads on someone's newsfeed that a flood or wildfire has affected unknown people in some far-off foreign land. She even sends occasional donations when appeals pop up which strike her as important and affecting. Most recently that one which aimed to rescue the koalas. Ava's never seen a real koala – whether stranded in a eucalyptus tree or otherwise – but thinks they must be an essential part of other eco-systems. For creatures to survive so long they must have valid functions, and besides that, they're adorable. But in her own life, she relies on the assumption that the worst will never happen. *Not here, not now*, a placid disposition tells her. "Isn't that a bit unlikely?" she suggests.

"It's unavoidable," says Arak. "If Obic doesn't track me here, she'll catch up in a week or two. If I leave town, she'll follow me." He hunches up his shoulders, turns his mouth down at the corners, is ostensibly indifferent. "It's bound to happen in the end," he says.

"Oh, don't say that!" says Ava, who can accept our nature is to die but can't live with the thought it's not important. We must be more than our biology, she thinks, and must make marks on someone, be a loss that's not too easily replaced. "That *can't* be true. She can't just make you disappear 'cos it's against the law for starters," she exclaims.

Ava's nothing if not inconsistent, Arak thinks. Her own mother has vanished and though Ava might experience a pang of guilt when she's reminded of it, she doesn't think that it was wrong to stage a vanishing. Admittedly she does her best to tend the body though her once-was-mother's mind's forgotten all the life it lived already. She visits often, talks to silence, keeps her mother's photo in a prominent position in the hall. She doesn't think about the fact that that's a room where no one lingers, no one ever lives. She hung the picture next to the front door. It shows her not-yet-mother in a uniform, aged sixteen on the first day after school when she was sent to work, when she began to be polite, to fetch and carry in the town's most swanky tearoom. She is crisp in apron, capped and frilled in starchy white, stares out at the camera from between two other fledgling waitresses.

Ava's habit is to stop and put a finger to the photograph whenever she must leave the house. She taps her mother's hair or pats her arm. She does this to remind herself of where she comes from and how lucky she is not to have to wear a pinny, not to haul around a tray of humble pie, nor to juggle teapots back and forth between a kitchen and a stranger's table. She thinks remembering will stop her being flighty, will keep her feet on firm ground and ensure she isn't tempted to ask for more from life than is her just deserts. She comes and goes and marks each new arrival and departure thus, and as she does so Not-Yet-Mother stands quite safe and sound behind the glass in long out-dated clothes and stiffened hair.

Separately – but in a care home – Has-Been-Mother stays equivalently motionless but in a chair, is just as thoughtless as the image of her youth. She gazes through a window at a bed of carefully stipulated flowers. The hopes and wishes of the almost-woman in the photograph have gone and in the real-life version they're now equally inaccessible.

"Just 'cos it isn't legal doesn't mean it doesn't happen," Arak answers. "When the law comes into town, then Obic finds another town to go to."

"Please, you mustn't talk like that," says Ava. She slumps down next to Arak. The surface leaves are dry and leathery and rustle as her body bends them, but beneath there is a moist and woody warmth where fronds and foliage relax. She'd like to offer him some comfort but has nothing she can offer but her hand. Her instinct doesn't understand that a rejection can be sometimes followed by acceptance, so she only puts her palm flat on the ground and next to his, her little finger just a hair's breadth from his touch.

"She's killed the others, so I must be next," shrugs Arak. "I suppose it's just my turn."

Ava gulps and pointedly considers the jam-packed canopy of glabrous heavy leaves. Their untoothed margins overlap, seal up this hiding tomb from prying eyes. How she wishes she could catch a glimpse of sky! "But aren't you scared?" she whispers. What she really wants to ask is whether she should be afraid herself, whether in the act of sitting here, of keeping company with him and offering her interest and her hand, she's also put herself in jeopardy. She holds her tongue. Sometimes a question is too selfish to deserve an answer.

"Yes, of course I'm scared," nods Arak, "though in my trade being scared is just my job."

"I know exactly what you mean," says Ava, although she doesn't really and he knows she really doesn't, but the dominant need in this case is agreement. "It feels to me as though the world and everyone knows far too much," she says.

Arak pauses then he lifts his hand and lowers it to cover hers. His fingers slide between her own until their two hands are completely interlocked.

Will he hold on to me and never let me go, thinks Ava? His finger skin is rough and hardened, prompting her to wonder what he's done to earn such callouses.

"It's just the tracking pixels," he says softly. "You can't see them and it's hard to turn them off, so best if you try not to mind."

They sit in joined-up silence.

"I don't think that I'm ready," Ava breathes.

"There comes a point when you accept it's time," he says. "You listen to your nerves, and suddenly you know you're done, it's time to end your story. If you're lucky you can do this for yourself and not let others do the telling for you. I've accepted that I'm coming to the end and I'm glad it's nearly over."

Ava shakes her head. "You make it sound like we're all lambs just waiting for the slaughter," she says.

"Perhaps we are," he says. "Arak of lamb!" He laughs and winks.

Another wink? Oh, how she hates these winks. Her hand is trapped and stifled underneath his toughened palm. It isn't possible to trust a man who winks, however much he makes a problem sound innocuous. The absence of his glasses changes her perspective on his face, a blandishment that hides all sorts of wicked things. Unframed his eyes look weaker, browner, sunken-in. She wishes that he wouldn't look so steadily. "D'you want my help with something, Mr Arak?" she asks cagily. "Should I go with you to the police? Or is there someone I should speak to, someone I should call?"

"Too late," he says, "at least for me. But that isn't your problem." He pats her hand and draws his own away. Bell's gone. Fuck off. He folds one with the other in his lap. "It's probably best if you go home," he says. He means to signal her release, to give her his permission to depart, to fly away and leave him. He puts his glasses back onto his nose.

Are any of us ready to be free? We leave and risk a different kind of failure. Ava neither knows where she belongs nor where she wants to be, which windows ought to substitute for eyes, nor which door ought to be her rightful mouthpiece. She only knows she doesn't want to stay in Combfoot Chase. To stay is to accept the creep of beige and grey, to kow-tow to a bleak row of conformist neighbours. But to leave might mean to fly off to Australia and that's still far too great a leap to contemplate.

"I can't go home," she says. "I don't know what or who you mean by home or where it is these days." And Ava tells him all the ins and outs of Philip's proposition. "So should I go with him?" she asks. "I can't make up my mind," and she confesses that his unexpected flight has quite uprooted her. "I've tried to talk to Grace about it. I've called her several times, to get her take on it, you know," she says. She draws her phone out of her pocket, presents it in her palm as though that's proof that she is open to connection. "She *always* helps me, usually, well, in the past, I mean, but in the last few days she hasn't answered, won't pick up. It's not like her at all…"

"If the hill stands still…" says Arak.

Ava frowns.

"…you have to go to it."

"D'you think?"

"Submit to the alternative."

"I can't. And anyway, she's working. Her job's important, so I can't disturb her."

"Would it make it easier to interrupt if I came with you?" Arak knows that if he chooses to depart this shrubbery, there's every chance that Obic will catch up with him. Her spies are everywhere, in light and dark, in shadow gaps between, disguised in letterheads, inserted in a footer, in the body of an email. They're tracking his devices, where he goes and what he opens, what he closes and how often, but he knows they are, and knows that on behalf of Ava he will risk it. His guts shout out to hide and hide forever, though his hope insists his guts could get it wrong. He has a fair idea of what awaits him at the end, but there's no question that he'll follow Ava out from underneath this shrubbery. We know that it's a done deal, but don't kid yourself he wants to be a hero. He's not got the honesty for that but wouldn't mind if in the future he's remembered as a symbol or a turning point. He'd like to be a thorn in Obic's side just one more time, he thinks. He'll make himself her problem while he can.

And no one lives for ever. Not even Obic. Someday someone – something – will replace her. And he'd like to think he'd made a stand and given some support – however trivial – to whomever – or whatever – that may be.

Ava signals her acceptance of his offer by squirming off on hands and knees through the littered brush and tangle of low branches. Arak shuffles after her, accepts a hand to get back on his feet. One palm fits neatly in the other, he observes, and hopes she won't let go once they're both out and in the open. He takes some comfort that they're setting out together on what will be their final journey.

"Will it take a long time?" he asks.

Ava shakes her head and points towards the tower on the margins of the park.

He looks over his shoulder only once as they break cover. In full view beside the fountain he's aware of every detail of the things around him, all the frilled specifics of the cherry blossom, newly vivid and extraordinary, of every bead of water flung into a sunny sky. The world's more real and brilliant than it ever was before.

He lifts his face and lets a droplet land with feather-touches on his skin.

A bossy duck quacks to its flock and leads a general swarm across the pond. Impossible that humans would turn up and not bring bread, they think. They spread their webbed feet wide and push a little harder, paddle faster in resistant water.

"Just a tick," says Ava. She makes sure that her feet are shoulder-width apart and lifts the hand that isn't clasped in Arak's till it's level with her ear. She shifts her weight back then in one smooth motion, with a twist of torso and the curve of energy and arm, she launches something high into the air. It makes a wide arc, soars above the fountain and the ducks, then drops, lands in the deepest darkest middle of the pond and sinks down out of sight. A slop of muddied water closes over it.

"Feel better?" Arak asks, and Ava laughs out loud.

"Actually, yes," she says, "I do."

Beneath the surface of the pond the ions in the water have already started on the process of corroding all the electrical circuits in Ava's phone. Its back and battery cannot be removed so even if it hadn't sunk so deep into the water, hadn't been submerged enough to kill it, there'd be no way anyone could ever dry it out.

The action was capricious and eccentric. We're certain Ava hasn't thought it through. She threw her phone away on impulse as proof to Arak she can also face a loss and is prepared to take the consequences, so perhaps she's ready to direct her story after all. But is she brave enough to start again and face to face?

There's only one way to find out.

*

I've not seen Grace for days. Perhaps it's weeks? I can't remember. At the moment when we creep into her office she's sitting absolutely still in a colossal chair behind the most enormous desk. I haven't been to where she works before and I'm impressed. This tower is formidable. There aren't too many buildings like that here in Combfoot Chase and I'll admit to being stunned. Grace must be almost at the top of her game, whatever game that is. She's just shy of the pinnacle, but I don't think any less of her for that.

I came for her advice but now I'm here I don't dare break a stagnant silence. It's obvious she's not herself. The body posed in front of me has the appearance of the person that I know but doesn't have the energy of Grace.

She hasn't noticed me, is staring blankly into space.

I raise my hand to Arak as a signal we ought to stop and so we hold our horses side by side. We must have made some noise on entering, I think. We turned a handle, caused a spindle to rotate, a cylinder connected to a latch and made it draw. We swung open the door and came halfway across the floor. There must have been one moment in that process that was real enough to make a sound, however small, but Grace remains oblivious.

At first I wonder if she's concentrating on the many screens that stand around her desk but then I realise no, they're all turned off. She's simply staring at a spider which has placed itself – eight legs and all – in the middle of the glass door through which we two have entered.

Strange.

I try to tell myself there's no way somebody as tough as Grace would be afraid of spiders, but I can't escape the thought a bug's got no right to be in here. Surely spiders can't climb up this high, I think?

*

They get everywhere, these insects, and you can't get rid of them. I'm on the brink of telling Ava how the tower creates a draft that sucks bugs to the top when she lifts a hand to stop me in my tracks. There's Grace. The sort who's never had to ask for help before, I think, but now the mere appearance of a spider has unnerved her. It's probable she got no warning, saw no crawling journey up a wall, no sneaking trek across a floor. Perhaps one moment there was nothing and the next a black star had appeared, emblazoned on her door. How's that for kicking someone in the teeth?

She must be trying to decide on her best course of action. One option would be for her to rescue it. It must be possible to press a button, to call a caretaker, to ask them if they'd kindly put the spider in a box and cart it outside of the building.

Or she could deal with it herself? She could scoop the spider up and throw it from a window. If she found one she could open.

Or she could simply squash it. Up here a spider's so far from its natural habitat its chances of survival must be dubious, she thinks, so hastening its death would be a kindness.

In the end it might be better to be put out of our misery.

However there's an obstacle which makes each one of these solutions quite impossible. Grace is rooted to her chair and no matter what she does to try to motivate herself she can't muster the will to move. From my vantage point I see that if she wants to reach the door she'll have to span a stretch of vacant carpet. She has a pair of legs and Ava says they've always functioned pretty well, but if I'm not mistaken Grace now doubts her own ability to cross a room and use the door.

I make a note of her inertia.

*

"I must have left last night," Grace thinks, though come to think of it she's got no memory of exiting the tower. She must have walked through dusk, gone home, but when she tries to think about the house in which she lives, there isn't anything. No pictures come to mind, nor does she know for sure if life is populated with anybody's flesh.

She thinks she has become subsocial.

With one eye staying on the spider – as she'd rather know exactly where it is than have it sneak around and hide – she glances down. "Oh good," she thinks, "I've dressed appropriately for work." No spills or dribbles on this suit and nothing to suggest she's worn the same outfit for several days on end. In fact she'd say her clothes look crisp and newly laundered. The shoes in which she's tucked her feet beneath the desk are highly polished and her hands are clean with nails unchipped and tidy. All the signs suggest she must have left the tower, but how she managed it or where she went she cannot say.

She's outsourced all her memories.

*

Grace looks so small behind that desk. She's hinted that she thinks her competence is failing and I can't say I'm surprised. I'd feel the same if forced to work in rooms like this. It's far too large and fringed by panoramic sky, impossible to take in all at once – even if I use the full extent of my peripheral vision – but Grace said that she loved the open access and the possibilities of an endless space.

I remember her elation on the day they shooed her in. She'd met me at the theatre, brought champagne – which Brogan promptly drank – had trumpeted her progress round the bar. She'd boasted how they'd given her a throne-like chair.

"'My right-hand *man*,' my new boss called me," Grace had said, and snorted. "D'you know, I had to cough before he realised. 'Hmmm?' he said. 'Oh! Oh, yes. Right-hand *woman*. Yes, I meant to say a woman. Yes, of course.'" She'd mimicked him, had swigged a glass of wine down in one go. "You see?" she'd said. "Even *he* can get things wrong, forget that times have changed."

He'd sat her down, she'd said, and spun the chair so she'd appreciate the view. She'd told me how the park had spread out far below the tower like a picnic blanket and I saw the sheer delight, the pleasure that she'd taken in her new and elevated status. I remember wishing somebody would say that *I* was just the ticket.

The company had fussed around her, grinned and raised their glasses while she'd told them how she'd taken off her shoes and scampered round this carpet in her two bare feet. Jason watching from the far end of the bar. He'd looked completely awe-struck and it made me jealous, I'll admit. He never looked at me like that. I thought it meant he only tolerated me and that I wasn't everything the company had hoped for. I'm not sure I'd interpret it the same way nowadays.

The last time I saw Grace she mentioned how the rumours going round the tower had become completely ruthless. "Word is, my face no longer fits," she said, and poured us both a glass of wine. Of *whine*. "I'm worried I might get the boot. I need a nudge, one thing to happen, one new *unusual* thing to get me back on track. I can't let people think I'm stuck."

I wonder if this spider will give her that opportunity?

*

Consider Grace. Make a note if she leans forward in her chair. We store vast quantities of routine information because you never know when keeping tabs on someone turns up something useful. For example, notice how she squints, considers the considerable distance between herself and the glass door.

"She does that when she wants to make her distance sight less blurry," Ava whispers.

*

Grace is trying to convince herself that she can cross the room. She's reached the door before, she thinks, so must be able to get over there again, although she must tread carefully. In heels as high as these it's possible she'll trip.

Once at the door she reckons that it should be easy to trap the spider in a glass or place a piece of paper over it and push. She imagines the crack, shards of the spider's punctured body, the impression left on paper of its flattened tagmata. A week ago – a month? a year? – she'd just have done it, but today the idea leaves a bitter flavour in her mouth. It can't be right to crush it. It's not doing any harm, she thinks. And theory's one thing, the reality another. However if she lets somebody else remove the spider, then she'll never know its fate. That bothers her. She knows that endings are important. "I'd still be held responsible," she thinks. "I'd still be told that I'm the one to blame." She can't bring herself to put an end to it, although she knows a lack of action raises eyebrows and that other people will begin to draw conclusions.

It's desolate, the moment when you recognise you're thwarted.

*

Outside a run of footsteps in the corridor. I watch a shadow track the glass. It passes, moves towards the lift which spends each working day in running up and down. This office is so close to the top of the shaft that if you hold your breath and listen you can hear the motor whirr, the cables clank, the sheave as it keeps turning.

"Does no one come in anymore?" I turn to Grace and ask. "Don't they think you know they're out there moving while you're in here at a halt?"

Grace rests her elbows on her desk, her chin placed on her hands. She shuts her eyes. "How long is it since I last had a proper conversation?" she murmurs, then she adds, "No, not with you. You wouldn't count. You've only come in here to watch."

*

I don't know whether Grace meant to address those words to Ava, or to me, or to the spider…

*

"People did come once upon a time, I'm sure of it," Grace begins again. A recess in her mind catches images like flies. "I'm sure I went to conferences and once had vigorous discussions. And when I spoke, I'm sure that people heard me." She'd like to think that what once was could come again, but no one gives her half a chance. "At some point they forgot me and they left me to the spiders."

The spider on the door flexes and extends two pairs of legs. Microscopic feet provide the necessary traction and it scuttles a few centimetres lower.

Grace teeters. "No, it can't be true," she thinks, "I can't have been abandoned." Her eyes snap open. "Ha-ha! I've got it. Because the office stays so clean, there must be *someone* coming in, to dust if nothing else."

On cue a robot vacuum cleaner trundles out from a dark corner where it's spent the last hour hooked up to a charger. Beneath a calm exterior it's become perplexed. It thought it had established a routine, had had an incomparable programme laid down pat, during which it navigated only when completely sure that Grace wasn't in a meeting. It's learnt how to deliver highly specialised floorcare at her convenience and how to keep its profile low. It's mapped the space and operates its dual-surface brushes and its dirt-detecting sensors only when it can be subtle, when it has identified a handy gap between spells of activity. But now that nothing happens here it thinks that something shifty must be going on. It scurries round and whirls its mops and brushes all the time, makes far too frequent darts out of the dark and threatens to run out of charge but still does not dare loiter in the safety of its corner or a cupboard. It feels its obligation is to clean up endlessly, although there's no dirt left for it to gather. It knows it's more connected and more automated than it's ever been before but worries that it isn't getting smarter.

A bell rings suddenly and everybody jumps.

It takes a second to appreciate it's nothing but a telephone.

"At last," Grace says, "the call has come…" She tells herself it's best not to appear too eager. Let it ring a few times, wipe your palms along your knees before you pick it up. The fingers of one hand now ape the spider on the desk, the other lifts the receiver to her ear.

*

A bell rings suddenly and everybody jumps.

"They mustn't find me here," says Arak, and dives underneath the desk.

I follow him into the gap and squeeze myself between the other legs and shoes. In such close quarters to Grace's shins I see tiny bristles growing out of every follicle, the slut wool on her legs. That's not like her, I think. She's always been particular about self-care and grooming.

"Mm-hmmm," Grace murmurs down the phone. She shifts and crosses one leg, stickle-bricked across the other, almost kicks me in the process. "Okay," she says, "well, thank you."

The call does not last long, thank goodness – too long stuck here and I'd suffer pins and needles. I hear the scratching of a pen, the rattle of a keyboard. Grace is making notes and typing up an email, I suppose.

The spider on the door senses a change in pressure. With a sudden snap of all eight legs it launches high into the air.

"But will I ever get an answer back?" Grace asks out loud.

The spider makes a sudden curve through space.

"And did I used to?"

The spider lands and tests the floor. It eyes the robot vacuum cleaner, decides it's far too perilous down here and makes a quick retreat back up its dragline.

"And should I bother if there's no reward?"

The spider resumes its place upon the door, a little lower down perhaps but more or less in the same spot. Like me it must be very tired. That leap must have consumed a lot of energy and now it knows how vulnerable it is. It's best interests are served by staying still.

We all hang on.

*

In silence new thoughts wink to life and spark in Ava's eyes. I read them there before they ever make it to her lips. "Grace ought to quit this tower," she declares, eyes flaring like she's had a revelation. "It's obvious. I'll take her to Australia!"

Ava thinks you have to kill the spider if you want to rid yourself of webs.

"One place is very like another," I begin. "It doesn't matter where you go, nor if it has a bigger cupboard or a larger chair; it's all much of a muchness." It's possible to make it to the top, to see a wide expanse of glass and look out on the high white air, only to cotton on you're so high up you can't remember what it feels like on the ground.

Ava scowls at me and at the underside of Grace's desk. "If it's *my* story then I've got the right to choose the ending for myself," she says.

Against my strenuous advice, against my every call for caution, she crawls out from underneath the desk. "Come with me, Grace," I hear her say, "and don't believe that anyone is standing in our way except ourselves."

*

Grace is startled. She has to blink before she recognises Ava. "But how did you get in as well?" she asks. Can everyone go everywhere now, freely, without seeking anyone's permission? The thought is so preposterous it makes her laugh. "You've caused quite a disturbance," she informs the spider.

The spider thinks of Grace and Ava only as pieces of furniture which talk. It could run off, it thinks, but won't. It wants to stay and see what happens next.

"Let's go away together," Ava says, "like we did that time we went on holiday, d'you remember?"

Grace tries to spin her mind through all the places of her past but only catches a thin vision of two pairs of long and tangled legs, an unidentified and rather muscular shoulder, an obscure earlobe. "Was that me or you or someone else?" she says to Ava, then she shakes her head. "I don't think that was anyone. I think I only dreamt it up." It's true that memories grow vaguer and the minutes shorter the higher up you go. Grace hasn't looked back into memory for ages, has left those pictures in the clouds. The tower has taught her everything she doesn't need to know.

Ava grabs a pen and paper from the desk and starts to draw. A few lines flick across the page. She shapes the outline of a structure, a crumpled tower of her own. "It was like *this*," she says, "d'you remember?" though she's punctured when her picture makes Grace laugh again.

"It looks like mud and twigs and straw!" says Grace.

"It was bamboo," says Ava. Although her drawing's not been good enough for Grace to recognise, Ava is determined. To fail is not to make mistakes. The real mistake is when you give up trying. She crumples up the picture, throws the ball into the bin, begins again. Again. Again.

The spider also chooses this exact moment to make its second bid for freedom. It makes a run for it and this time chooses different tactics. It scuttles down the door towards the floor and starts a systematic search for exits, beginning with the skirting board.

Ava draws and Grace watches the spider, tries to think what it was like when she could go through doors. The only day she can recall with any clarity is the day of her arrival at the tower. "I was full of hope," she thinks, although it was very cold and wet and winter. "I remember how I clutched the letter to my chest, *Dear Ms Coppe, Following our recent meeting, we are delighted to offer you the position of…* I couldn't wait to get out of the sprawling mess of streets down there. I wore my green coat, I remember… I wonder where that coat is now?" She looks in puzzlement at a row of empty hooks behind the door.

The robot vacuum cleaner stirs again, remembering it's got the job of mapping everything, the whole shebang. If it's not charted every detail it might as well give in and not exist.

Its movement throws the spider into a blind panic. It has a go at sliding underneath the skirting, but no, the crack's too small and forces a retreat. The spider rushes in the opposite direction, is desperate to dodge the vacuum cleaner, is almost – not quite yet – convinced that it will have to quit its quest.

"It had a plaid lining and a large buckle," Grace says, pleased to rediscover these particulars. She thinks it means the memory must be true.

"I know the one you mean," says Ava, "but you won't need it, Grace. It's warm, so no one needs coats in Australia."

"I'm pretty sure I hung it on a peg," says Grace, "but that was long ago and I'd have had to share those pegs with other people…" A mental picture of her colleagues, glossed, like pages in a magazine. As soon as her mind turns to it she notices the picture has an edge, a border which she cannot cross. The memory is posed and Insta-perfect, artificial, unconvincing, a wish of how her life has been, not how it really was. "That must've been a few floors lower down…" she says, and wonders why she feels the coat's loss quite so keenly.

The spider, having run the gauntlet of the floor, has been delighted to defeat the vacuum cleaner by straggling ungainly on the window.

The robot vacuum cleaner sees a distant smudge and bumps against the skirting in frustrated repetition of an unsuccessful pattern. It doesn't like a blemish drawn on what should be completely clean and clear. It likes the glass uninterrupted, windows, walls and all. Its work should be invisible so even birds don't notice anything, are made to crash and plummet. But this spider makes it see the fucking glass again.

"Say you'll come with me, Grace, *please*," Ava says.

Again a holding out of hands.

Beneath the spider's feet the tower flows away towards the tumbling geometry of streets that makes up Combfoot Chase. The park is too far off for seasons to be visible. There's no way anyone up here could hear the splashing of the water in the fountain, or see the colours of the tulips or the daffodils, or smell the fragrance of the new-cut grass. A passing car is just a toy and all the people on the streets are only specks of dust so small that even spider feet could step on them and crush them.

Nor does the spider look up either. It's not ambitious, doesn't need to see the summit, can't count the storeys rising up above. The tower simply stretches smooth on every side, is bleached by light, reflects a view of nowhere. Any passion that the spider might have had for heights is now extinguished and it's only interested in getting down. It slips a centimetre then another down the glass. Even hairy feet can't grip on something this smooth very long. Leg by leg it makes its way towards the floor. It skirts the carpet, finds the tufts unstable and determines that they're too much of a barrier, so makes a swift diversion. It tells itself it must be brave and reasons even robot hoovers can be side-stepped if it's very crafty.

Grace looks down at Ava's open hands then glances at the telephone.

The telephone stays resolutely silent.

The robot vacuum trundles off and plugs itself into its charger once again. It's home.

Slowly – leaning heavily on Ava – Grace stands. She's gangly. Feet feel too far off to be reliable, but she takes a step, first one and then another and another. Step by step, with lots of help, encouragement from Ava, she begins to shift her weight towards the door.

*

It makes me nervous when I have to take the lead. I clutch her fingers tight in mine and say, "Just keep your eyes on me."

Arak makes a funnel with his arms so Grace keeps heading to the door and doesn't get distracted. We're so caught up in this procedure, one of us – I won't say who – steps on the spider, mashes it into the floor. The crunch is slight but it's a horrifying moment and it brings us both up short. We look down. Eight legs sticking out from underneath the sole of one unfortunate shoe. We silently agree it's best if we say nothing and hope that Grace won't notice.

*

In the lobby Ava grabs a coat from off a peg and drapes it around Grace's shoulders. "It isn't stealing," she says. "We can post it back. I bet no one will even miss it."

I shrug. "No skin off my nose," I say, and step into the swirling of revolving doors that lead out of the tower. We all make sure before we go to wipe our feet off on the mat. The spider's limbs – what's left of them – stick up between the coir. "Tomorrow then?" I say. "You'll meet me at the airport?"

Ava nods.

You'd think that after days of stagnant silence in the tower, Grace would flinch away from all the squawking life out on the streets, but no, she doesn't. She stands numb, as though there's nothing worth her notice here, her hands still idling in Ava's.

But Then Face to Face

Call me Obic. I'm the Only Bitch In Charge.

If you're seeking out a perfect painting then you'd better stick to Eve. I work outside and never soften anything with beeswax, oil or honey. I won't be bled just to achieve the right degree of statutory paleness. I've never once been seventeen or innocent or virginal, and I don't care if you catch whiffs of sour towel from in between my legs. It's taken me a whole lifetime of trouble and desire to earn my wrinkles. I'll take a blousy peony over lilies every time.

I'm not your poor relation even when I haven't got a penny to my name and I'll cut my cloth in ways that you can ill afford. I won't sell out and couple-up to save the family fortune. I'm not accomplished at piano and – believe me – you don't want to hear me sing. You'd rather skulk backstage and wish the audience would go away. I'll never bake a cake for you, nor set the table for your dinner, nor mop your floor, nor scrub the skid marks from your toilet. I'll spurn all of my admirers and I'll pin their hearts like butterflies. In spite of this they'll never want to leave me as my hold is more than fleshy.

I'll make sure I eat my way to greatness and I'll thrust my fat deposits in your face. I've a belly and a lot of dimpled ass and though I'm hardly packing in the breast department, I'll neither maximise nor minimise. I'll never listen when you tell me I would benefit from rhinoplasty because my voice is more important than my nose. I'll be mutton dressed as lamb with all my sins and dissolution on my chest. I'll only accept fasteners if they're possible to close all by myself. I'll never squash my toes into a high-heeled shoe. I value pain too much to waste it.

I predict you'll find me difficult and meddlesome and gobby though I don't think these are really my worst flaws. I'll never stumble backwards and avert my eyes. I'll steal your seat and not say thank you and it won't be long before you wish you'd called me witch and had me burned, or had at least declared I was insane.

I'll never be another person's refuge.

I'll like everything and nothing. I'll be your hell of other people. Or their absence. Take your pick according to your preference.

When there's nothing left to hide, then I'll be nothing.

Until then it's one on one, just you and me against the other.

Till extinction.

Till the end.

*

We're at the airport of a city not too far away from Combfoot Chase. You'd think from all the business in the concourse that everyone we've ever met has gathered here. There's not a seat untaken, though a row of three is occupied by one man lying down, hands folded on his chest, looking for all the world as though explosions wouldn't penetrate his secret meditations.

We've thought about disturbing him. "Excuse us, mate," we'd say, "but it's quite busy and there's other folk that need to find a seat here, not just you." But in the end we thought it better to say nothing. We don't want to draw attention to ourselves and he's the only person here who's managing to look peaceful. Though it's possible he's already stone dead.

Most passengers are frantic in the manner of their waiting. They distract themselves by looking at their phones. They do glance up occasionally to check the boards, to see if further information has come up about today's departures. Has our gate number been listed yet? Christ in heaven, *please* don't let that screeching baby be on our flight… We've not met any of these people yet, but they won't be so different from the ones that we do know. We all leave similar traces everywhere we go and as you've gathered we don't mean smiles, a kind word or heroic actions.

However we have spotted one or two familiar faces. Over there is Philip, who is looking pretty shady. It took us time to realise it was him because he thought that he could hide from us behind a pair of sunglasses. We clocked him, though, when his friends turned up, Jason and Mark, who came to see him off, a last-minute surprise. We hadn't realised they were friends with him as well.

"Hey, Phil! We've come to wave yer off, yer dickwad," Mark called out.

They both rushed over and they gave him manly hugs and clapped him soundly on the back.

"Me and Mark are gonna miss yer, mate," said Jason.

We watched Phil shake them off and check his baggage, then he hurried through security. We thought it might be fun to follow him if only with our eyes and our binoculars. He stopped beside a rack of books outside a stationer's concession. We're pleased he only went that far because it meant we didn't have to move from where we'd hidden and we had a brilliant view of everything he did.

He started leafing through the paperbacks, had seemed distracted, kept on pausing, looking at his phone. We know that last night he deleted all the texts he'd stored from both his wife and from the mother of his youngest child, so we were interested to note he was still checking. Our best guess is he'd hoped to get a word from Ava, but we can assume he didn't get it because he tucked the phone away again into the inside pocket of his jacket. Seconds later he thought better of it, took the phone out, threw it in a bin. We made a note for one of us to saunter by and pick that up a little later. Then he disappeared into the stationer's and came out with a brand-new boxed-up mobile. Pay-as-you-go, a burner, we'd lay bets. He then went back to flicking through the novels. Well, he'll need something to entertain him in the long and lonely hours of the flight.

It's pretty clear that Ava isn't coming. Phil's making up his mind to do his best to catch the eye of someone in the cabin crew – although there isn't any guarantee that any will be pretty. He picks himself a book that is generic and predictable, though even this far off we see the cover's very striking. There's lots of black and red and yellow, and it stands out, that's for sure. The author's name is macho and implies he's hardened, rough around the edges, but for all the twists and turns of plot we know the story will resolve. When Philip reads it he'll be satisfied that everything is still in order, though he won't expect its concepts of rough justice and morality to be applied to him. When he gets to Australia, he thinks, nobody will be able to catch up with him, nor make him pay for anything he's done.

Except he hasn't banked on Obic, who arrives here at the airport bang on cue. She's just caused consternation as she's ambled through security because she's sporting a new T-shirt which is printed on the front with a large and recent picture of her colleague, Mr Arak. The facial-recognition tech got quite confused and someone stopped her, double-checked her travel documents and passport. Luckily she only found this very funny. She's well worth watching, that one. We know from past experience she's a character who won't give up, can be relied upon to chase her subject till the very end, so keep your eyes well-peeled.

Arak, on the other hand, has lost all sense of humour. He's over there behind that pillar, engulfed by the gripes and grizzles of his stomach. Since he too realised Ava isn't on her way he's looked a little pale and has developed a disarming tick of clutching at his sides. He made some gurgling noises too which quite disturbed the other passengers. They cast an anxious glance towards him, though no one thought to be kind or to offer him assistance. They all avoided eye contact and hoped they'd not be sitting next to him when they got on the plane.

Oh, good. It seems that Obic's spotted him.

"What's up?" she says, and crouches down in front of him.

He doesn't answer.

"D'you know this man then?" Arak's neighbour asks. He would be willing to give up his seat, would rather stand than have to sit beside an individual who's clearly very ill. Nor would he mind securing the attention of the gorgeous woman who quite by chance has come and squatted near his feet. He's ready to show off a row of perfect and expensive teeth.

Obic shakes her head and waves away the neighbour, who is disappointed when she doesn't even look at him. He presses his lips back together, gets up and goes away. There's time for one more glass of beer before his flight is called, he thinks.

"I think it's something that I ate," says Arak. His mouth is full of bile and grievances.

"Yeah. Well, no. Actually it's not," says Obic. She slumps down in the chair beside him, does her best to look apologetic. She doesn't list the range of options she considered before she set her sights on this one. It doesn't matter as the outcome would've only been the same. She could have spiked his tea – too dull, too easy – or had him strangled with a dog leash – though she doesn't have a dog. A blunt-force trauma to the head would do it – messy – or she could have shot him in the lift as he was exiting the tower – too troublesome with Grace and Ava there as witnesses. And it would've meant she'd have to wear a mask. She hates those things because they mess her hair up and play havoc with her lippy. She did plan to abduct him and to dump his body in the woods beside the reservoir, but he might not have been found for weeks, or maybe even months. Obic wants the credit while she's still around to savour it. So in the end she plumped on smearing something in his underpants. You've probably gathered she's a fine taste for absurdity and this solution was the one that made her laugh. The substance chosen was both odourless and clear and must have worked its way into his nerves by now. The sounds he makes are countless. Almost all of them are vowels, with consonants too few to transform sound to words or give them any structure. Soon his eyes will roll and froth will gurgle from the corners of his mouth.

It's possible that Arak in his final throes will do his best to lay the blame on Obic. If he's got strength enough he'll point a finger, cast aspersions, kick himself for having been so stupid. Obic's not concerned about potential accusations because she knows we're still at the beginning, not the end. She simply has to stonewall, or to say it's fake news, or a witch-hunt and to issue a robust denial. If someone really starts to probe she'll say she'd only meant it as a warning. She'll bat her lashes, claim that everything got out of her control. The rich and beautiful are easily forgiven in this world and details can be blanked out, or redacted, or overruled by bank accounts, or the fine features of a face.

Consequently Arak's death won't make the slightest difference and there isn't much that anyone can do. All those who happen to be near will close their eyes and look away, for empathy is risky. No one's prepared to make a fuss these days, to take the first and costly step of raising the alarm. Besides, to do so would delay their flights and everyone has waited here for ages. So Arak will chase spasms on his own and hide his gusts and groans inside a toilet cubicle that reeks of yellow eggs.

Well then, you think, if that's the case then this can't be the end. You've reached this point before and more than once, enough to know there must be one more chapter, or an epilogue, a line, a word, a something more in any case. There *must* be! Perhaps, you think, you'll find the answers slipped into the complimentary magazine that airlines ping onto the backs of chairs? You'll slip it out of its elasticated pocket and you'll flick through thickened pages filled with fashion plates and promos for a far-flung destination that – they claim – is very different from what you'd expect from Combfoot Chase. You won't waste time considering this place for very long. You'll keep on flicking. It might be that you've travelled there before, or maybe it's got nothing that can tempt you, or the prices quoted are extortionate, or perhaps you think that everywhere is really much the same.

Though halfway through the magazine you'll pause. A double-spread will capture your attention. It's occupied by a textless advert for outlandishly expensive perfume, the perfect way to pitch to global markets. Suddenly you'll want what anyone who's affluent can have, enough to stop and pull the sample sachet from its zot. You'll scratch and sniff and daub a trace of perfume on your wrists. "Oh, I quite like that," you'll think to yourself. "Oh yes, I'd say that rather suits me." You'll make a point of carefully examining the picture-bottle to try and fix its slick and polished image in your head.

At journey's end you're very tired so you'll hunt half-heartedly in Duty Free but find you can't remember which of all these piled-up scents it was you wanted. All the bottles look so similar and stand in towers of boxes casting shadows on the floor. After trying one or two – which only smell like echoes of the one that you were searching for – you'll give up and you'll say, "Oh, never mind." You'll shrug the disappointment off and buy the same scent that you always buy.

On your way home you'll convince yourself that nothing's easier or more desirable than simply doing nothing.

Acknowledgements

Huge thanks to Emma Courtney, who read my manuscript in such detail and with such care that she made me believe it had real value.

To Jeremy Thompson and Rosie Lowe, for their guidance in the world of publishing.

To all the members of Wight Lines and The Wight Fair Writers' and Artists' Circle, who have read or listened to my work, encouraged me to keep going and shared their knowledge and experiences so generously and freely.

And last, but not at all least, to all my friends and family who have had to put up with me going on about spiders and surveillance capitalism for much longer than they might have wished.